Praise for Intentional

"Throughout this intelligent and perceptive novel, Arbor traces with strength and delicacy the many strands leading up to and away from a suicide." — *Kirkus Reviews*

"A thoughtful, sensitive but never saccharine exploration of what suicide leaves behind." — *Kirkus Reviews*

For Grace,

It's such fun in our writing group.

love,

Lynn

INTENTIONAL

A novel

LYNN ARBOR

INTENTIONAL

Copyright © 2015 Lynn Arbor
All Rights Reserved.

No part of this book may be used or reproduced by any means,
electronic, mechanical, graphic, or by photocopying, recording, taping,
or by any information storage retrieval system without the written permission of
the author or publisher, Spring Forward Books,
except in the case of brief quotations used in critical articles or reviews.

This book is a work of fiction. Characters, names,
places and events are the product of the author's imagination.
Any resemblance to persons living or dead is purely coincidental.
Although every precaution has been taken to verify the accuracy of the
information contained herein, the author and publisher assume
no responsibility for any errors or omissions.
No liability is assumed for damages that may result from the use
of information contained within.

"My Favorite Things"
By Richard Rodgers and Oscar Hammerstein II
Copyright © 1959 by Williamson Music (ASCAP), an Imagem Company,
owner of publication and allied rights throughout the World
Copyright Renewed
International Copyright Secured   All Rights Reserved   Used by Permission

Cover design by Lynn Arbor and Nancy Massa

ISBN 978-0-9862206-0-9
ISBN-10: 0986220604

Library of Congress Control Number: 2015900129

Spring Forward Publishing

First Edition printed in USA

*Although this story is fiction and the setting is in 2012,
the impetus for writing about suicide comes from
my memory of a friend who left us without saying good-bye
nearly forty years ago.*

TABLE OF CONTENTS

PART ONE—SURVIVED BY 1

  1. Lily 3

  2. Fred 17

  3. Robert 25

  4. Lily 34

  5. Christina 35

  6. Grace 42

  7. Rose 47

  8. Carlos 54

PART TWO—SURVIVING 57

  9. Lily 59

  10. Robert 68

  11. Lily 77

  12. Rose 82

  13. Lily 85

  14. Fred 87

  15. Lily 91

  16. Robert 95

  17. Grace 100

  18. Lily 105

  19. Christina 110

  20. Lily 115

  21. Grace 117

  22. Fred 121

  23. Rose 130

  24. Christina 132

  25. Robert 137

  26. Lily 144

  27. Grace 150

  28. Lily 157

  29. Fred 162

  30. Christina 163

  31. Carlos 167

  32. Lily 169

  33. Rose 175

  34. Lily 179

  35. Christina 191

  36. Fred 193

37. Robert 198

38. Lily 200

PART THREE—SURVIVORS 203

39. Robert 205

40. Christina 209

41. Lily 213

42. Grace 215

Acknowledgements 221

About the Author 223

*This book is dedicated to those
who've lost a loved one to suicide,
and to the memory of those
whose path became too dark
to continue life's voyage.*

Yesterday Morning My Friend

Being alive today I am busy
baking a cake (I never bake anymore)
a yellow cake made orange with juice
and stirred with a rust-bleeding
slotted spoon (is it poisonous?)
and poured without thinking into
an angel food cake pan (is that symbolic?)

being alive today my hands pull away
sweat-stained sheets (I suppose
I should wash more often) I give them
extra softener because they are coarse
and last night they (or the night?)
rubbed against my skin
not letting me sleep

being alive today I am busy
doing meaningless valuable tasks
and thinking about my friend
a housewife
who shot herself yesterday morning

Poem written in 1976 for my friend Mel

PART ONE—SURVIVED BY

LYNN ARBOR | 2

1. LILY

At 11:00 a.m. on Friday, October 5, 2012,
Lily Cummings got a text message: *I love U. Be*
She texted back: *I love you too. Be? Be what?*
There was no reply.

Twenty-two hours later, Lily stood staring at the smashed doorframe into Dust Steward's bedroom. A name dug up from her childhood repeated in her head—*Corinna Dustina Malibu Jones, Corinna Dustina Malibu Jones*—like an earworm of a song that wouldn't shut up. It started after the phone call from Dust's mother on Friday night and rhymed her into a fitful sleep, then it woke her before the birds started chirping. Between the internal chants, her brain was jumping around finding memories, tracking down stray thoughts, distractions, and diversions, and herding them to the front line of her attention. She was stuck, immobilized. If she stepped over the threshold, it would all be real.

It was Saturday morning. She should be meeting Dust at the Royal Oak Farmers Market where they'd wander around stands weighed down with autumn's abundance. They'd eat fried egg sandwiches at their favorite table beside the Market Cafe and catch up on each other's stories. But Dust canceled last week, said she wasn't feeling well. This was the second Saturday they had missed. Two weeks. The beginning of never again.

If she couldn't be at the market with Dust, then Lily wanted to be asleep. She wouldn't even mind having a nightmare with boogiemen lurking in shadows making her cower; she'd wake up spooked in her bed, but life would still be intact. She wanted to be somewhere else, anywhere, just not here.

Not here.

Lily couldn't move through the door into Dust's master bedroom suite, but she couldn't move away either.

This wasn't one of her many phobias, like standing at the top of an escalator and deciding not to get on, or avoiding boats and airplanes. It wasn't fear. It was anguish.

The bucket that she'd brought from home was loaded with spray bleach, paper towels, a black trash bag, and orange rubber gloves. She clutched its handle so tightly her knuckles ached. She squeezed the handle, but still she didn't move into the room. Why did she volunteer to do this? Why? She knew why. If she didn't do it, Dust's mother, Christina, would, and Lily couldn't let that happen.

Frozen in the doorway, she tried to remember the last time she saw Dust, scratched around inside her memory and found details—an image. It was the day that Dust gave her the official tour of the new addition, "official" meaning that the bed was made and no one's underwear was left where it landed. After months of architects and contractors and carpenters and plumbers and decorators, it was finished—a bedroom suite bigger than the entire houses that she and Dust grew up in. Beneath the master suite there was a new family room and kitchen. Lily had seen the addition in progress, from the hole in the ground where Dust's garden used to be, to the framing and drywall installation.

***

On the day of the tour, the temperature had been perfect—warm, but not too warm. Standing beside Dust in the open doorway of the master suite, Lily had sucked in her breath. The bedroom was serene and beautiful with off-white carpet the color of bleached beach sand and walls the pale aqua of a travel poster sky—like a honeymoon paradise in the Caribbean. A breeze ruffled the sheer curtains in the open bay window, where two bulky white slipcovered chairs were waiting for someone to curl up with a good book. The king-sized bed was puffy with down pillows and a white duvet. If she'd been young enough to get away with it, Lily would have taken a running dive into that cloud of a bed.

"Welcome to conspicuous consumption," Dust had said, twirling her arm into the bedroom, like a model at the Detroit Auto Show inviting you to partake the wonders of the latest Hummer. Her words were sarcastic, but the break in her voice made Lily look away from the beautiful room, back to her friend's face.

"We don't have to do this," Lily said. "Let's just go have coffee."

"Where, Lily? Robert's gymnasium of a kitchen?"

"We could go into town. Starbucks. Leo's Coney. My house. Anywhere. We don't need to do this."

"No, come on," Dust said, and she led Lily across the room to the French doors that opened out onto a balcony.

"Nice," Lily said, stepping outside. Then she questioned herself: should she be impressed? She was, but should she show it knowing how unhappy Dust was with the addition?

"You can have coffee out here on warm days," Lily said, working hard on a cheer-up mood. "You can sit out here on a chaise and do the *New York Times* crossword puzzle." That was good. Dust loved puzzles.

No response.

"So is this a deck or a porch or a balcony?" Lily asked, trying to find a verbal edge to lighten things up.

"It's a whole lot of dead cedar trees," Dust said, as she walked over to the railing. "Remember the magnolia, Lily? I planted it when we first moved into this house. Remember how beautiful it was in bloom? It was so tall I could see its flowers from our old bedroom when I woke up in the morning. They just plowed it over like it was nothing. Nothing important."

"I'm sorry," Lily said, and put her arm over Dust's shoulder. "I know you loved that tree and your garden. But maybe next spring you could put big pots out here on the dead cedars and grow some vegetables."

Dust pointed to another spot beneath them. "That's where my compost bin was. After all these months of construction, I still feel weird, guilty, putting potato peels and apple cores in the trash. They could be decomposing with leaves and grass clippings. They could be making compost—vegetables enhancing the soil to grow more vegetables. There's a beauty to it. I thought about doing some red worm composting in a bin in the kitchen." She laughed then, but it wasn't joyous. "Can you picture Robert's reaction to a bin of worms in the house? He doesn't even like me the leave the toaster on the kitchen counter. Besides, the vegetable garden's gone, so what's the point?"

Dust seemed so depressed that Lily wanted to say something to make her laugh.

"Hey, here's another idea," Lily said. "You could get a big rope, tie it to the rails and escape." Dust smiled at that, then led Lily back inside.

The highlight of the tour was the master bathroom, where Dust had pointed at the mahogany shelves stacked with perfectly folded towels—Martha Stewart would approve.

"The interior decorator folded the towels," she said, her tone flat, lacking any interest or enthusiasm.

A mahogany vanity was topped with granite and two thick glass bowl sinks. A bidet was next to the toilet.

"A bidet for God's sake," Dust said. "Does Robert think this is Paris?"

Granite—a gorgeous brown and blue abstract—lined the back wall of the shower.

"It's called Blue Louise," Dust told Lily. "Most granite doesn't do that swirly pattern. When granite's under heat and pressure, it becomes metamorphic rock. The pressure causes the minerals to stick to each other. That's what makes those lines of color."

Dust was more interested in how the granite was formed than the fact that it was on her wall. Every other wall in the bathroom was covered in pale aqua glass tile, floor to ceiling. It shimmered like water.

The problem, Lily knew, was that Dust didn't want this fancy bathroom or any part of the new addition. The new master suite addition—bedroom, walk-in-closet, a bathroom big enough for a party of twenty to stand around inside waiting for their turn to use the facilities, and the dead cedar balcony—were Robert's ideas, as was the new kitchen and family room below. Two years ago, he began dreaming of moving out to one of the suburbs where treeless acres were filled with supersized houses, houses with two-story entries emulating cathedrals and with turrets fantasizing themselves on castles, no moats though. The thought of moving into a monster house appalled Dust. She liked their old house with its odd-colored red brick and drippy mortar. She liked the treed neighborhood where lots were small but adequate for a modest vegetable garden. And what about their daughter? Grace was happy here.

If Dust wouldn't move, Robert wanted to remodel. He gave in about moving, so he told her she should give in on the addition. Dust told Lily how she'd suggested that they save their money for Grace's education. She'd suggested that they buy land and plant a thousand trees, a gift to Mother Nature. He just laughed at that.

She threw adages at him: *bigger isn't better, less is more, think of the greater good*; but they were whiffle balls that bounced off his forehead leaving no impression. The remodeling began.

For years Dust had talked about—more like fretted, stressed and fumed about—greed destroying the planet. She wanted to leave a small carbon footprint. In Dust's favorite fantasy she lived in a tiny cabin in the woods. Simple. Plain. A wash pan on the counter to splash her face would be just fine with Dust. An old tub with an orange teardrop-shaped rust stain beneath the faucet would be just fine with Dust. An outhouse with a moon in the door would be fine with Dust—well, maybe that was exaggerating a bit. Robert could afford to buy her that cabin in the woods, but that wasn't the point. The footprint was the issue.

Sometimes when Dust got up on her soapbox about small footprints, Lily said, "It'll never happen with your size tens." Then Dust would laugh, or she'd give Lily a friendly little swat and continue her diatribe.

Lily had been over many times during the building stages of the addition. Not once, not at any point, did Dust seem happy about it. When carpenters and painters and siding people and plumbers and roofers were there, Dust left. She volunteered at the Detroit Medical Center where her mother Christina was a nurse, she helped out at Grace's middle school, or she spent her time at the nursing home visiting her grandmother. She might have gone to work for the EPA or the DNR, but that would be a kick in the teeth to Robert's political career. She was already useless as the candidate's wife—shy with strangers, which was probably just as well. If she did speak up her opinion would clash with his politics.

When the addition was done, when the pillows were on the bed and the towels were folded on the bathroom shelves, Dust gave up the rant. She slept in the bed and showered in the bathroom. Lily hadn't asked her about the bidet.

Knowing how unhappy Dust was with the addition, Lily wondered why she gave her the tour. Why?

"It's all so beautiful," Dust had said on that day of the tour. "I thought that when it was done, I could accept it. So many people struggle with too little. Why would having too much make me so unhappy? I should probably be grateful."

But she wasn't grateful; she was upset, angry. She hadn't accepted it.

***

Now Lily wondered if the tour had been about Dust sharing her loss. Maybe it was like showing your best friend the stump where your leg was amputated, or opening your shirt and revealing the red oozing line where your breast used to be. No, that wasn't the right analogy; it was more like surveying a subdivision where the family farm had been. The beautiful addition was there, but what had mattered most to Dust was discarded.

Lily stood staring in at the bedroom, still gripping the bucket handle in her hand. She'd love a room like this. So what if the bed wasn't made, she hadn't made her own bed this morning. The last time she saw this room, the decorator had just finished fluffing the pillows and had placed an orchid on a nightstand. Now, unlike during the official tour, dirty clothes were scattered on the chairs and black sock fuzz freckled the off-white carpet. It looked lived in. Lived in? The smashed door into the master suite and the smashed bathroom door twenty feet across the enormous room didn't fit into the fantasy.

***

Stalling. Stalling. Letting her thoughts wander to other places and another time, Lily was seven again, sprawled out on her front lawn with Dusty, her best friend and next-door neighbor, watching clouds morph into animals while they created new names for themselves. Dusty hated having a name that ended with a Y. She said it was too sissy and that was that, forever after Dusty was Dust. Being a loyal and supportive friend, Lily dropped her Y too. Lily didn't want to be a sissy either, although everyone knew she was. Briefly Lily was Lil. Dust and Lil would be their new "go by" names. They needed full names too, names they'd use for important things like pretend passports and make-believe driver's licenses. Lily had no trouble remembering the full name they made up for Dust: Corinna Dustina Malibu Jones—way more exotic than Dusty Ann Jones.

Thirty years later, Lily still remembered the name—maybe because it rhymed. Corinna Dustina Malibu Jones. Malibu? *Malibu* was more significant than just an interesting feeling word in the mouths of two little girls. Dust's dad took off to Malibu to surf and be a free spirit during most of her childhood. Sporadically he'd pop home for a teaser visit with his wife and daughter, which Lily felt was more sadistic than just being gone forever like her own mother. Every time Jay Jones showed up next door, she'd be on the lookout for her mother to return home too, which would explain why she thought his brief returns were cruel.

The girls were bonded in their loss—one with a rarely seen, exotic father and one without her mother. When Lily was little, she imagined their wayward parents—Dust's father Jay Jones and her mother Wanda Abbott—playing, laughing, chasing each other, and building sand castles on some faraway beach. Lily's mother disappeared when she was eight, but by that time Jay had already been popping in and out of Dust's life for years. Jay came back, but Wanda never did.

Funny, Lily couldn't remember her own made-up name. She'd have to ask Dust. With a sting like a wet-handed slap in the face, it hit her again. She couldn't ask Dust anything.

✳✳✳

Motionless, Lily stared across the room at the bathroom door, or anyway, at what was left of it. She should turn around right now. Leave. She didn't want to see it. But at the same time it was like driving down the expressway when you see an accident ahead—ambulances, crushed cars, and someone lying on the road. You don't want to be a gawker, but as you get near you slow down anyway and see what you didn't want to see. Lily moved slowly across the deep, squishy new carpet toward the bathroom. Dust wasn't in there. They had taken her body away yesterday afternoon. Lily knew that, but she was afraid of what was left.

She sidled up to the bathroom door slowly, as if approaching a big dog foaming at the mouth. When she got to the splintered door jam, she stared down at her feet. She looked at the marble floor, trying hard not to see too much. Chunks and shards of wood were scattered where the police broke the door down.

Then she saw the blood.

Corinna Dustina Malibu Jones. Corinna Dustina Malibu Jones. If the words in her head were chanted loud enough she could squelch her screams.

Dust's pink rosary was half in and half out of a gummy, black, O-positive pool on the floor. Lily stepped over the shards of door and into the room. She tried hard not to see anything but the rosary. Dust always joked that she was a bead Catholic, never devoted to her childhood religion like her mother was. When she married Robert, their wedding was in the Presbyterian Church where his great-uncle was a deacon. But still Dust loved holding the beads in her hands, feeling their shape and reciting words—any words would do. Lily remembered how Dust would sneak her mother's rosary up to her attic bedroom and chant or mumble what she thought sounded holy as she squeezed each bead. Eventually Christina bought a new rosary for herself and gave her daughter the pink one.

Lily knelt down and tried to lift the rosary up out of the blood. She tugged gently—afraid of breaking it and having pink beads fly around the room—but the dried, clotted blood clutched it. She yanked with her eyes closed. Suddenly the rosary came free, whipping up flecks of Dust's blood onto Lily's arms. She wailed. A wounded animal was inside her howling. She heard the noise and couldn't stop. She remembered the breathing instructions when she'd been in labor with her twins. Deep breath. Blow out. Deep breath again. You can't scream and take a deep breath at the same time.

Then it was quiet.

Tears blurred her vision. Blurred was good. She took the rosary across the huge bathroom—that she had once envied, but now she saw it as Robert's preposterous self-indulgent vanity—to the vanity, dropped it into one of the two glass-bowl sinks, and turned on the hot water. The water turned pink. She told herself think strawberry Kool-Aid, as the hot water hit the crusted blood, and black clots broke loose and floated among the beads. Her eyes were so wet she could barely see as she took the bleach bottle from her bucket. She pulled the spray trigger and shot into the sink—shot and shot and shot—killing something terrible. The smell of bleach stung her eyes and nose and lungs.

Lily brushed her forearm across her face, clearing away the blur of her tears. She saw her face in the mirror: her cleft chin, her brown eyes, summer's faded highlights in her brown hair. But there was more in the mirror. She saw the opposite wall of the bathroom behind her.

Reflected in the mirror she saw long hairs stuck to the wall, glued on with ugly gray gunk. Brain matter. Dust's brain matter. She saw the shattered glass tiles where the bullet exploded through her best friend's head and hit the wall. Sounds came from Lily that she'd only heard in movies—sounds of women screaming in grief, shrouded in black as they followed a coffin through a white-washed village, wailing in shock and pain—then her throat contracted, stomach contents pushed up into her neck. She rushed to the toilet, bent over, saw blackened red blood splatters on the seat, and swallowed hard. She wouldn't vomit. She told herself that the smell of blood and bleach was bad enough. Then she threw up. The toilet had a round two-phase flusher on the wall. She wasn't sure about the fancy flusher. Was vomit a big button or a small button item? She pushed the big button.

Lily rinsed out her mouth in the second sink and splashed water on her face. She was about to reach into her bucket for the paper towels to dry her face, respecting the perfectly folded towels on the shelf, but then she stopped and wondered what Dust would want her to do. Paper towel? Dust loved trees and some tree had died for that paper product. The towel might have been a twig. So should she use a Martha Stewart towel? They were so perfectly folded. Paper towel? Martha Stewart towel? She wiped her face on her sleeve.

The blood—massive quantities of blood—dominated one side of the room, where a dark pool had spread onto the floor. Dried drip tracks ran down the glass tile wall with bits of brain and skull bone sticking in the grout. It could have been anyone's brains and blood—a bear's or a tiger's or some other big vicious animal—but those long hairs belonged to the friend she'd known longer than any other friend, since they were tiny toddling little girls. Dust always had long hair. Her hair, her best feature, was natural and long always. Sometimes it changed position: pig tails or piled on top of her head or in a ponytail or braids. She was what they called a strawberry blond when she was little, but her red hair was nothing like the color of a strawberry, it was more like orange sherbet. By the time she started middle school, it had darkened to the color of teak, an endangered wood, Dust had told Lily. An endangered species, Lily thought and was crying again.

The expensive bathroom door had three inset panels. Robert had selected the best hardware available, but then yesterday morning Dust had installed a new deadbolt lock. A cordless drill, a nail, a hammer, and a pencil were piled on the granite vanity counter. The empty box from the new lock was lying beside one of the sinks. Lily picked up a plastic bag from the hardware store and found a receipt dated a week ago. A week ago? A week ago, Dust had canceled their Saturday morning breakfast at the farmers market. She said she wasn't feeling well. Lily offered to buy her produce and bring it by, but Dust said that she didn't need anything.

Lily checked the time on the receipt. Dust was at the hardware store when Lily was alone at the farmers market.

Lily figured that by adding a new bolt to the bathroom door, Dust was protecting her daughter Grace and her husband Robert. She was making sure that no one could be blamed for her death, and that only the police would find her. One of the door's wood panels was shattered where the police bashed it in. Lily could picture them reaching in to unlock the new brass deadbolt. There was no question that it was a suicide.

Beside the drill, Dust's cell phone was clean and unsplattered. Without questioning why, Lily stuck the phone in her jeans pocket.

***

When Lily's home phone rang during dinner the night before, the caller ID read, "Local caller," and she hesitated, figuring it was probably a political pitch or some robocall making it impossible for her to say she was on the *no call* list. She almost didn't answer. It was strange that she did, considering that she never answered the phone during dinner. Normally she'd let it go to the recorder.

No one said hello; there was just a strange, muffled gurgling sound on the line. Lily was about to hang up when she heard a sniffle, then Dust's mother Christina's voice, with words spilling out in a blur of high-pitched sobs, words that didn't belong together. *Dusty. Shot.*

What?

Dust had locked the door of Robert's new master suite and then she locked herself in the bathroom with two of Robert's guns. (Why two? In case one didn't work or she couldn't figure it out?) Fred Williams, Dust's next-door neighbor, was in his garden when he heard the shot and saw the flash in the bathroom window. He called the police. Grace, Dust's thirteen-year-old daughter, was at school. Robert was off campaigning somewhere. It had been on the news. Suicide wouldn't normally make the news, but Robert Steward was a state senator who was running for the US Senate. It was a month until the election.

When Lily drove home from work earlier that evening, she'd been listening to NPR on the car radio, and then she didn't turn on the TV while she started dinner for her husband and their teenaged twin sons. She liked the quiet after listening to people with insurance claims all day. News that people in the Detroit Metro area had been hearing for hours was new news to Lily.

On the phone, Dust's mother said, "She didn't leave a note, Lily. Why would she do this? How could she do this to Grace?"

Lily was too stunned to speak.

"I have to go clean that bathroom," Christina said. "Grace can't see it like that, like that, with her mother's...Oh, Lily..." Lily heard Christina's hard breathing on the line, and was afraid Christina would have a heart attack. "Robert can't do it," Christina said, her voice breaking, "I think he's in shock. I have to go clean it before they see it."

"Christina, stop," Lily said. "I'll do it."

"No, Lily," Christina said. "I don't want you to have to see it, I don't want you to have that in your memory."

"Don't the police do something?" Lily asked.

"I wanted to ask Robert," Christina said, "but the thought of talking about it to him, he was already in shock I think, barely speaking, just barely speaking. I didn't want to make it worse by talking about cleaning up."

So Lily had volunteered herself. She didn't want Christina's last memory of her only child to be a death scene. Christina had been a second mother to Lily and her sister Rose, really a first mother, after their own mother had disappeared.

Lily had volunteered to clean. She hadn't thought it through. She got trapped in a moment when her brain was stupid and in shock. What did she think it was going to be like? Cleaning up a flooded basement? Cleaning a child's vomit off the carpet? This was the worst thing that had ever happened to her.

But worse, worse, it was the worst thing that had ever happened to Dust.

Why didn't she take pills so they could pump her stomach? Why not cut her wrists so they could stitch her up and save her? But Dust wouldn't do it that way; Dust had always been fearless and impulsive. But she bought the lock a week ago? She hadn't been impetuous. She'd mulled it over, planned. She didn't want anyone to save her. She didn't want to take it back. She didn't want to cry and apologize. She didn't want to say, "I'm sorry, I won't do it again."

There was a cruel finality to her exit choice.

***

They were seven years old, Dust and Lil with their newly eliminated y's, blowing up a big pink balloon for a Brownie Scout project, taking turns blowing in big gulps of air until they thought they might faint. When it was fat and round, Lil tried to tie off the end, wrapping the little flappy mouthpiece in her fingers the same way her dad knotted balloons. Half the air escaped. They took turns blowing it up again. Air whistled out and they blew it up again, then, team that they were, they worked together. Dust squeezed the little rolled end shut, while Lil tied it tight with a string.

They stirred up a flour and water glue, then carefully lay papier mâché strips of newspaper all over the balloon. The first layer of soggy paper hid the pink of the balloon. They got out the poster paints, green and blue and brown. EARTH!

"This is so cool," Dust said, and squealed with delight. She was bursting with happiness, bouncing on her bed, and then jumping around her attic bedroom. Suddenly she hugged their masterpiece like it was a teddy bear. BOOM! The world exploded all over her.

Lil lost it. It had been so hard blowing up that big balloon, so hard that it hurt her chest. "You wrecked it!" Lil screamed. "You're such a dork! It wasn't even all the way dry yet. You destroyed the Earth! Your name shouldn't be Dust. It should be Dirt. I'm going home. I don't want to be Lil anymore. I'm putting my Y back on. I'm Lily, like a flower and you're dirt! I'm outta here!" She stomped across the attic bedroom, but when she got to the stairs she glanced back. Wet sticky paper and pink balloon fragments stuck all over Dust's chest. Ragged pink scraps and newspaper clung to her cheeks and splattered her red hair. Tears ran down her face.

She knew Dust would never yell at her if she did something stupid. Dust would help her clean up the mess. Lily went back to Dust.

"Okay, so well, I'm sorry. That was very mean," she said, as began picking gluey paper out of Dust's long hair.

"I'm sorry I popped the balloon," Dust said, with her bottom lip quivering and tears rolling down her cheeks.

"It's alright. It's just a stupid balloon," Lily said. She wasn't sure she meant that, but she wanted Dust to stop crying. "But I meant one thing I said, I want to be Lily. I want my Y back on."

"Okay," Dust said, "but Lily, you said my name should be dirt. Don't forget, if it wasn't for dirt, there wouldn't be any flowers."

If there wasn't Dust, could there be Lily?

***

So here she was again. Dust did something stupid and Lily was cleaning up the mess. Robert could have hired someone to clean the bathroom. Probably. Surely. But Lily knew she was the one who should do it. She was guilty. If she'd been a better friend, if she'd been paying attention, she would have known Dust was in real trouble. Lily knew Dust was unhappy. Last spring Dust told her she wanted to leave Robert, but Lily thought she meant divorce. Not this. Not leaving everyone. Not leaving her.

She should have known.

For most of their thirty-seven years, they were good friends, close friends, best friends. They had each rescued the other in so many ways, so many times. There were years when their lives took different directions and they drifted apart, like when Dust was away at the University of Michigan studying ecology and environmental science. Before her first semester at Oakland Community College began, Lily was pregnant with the twins and she and Jagger Cummings got married. There were those times of separation when Lily and Dust were on different paths, but their roads always lead back to each other.

The farmers market was open on Saturdays year-round. Dust and Lily were there, every week, even when local produce was down to cabbages and hard squash. In the winter when the farmers sold lemons and out-of-season vegetables, they labeled them with bright pink sheets of paper: *Grown in California* or *Grown in Florida.* Between market Saturdays Lily and Dust texted or talked on the phone.

Now she wondered, how could she think they were close when she had no idea that this could happen? But then, there were things she hadn't confided to Dust in the last few years. There was so much she could have said that she didn't—secrets she should have told. If she had talked about her secrets, would Dust have felt free to tell her what she was planning? Mostly their talk skidded around on surface drivel and inconsequential things—like the house remodeling. But was that only inconsequential to Lily? If she had taken her friend's concerns seriously, would she still be alive?

Lily looked at all the blood and felt more screams in her throat, but stifled them. She walked over to the sink, picked up the rosary, rinsed it off, wrapped it in a paper towel, and took it with her when she left the scene. Robert would have to hire someone to clean up.

2. FRED

Fred Williams was grateful that it was Saturday and his wife Margaret could be home with him. Her pale cheeks were blotchy red from tears. He'd seen Lily, Dust's friend, go into the house next door with a bucket.

"Sweet Jesus, Margaret," he said. "She's going to go and clean that bathroom. Oh, sweet Jesus."

He'd gotten his emotions in check, but Lily's screams coming from next door triggered his pain and his own tears were running again.

He hadn't slept all night; their bedroom was haunted by Dust. Awake in the dark, he kept replaying seeing her yesterday morning (he was probably the last person on earth to see her alive) when she'd come out onto her front porch. He'd called out hello and she waved, but abruptly turned and went back inside her house. He thought, she must be busy today, no time for a chat, and felt disappointed. It seemed like their visits had gotten so rare lately.

He'd been weeding the flowerbed that ran between their yards, something they often worked on together. Originally the strip of garden was only in his yard, but years ago, she dug out some of the lawn in her yard and they merged the beds. They had long conversations about what plants would survive in their changing climate. They made dozens of shopping trips out to Telly's Nursery. She'd come over and sit on his front porch to have a glass of iced tea, a cup of coffee, or occasionally a beer with him, or sometimes he went to her house. Several times she brought her friend Lily over to check out his garden.

Years ago, he'd taught her the best way to plant tomatoes. Pluck off the lower leaves of the plant and bury the stem in a deep hole, burying several inches of the stem of the tomato plant. New roots would grow along the buried stem making the plant stronger. She was a natural gardener, absorbing any tips he had for her like bread sopping up a dippy yolk on an over-easy egg.

How long had it been from the time he waved to her until he heard the gunshot? An hour? Two? By then he'd finished weeding the beds and was raking up oak leaves. Rain was predicted later in the day and ominous clouds darkened the sky. He'd been looking over at her house when a flash of light and the loud crack of a gunshot came from the upstairs bathroom window.

***

Fred Williams was home all the time now. He'd taken an early buy-out from Chrysler four years ago when the auto company was about to go under. He knew, as everyone did, that if you didn't take a buy-out when it was offered, within days someone would hand you a pink slip. You'd be terminated, let go, laid off, fired. He had been fifty-six years old then. Who can find a new job at fifty-six, or now at sixty, still too young for social security?

Once he got over feeling hurt and sorry for himself, he realized that he loved being home. He liked fiddling around and moving plants from one spot to another. A few times every year, he and Dust would toss their shovels into the back of his minivan and drive to the tall piles of compost that the combined cities of Southeast Oakland County made from the bagged leaves they collected from the curbs on trash day. They worked together shoveling rich black compost onto a big tarp he'd spread in the back of the van. Then, back home, they added the free municipal compost to all their flowerbeds. Because of their concern about street salts and unknown content in the municipal compost, they only used their own homemade compost in their vegetable gardens. He had a tumbler, and she had a bin until Robert got rid of it to make way for the addition.

Money was an issue, but Fred's wife Margaret still had her teaching job at the high school, and he'd made good money at his engineering job back when he was working. They had always been careful about their spending, so their savings were in good shape.

The happiest part of his day was spent talking to Dust. She was like the daughter he never had, but if he and Margaret had had a child, he would have liked one just like Dust Steward. Theirs was a typical suburban neighborhood, where unless you had children and knew your neighbors through PTA and play dates or kids events, you didn't know the people on your block. You might converse with the neighbor next door over the fence, or give a wave when you saw someone mowing his or her lawn. But to really know the folks around you, that was rare.

He knew Dust.

They may have been the only two people on the block who didn't leave every day for work or school. They were both home full time. Loneliness was swigged away with cups of coffee and talk. She'd gotten a degree in environmental studies from the University of Michigan. The past two summers they mostly talked about the weird weather and climate change. "Robert calls me a tree hugger," she told him years ago, and then laughed, "He's right. I hug trees. I kiss bark."

He often wondered how that sweet, smart girl ended up married to a conservative politician. He sometimes tried to imagine what she saw in Robert. Oh sure, he was good looking, but Fred thought she wasn't the type of person to be sold on a pretty face. And how did they even have a conversation? Maybe they were like James Carville and his wife Mary, Mary something, he couldn't remember her last name. There were times when he'd heard loud arguments coming from Dust's house or back yard. He never asked Dust about her relationship with Robert, figured it was none of his business, and mostly he didn't want to offend her, but he was always ready to listen if she ever wanted to talk about it.

In late August, Robert—handsome, dark blond, charming, with his perfect white teeth posing his political smile—stood at Fred's front door, and asked if he could put a sign on Fred's lawn, "Robert Steward for US Senate." He wanted a head start getting his name visible around the state, starting on his own block. There was a uncomfortable moment. What could Fred say? Dust was his friend, but there was no way he'd put Robert's sign on his lawn. He didn't agree with Robert's politics, and he hated Robert's new addition on the house.

The addition was enormous, much bigger than the square footage of the original house. Fred wondered how the hell he got away with it. There were limits, city restrictions—lot-to-house ratios that had obviously been waived. A bit of political maneuvering, undoubtedly. Robert had wanted the addition to be brick, but it would be next to impossible to match the old house, so the addition was wood-sided. The builder had left the brick wall that had been the back of the old house exactly as it had been. The old kitchen window and the storm door were still there. Fred thought the brick walls inside the master suite and the new kitchen and family room looked good, but he'd never say it out loud. He preferred to hate everything about the damn addition. It came right up to the setback along his side yard, ran twenty-five-feet deep into the back yard, and was two stories high, all legal according to the city.

Fred knew, even as construction began last spring, that his vegetable garden was about to have one final bleak summer. His neighbor on the sunrise side of his yard had a dense maple that blocked morning light from his garden. Now Robert's addition on the sunset side cast a solid dark shadow over most of Fred's compact, city-sized lot. His own garage sat in the only spot in his yard that might still get full sun. This was his last year for tomatoes. Without a garden, how would he spend his days?

Finally, Fred said to Robert, "Sorry, I don't like putting holes in my lawn."

That was ridiculous. In July, Fred's lawn was fried from no rain in weeks—June and July were rainless and hellishly hot, like none he could remember in all his sixty years. His lawn turned beige and looked like short, mown hay. He watered it a few times then not much, just enough that the lawn would go dormant but not die.

Hundreds of homes were destroyed by big fires in Colorado, New Mexico, and California. Michigan's upper peninsula had the third largest wildfire in a hundred and forty years. Back in March, the temperatures all over the state shot up into the high eighties, almost ninety degrees. Folks around town loved the warmth, loved being out in their shirtsleeves in early March. The farmers got the downside when the heat wave teased out the apple and cherry blossoms, but then a freeze hit and decimated the flowers. Apple farmers lost 90 percent of their crops. Cherry farmers and the folks who made cherry jams and other Michigan cherry items had to import their fruit from Washington and other states or combine the cherries with cranberries. Corn crops all over the Midwest had fried and died from drought.

Two of Fred's neighbors' lawns had turned a brackish gray with tufts of dead grass that looked like an enormous dead animal's mangy, decomposing skin. Those lawns never revived, even though it rained in late July and August. Fred's grass greened up again, but still he felt foolish pretending to Robert that he had a perfect lawn.

***

Next door, Dust's friend Lily screamed again and his internal rants were doused by the sound. He wished for a cigarette. He hadn't smoked in years, but now he wanted the taste of nicotine and the smell of smoke wafting past his nostrils.

When he heard the gunshot yesterday—yesterday, probably the saddest day of his life—he threw down his rake and ran into his house, hit 911 on the phone, and shouted at the police. Then he rushed to his desk and fumbled through a cluttered drawer until he found the key with the green plastic tag—Dust's key. She'd given him a key that she had made especially for him, asked him to check on the house whenever they were out of town, and keep it in case of an emergency. An amazing thing, he thought, she'd give an African American man the key to her house, just like that. He'd grown up in the northern Detroit suburbs—always lived in upper-middle class mixed neighborhoods, sometimes his family was the only one that made the neighborhood mixed, and sometimes there was trouble. But no white person had ever given him their house key. Well, his in-laws gave him a key, but that didn't count, they were his in-laws.

Two police cars were pulling up just as he ran out his side door. He hurried over with the precious key and handed it to one of the cops. His hands were trembling and tears ran down his cheeks. He gestured toward the second floor of the new addition. "Upstairs," he said. "Bathroom."

The cop studied Fred suspiciously, absorbed Fred's polished black skull, his white goatee, his tears glossy as varnish on his matte black cheeks, then took the key and opened the front door with his gun drawn. They told him to go back home and stay inside.

He stayed outside, hoping that she was alive. It hadn't crossed his mind that there could be a burglar or some thug in the house who shot the gun. He couldn't see her side door from his house, and yet he didn't expect some villain to run out being chased by the police. Somehow he knew—without knowing where the knowledge came from—that she was alone in the house with the gun. He stood in his yard watching, thought about going inside and calling Margaret at work, didn't move, waited. Saw a couple neighbors come out onto their porches. Waited. Then audibly sobbed when a medical examiner's van pulled up. He didn't move, stood rooted until they came out of the house with her body on a gurney.

Within minutes, TV news vans filled the block. Robert Steward was a candidate for the US Senate, a current Michigan state senator, whose wife committed suicide a month before the November election. One of the reporters spotted Fred standing there and came running over brandishing a microphone like it was a sword to stab him in the mouth or heart.

"Can you tell us what happened?"

"How does it feel to have your neighbor shoot herself?"

"Did you know the senator's wife?"

Fred just shook his head in disgust. Vultures.

As he was turning away from the interviewer, a truck pulled up. Six foot green blades of grass were painted on its sides and "BE GREEN" was written in yellow letters. The name was a misnomer. Dust called it The Poison Truck. Dust didn't want poison on her lawn. She didn't want poison and fertilizers washing down into the water table. Robert poisoned the yard anyway.

Robert Steward was an odd man who'd pick a stray hair from your shirt as he spoke to you. Of course, Robert didn't do that to Fred, since he kept his head shaved clean.

Robert was obsessive about weeds in the lawn. Would Dust kill herself over chemicals on her lawn? Or over the sprinkler system running every day? She didn't want to waste water on grass. During the drought in July, she told Fred that she was embarrassed by how green their lawn was—an oasis in a desert—compared to all the neighbors. They lived on a sand bar, pushed along by ancient glaciers. In other parts of Oakland County, the ground was thick sticky clay. Their soil was sandy; water drained right through. Most folks on the block had given up watering when they remembered their bills from the summer before, hot then, but this year was the worst ever. Robert said they could afford to water, so he'd run the sprinkler as much as he wanted. Dust said, "He thinks that just because you can afford something, you should get to do it."

Did she do it because whatever she thought or wanted was irrelevant to Robert?

The chemicals stunk from the Be Green spray. They hurt your nose and burned your eyes. The young man—without any protection from the chemicals—walked back and forth across the lawn with poison misting out in front of him. The reporters hurried back into their vans. Fred could say that this was the only time he was ever glad to see that truck.

One persistent reporter pursued him anyway, holding out his microphone. "Sir, I can see you're upset, you must have been close to Mrs. Steward. Was there any sign, any clue that you knew of, that she was going to do this?"

He moved away from the reporter and his cameraman. He wasn't going to say a word. *Hell no, I had no clue that she was going to do this,* he wanted to shout, but then he'd get trapped in a conversation, his face would be on the news. He didn't want five minutes of fame, always hated it when he watched the news and some tragedy brought out all the neighbors wanting to give the reporters their two cents of useless opinion, or carried-on with their grief in a public performance piece.

Fred ignored the reporter and took his anguish back inside his house. He was walking across his living room when there was a knock at the door. *Damn persistent reporters,* he thought, but looking back toward the door he saw a police uniform through the wavy glass side panel by his front door.

"I was just wondering," the cop said, when Fred opened the door, "you wouldn't happen to have emergency contact numbers for the Stewards, would you?"

Fred did. When Dust gave him the house key, she gave him a list with her cell phone number and Robert's, her mother's phone number and address, and her friend Lily's information, just in case there was an emergency. Fred found the list and gave it to the cop. The cop copied some of it into his notebook, said, "Thank you," and turned to leave. He stopped, turned around, and handed Dust's key to Fred. "Thanks," he said, and left.

Now he wondered how had he known, how had he been so sure that no one else was in the house with her? She'd been different this fall, quieter. Since last spring, she always wore that big pink hat when she was in the yard, even when it was cloudy. He hadn't thought about it until now. What was wrong, what was missing for the past few weeks was the pink glow that hat gave her. When she was outside, which had been rare lately, she didn't have the hat on.

***

Another scream came from the house next door. It was chilly out, so all the windows and doors were closed, and still Lily's cries pierced the panes. Margaret got up from her chair. "Maybe we should go for a drive, what do you think, Fred?"

"I'd rather stay here, if you don't mind, Margaret," he said. Maybe it would be a kindness to take his wife out of the house, but he didn't want to block the anguish coming from Dust's bathroom. Lily's pain was his, too.

Margaret brought him a cup of coffee and placed it on a coaster on the table beside him. He smiled at his wife, reached for the cup, and saw the gift that Dust had given him a week ago. He'd heard or read somewhere that people planning suicide give their things away.

3. ROBERT

Robert Steward focused on a spot of white lint on the sleeve of his navy sport coat. He picked it off with two fingers and held it—rolling it around absently—while he spoke. He was in upscale Franklin, suburban metro Detroit. He wore a navy sport coat, red tie, and gray slacks; his other option here was a suit with a vest. He'd just spent weeks glad-handing in farmland—the vote-rich, juicy red, rural acres of the state—where he wore khaki pants or jeans and plaid shirts. Play to your audience.

He was the only one standing. The heads of twenty women and six men were upturned listening in rapt attention to each word he spoke. Some were sitting on the floor with their chins tilted even higher than those on upholstered chairs or on the floral printed sofa. He was speaking at a private gathering in a supporter's home, where he'd just ended his usual speech and asked for questions, when he saw his campaign manager Chuck stand up at the back of the room. Chuck put his cellphone to his ear and walked out to the foyer.

His host—the owner of this beautiful, bountiful, sprawling home on a lush rolling acre—wanted reassurance that if elected to the US Senate, Robert wouldn't raise taxes.

"Check my voting record, Harry. As a state senator, I've been very clear. No tax increases."

The room was filled with enthusiastic clapping. Robert delighted in applause; it was audio love, audio affirmation, and audio agreement with his philosophies.

"We have been overtaxed, overregulated, the government is…"

Just then Chuck came back into the living room and raised his hand like he was a school kid wanting to tell the teacher he had to go to the lavatory. Robert stopped, midsentence and just stared at Chuck. Heads turned following Robert's gaze.

"I'm sorry, folks," Chuck said. "The senator has had a family emergency. I'm afraid he'll have to get back with you at another time."

As Robert made his way through the audience—all of them cooing condolences even though they didn't know what the bad news was—he wondered if something happened to the cruise ship his parents were on in the Mediterranean. What if something happened to his daughter Grace? At thirteen, he thought she was getting too tall to continue the gymnastics classes much longer. Could she have broken a leg on a balance beam, or worse, landed on her head or neck? Paralyzed or brain dead? He started panicking. He walked down the front sidewalk beside his campaign manager. When they were out of hearing range of the voters, he stopped and touched Chuck's elbow.

"What? What's happened?"

Chuck chewed at the inside of his cheek, then said, "It's bad, Robert. It's your wife."

His wife? He'd been home the night before, but he mainly remembered being exhausted. After weeks of campaigning, endless weeks of traveling through rural Michigan until all the diners and all the bad coffee and all the overweight waitresses and all the overweight patrons had became one big indistinguishable, over-weight blur. In the farm towns, in the quiet country communities, out to the far reaches of the state, into the thumb and into the Upper Peninsula, into all the promising red districts, he'd talked and talked and talked. He gave his speech so many times that the words flowed out of his lips like the Pledge of Allegiance.

In remote towns, the only option was sleeping in worn-down raggedy-ass motels or clustered musty cottages, where he'd lift the bed's sheets checking for bugs or mouse turds or some stranger's curly pubic hairs. Quiet country, where night sounds—crickets and an occasional heavy truck—kept him awake. When he found a chain motel, he still entered his room shooting Lysol and checking between the sheets. Robert was on the road for weeks, then only home for a few days before packing up and heading out again like Willy Loman or a Bible salesman. Only he wasn't selling Bibles, he was selling Robert Steward.

When he finally got home late Thursday night, he was so exhausted, he thought he might collapse. He yearned for sleep in a bed that he didn't have to inspect, but when he walked into his new bedroom, all he could see was sock fuzz, black sock fuzz scattered all over the new master bedroom carpet, sock fuzz and dirty clothes in heaps on the chairs and on the floor. He'd come home tired and looking forward to doing nothing but relaxing in his beautiful, clean new space. The sock fuzz made him irritable. The sock fuzz was his; he knew that. He doubted that Dust owned black socks, but he'd been gone for two weeks this time and she never vacuumed the carpet. As his daughter joked, he was a fuddy-duddy, he liked things picked up and put away. It didn't seem like a lot to want. He pulled his weight so Dust should too, especially when he came home with every cell in his body burned-out.

"What about my wife?" he asked Chuck. Chuck hesitated, his eyes scoped around uncomfortably, before he said, "She shot herself." He reached out like he expected Robert to tip or fall or collapse, but Robert stood firm, so Chuck added, "She's gone, Robert."

"Gone? What do you mean gone?" Gone. Gone? That couldn't be right.

Chuck had driven them both to the campaign event. He opened his passenger door for Robert, and Robert slid onto the seat suddenly numb and as still as a yellow-green sky before a tornado hits. Chuck drove slowly out of the residential neighborhood, then the car lurched forward and sped up, weaving through traffic. Rushing wasn't necessary. She was gone with all the terrible implications of goneness, but speeding somehow seemed appropriate.

They stopped at a red light.

With his eyes on the traffic light and as though talking to himself, Chuck said, "A wife dying from cancer can get you sympathy votes, but a wife committing suicide is sure as hell a career killer."

"What?" Robert said. "What the fuck, Chuck! What the fuck!"

Chuck flushed, embarrassed.

"Oh, man, I'm really sorry," he said. "That was an awful thing to say at a time like this. Stupid. I mean it. I'm really sorry."

Robert didn't respond. He turned his head away from Chuck and stared out the passenger window without speaking for the rest of the drive.

His house was on the corner of the block; two police cars were parked on the side street. A FOX NEWS van was parked in front of his house. NBC LOCAL 4 NEWS was in front of Fred's house. CBS 62 was across the street. ABC 7 ACTION NEWS was parked two houses down. Neighbors that were home on that Friday afternoon were out on their lawns wondering what was happening.

When he stepped out of Chuck's car, the reporters closed in. Usually he felt a thrill when he had a chance for an interview, but now the reporters were sharks smelling blood. "Senator!" "Senator!" "Senator!" shouts were coming from all directions. "Was your wife unhappy?" "How do you feel, Senator, at this awful time?" "Senator, has this changed your opinion on gun laws? Do you regret keeping guns in your house?"

"Please," he said. "Please, not now."

A cop came down the sidewalk and walked beside him back into the house. Chuck followed.

"The medical examiner has already been here," the cop said, when they were inside the foyer. "They've taken her body. Senator, don't go up there until someone has taken care of it. There's cleanup companies that take care of this sort of thing. You shouldn't see it, Sir."

"Thank you, Officer," Robert said. "What about my daughter?"

"We got a hold of your wife's mother. She's picking up your daughter at school and she's taking her to her place."

The cop told him that the guns had been confiscated; they'd be checked for ownership and licensing, and returned to Robert after the investigation. Then the cop left, and Robert was alone standing in his foyer with Chuck.

"Maybe we can salvage this, Robert. Maybe we can say she was crazy. People don't do this kinda thing if they're in their right mind. I'll see what we can come up with. Maybe it'll be okay."

Robert looked at Chuck with disgust.

"Okay?" Robert said, "My wife is dead. You think you can make that okay? Write a slogan? Put up a billboard?" His voice was deadly calm. "Go away, Chuck. Just go away."

Robert turned, walked through the old house to his new family room addition, and dropped himself in a heap on his new black leather couch. Chuck trailed behind him, and then with a presumption that rankled, went across the big new space to the open kitchen. He'd been here for meetings and he seemed assured in where he was going. There were so many cabinets, but there was only one that mattered, the cupboard where the alcohol was kept. Chuck found a bottle of scotch, opened other doors searching for a glass, then poured a shot and took it and the bottle to Robert. Robert took the glass without comment or thanks.

Chuck left the room—Robert heard him upstairs nosing around—obviously on a reconnaissance mission.

When Chuck came back into the family room, he said, "The cop was right. Don't go up there, Robert. It's really bad. Do you want me to find a cleanup crew? I could make some calls?"

Robert felt the tornado in his gut, spinning and black. He was startled by how much he hated him, how much he just wanted him the hell out of his house.

"Chuck," Robert said, pulling it together, "I need to be alone right now. Could you have someone bring my car home from the campaign office?"

He reached into his pocket for his keys, tossed them across the room, and was surprised when Chuck caught them. Why? He'd always seen Chuck as competent, helpful, maybe even a friend. Now he all he saw was an insensitive man, a jerk that could catch keys tossed across the room.

"Sure, no problem," Chuck said, and walked out of the room poking at his cell phone.

Robert didn't want to speak to anyone or hear anyone moving around inside his house. This wasn't digesting right. This thing, this terrible thing was caught in his throat, and he couldn't breathe, let alone talk.

Then Chuck was gone and Robert was alone. The street settled down to normal. News vans were off seeking other excitement and neighbors were back inside their houses. Maybe Chuck said something to the reporters?

Robert felt numb, devoid, empty. It wasn't true. Dust wouldn't do this. He stared into the cavernous space of the family room and waited for minutes to pass. Something happened in this house. Something terrible.

Thoughts bombarded him. Questions. Why? Why now? Why a month before the election? He knew he couldn't take Detroit, and most likely wouldn't win any of the Detroit Metro area either, but all that outlying land and the small towns in the state had promise. He stopped then, embarrassed that even in the privacy of his own head, he was thinking about winning the election when his wife was dead.

Winning. He remembered how he'd won her. Tactics. Play to your audience. He remembered seeing her for the first time in a crowd of students. A tall redhead, not what you'd call beautiful, but she was interesting, intriguing, and special in some way that he couldn't describe. Pursuing what he wanted—single-minded and purposeful—scrambling around people, pushing them aside, *excuse me, coming through.*

How do you win a girl? Care about what she's interested in. Pass out flyers. Carry banners. Do whatever you have to do. Just get the girl. Win.

He won the girl and now she was dead.

No. It wasn't true. Dust couldn't be dead. He just saw her this morning. He tried to picture her. Couldn't. Why couldn't he remember what she looked like four hours ago? He remembered exactly what she looked like sixteen years ago as he charged through the crowd to win her. Her red hair—shiny and healthy in the sunshine—was draped over her shoulder in a long braid. Up close: green eyes, not gray or hazel, but green. Freckles. Bottom teeth tangled and crowded. A fussy guy even in college, he was surprised at his attraction to her imperfect teeth.

This morning he got up before Grace left for school. He got up, showered, and raced out to a breakfast meeting in Bloomfield Hills. He remembered talking to people in the restaurant, but he couldn't remember talking to or even seeing his wife. Did he kiss her good-bye? He couldn't remember. He didn't remember speaking to her at all and now she was gone.

How could she do this to him? How could she do this to Grace? How could she do this, period? Why?

Grace? Grace must be devastated.

He put the glass with the scotch down on the coffee table. He'd have to go to Christina's and see Grace. Couldn't drink now. What if he got pulled over for drunk driving while running for the US Senate? Scandal. He held his head in his hands and stared at the scotch, wanting it. He waited for the doorbell to ring and his car to be delivered to him. The longer he sat there staring at the scotch, the more he congratulated himself on his self-control and the more he wished someone from the campaign office would hurry and bring his car home. No, he didn't. No car meant he didn't have to face Grace yet. He wanted to hold his child and console her. He wanted hugs back. But what would he say to her? What good could he do Grace when he didn't know what to say to himself?

Eventually the doorbell rang, and a girl from the campaign office was standing there teary-eyed holding out his keys. He couldn't remember her name, and he was usually good with names, an asset in politics. This girl, who he saw every day when he wasn't out somewhere campaigning, had a name that was blocked somewhere in his brain. He thanked her. She hugged him, then ran off, and got into Chuck's car. Chuck stuck his hand out of the car window and raised his fingers in a sullen wave.

When they were gone, it was time to go see Grace. He wanted to stall, but his mother taught him to eat the peas first. Do the hard thing first and then it's done. Get it over with and then you can have dessert. Dessert? There was no dessert involved with this. Do the hard thing. Do another hard thing. All he could see in his future were hard things. Peas. His future was all peas and no dessert.

He drove, unconscious of turning corners and stopping at lights, and when he arrived at his mother-in-law's condo, he couldn't imagine how he got there. He rang her doorbell and heard movement inside. Christina opened the door and took his hand, led him inside, and hugged him. He felt the quaking of her body, felt her pain, and stood there holding her and crying.

"Why?" she whispered into his navy jacket. "Why would she do this?"

Grace, a shorter, young version of his wife, stood a few feet away from him. He went to his daughter and hugged her, but she was a tree—rigid, and she didn't hug back. Her arms stayed at her sides, stiff and flat. She was an Irish River Dancer. Maybe her feet would move, tap dance, but her arms stayed rigid at her sides. Her motionless feet were mute too. He hugged her and patted her hair. He kissed her cheek. *I'm trying, goddamn it, I'm trying.* Was she angry with him? He didn't do it. Dust did it. But Grace was being the recent Grace. Dust would say, "She's thirteen. Thirteen's a pain in the ass." Maybe it was hormones? How could hormones turn off emotions? Exceptions: bitchy, irritable, sullen. Six months to go until she was fourteen. Did the bad attitude end at fourteen?

"Do you want to stay with your grandmother for a while?" he asked and glanced at Christina.

Grace nodded, and he was ashamed that he was relieved.

Suddenly she leaned into him and moved her head so that her ear was pressed against his chest like an old doctor without a stethoscope. She was listening to his heart, like she did when she was two and six and eight and twelve, just like she'd always listened to his heartbeat until she turned thirteen.

"It's beating," he said. "I'm here. I'm still here."

Her arms came up and she hugged him.

He didn't stay long. Didn't have the coffee that Christina offered. He had to be someplace. He had to be home on his couch. He had to leave them. He had to be by himself. He needed to not think, not talk. He wanted to be sullen and thirteen.

When he came into his house, the phone was ringing. Then his cell phone vibrated in his pocket. He turned the sound off on the house phone, and left his cell phone in the front hallway where he couldn't hear the insistent buzzing. His car was in the garage. If someone came to his door, he wasn't home, wasn't answering. He didn't want to talk to anyone. He turned on the big TV in the family room.

"Too big," Dust had said. "Too big, it'll use too much energy. And where does electricity come from? Coal. And what does burning coal do? It puts carbon in the air."

"Read the damn label," he'd replied. "It's an energy saver. Read the damn label."

He adjusted the volume until it was almost painfully loud. He couldn't hear any phones and he couldn't hear his own thoughts. If someone came to his door, they'd hear the TV blasting, but he decided he didn't care. He was hiding out. He sat on the couch and drank the scotch. He wasn't going anywhere, wasn't driving. He drank.

***

When Robert woke up it was morning—gloomy and gray—but still morning, and he was still on the couch in the family room. He must have fallen asleep, or maybe he passed out. When did he turn the TV off? He was on the leather sofa curled in on himself, trying to shrink into the smallest nonentity he could become, and not spill the glass he'd just filled with more scotch. He vaguely remembered hearing knocking at his front door, then Lily was standing in front of him saying something about using the key Dust gave her, saying she was afraid he was in trouble, turning the TV off, *oh yeah, Lily turned the TV off*, then she said she'd take care of the bathroom. Now he heard her upstairs wailing and screaming. He didn't want to hear her, but if he put his fingers in his ears he'd have to put the scotch down. He stared blankly at the bottle of expensive scotch from his great-uncle

Rob's stash. He must have been staring for a long time. The screaming had stopped, and Lily was standing in front of him.

"I'm sorry, Robert. I can't do it," she said.

Do what? He was confused. But then he realized why he heard her screaming and felt something breaking apart inside his chest. Suddenly he was blubbering and incoherent. He heard himself saying words that even he didn't understand. He was drunk. Half the bottle of scotch was gone. He hadn't eaten since breakfast on Friday. What day was it?

"It's Saturday," Lily said.

Had she read his mind or had he said that out loud? She sat down beside him on the couch and held him. His crying set her off again and they held each other.

Lily pulled away from him and sat upright. She said, "You need to eat something," and headed back across the room to the kitchen. He watched her. She didn't know where anything was in the new space, so she spent some time opening and shutting cupboard doors until she found the coffee and filters. She made a pot of coffee and fixed him a peanut butter and jelly sandwich, put it on a plate, and delivered it to him.

"I can't eat," he said, then picked up the sandwich and ate it. He was hungry now, and wanted another sandwich, but felt guilty for being able to eat.

"Did you talk to Grace?" she said. "You need to go over there and hug your girl. She needs you to hug her, Robert. Her mother's dead, she needs to see you and know you're okay. My best friend is dead. I'd like to have my daddy hug me right now."

"Lily," he said, when he could get a word in. "I went over last night. Grace is going to stay with Christina for a few days."

She seemed surprised.

"Oh," she said. "Well, good."

She got them both coffee and made him another sandwich. Did she know he was still hungry? Maybe she was trying to counteract the whiskey, which she removed from the table and returned to the kitchen. She stood motionless, confused, opened several doors, and then just stuck the whiskey in one of the many empty cupboards. He made a note in his mind, third door from the sink—scotch. He watched her pick up a wad of paper towel on the kitchen counter. She brought it to him.

"She had this in the bathroom with her," she said, speaking softly. "Would it be okay if I took it to Christina? It would mean a lot to her."

Robert didn't speak, he just stared at the pink rosary nestled in the paper towel and nodded.

4. LILY

Everything in Lily's visual path was overlaid with the image of Dust's blood. The strawberry jelly on the sandwiches she made for Robert screamed red under the dull knife, and she felt queasy. She made him coffee and sandwiches—it was a duty she could perform—but she couldn't clean the bathroom. No one who loved Dust should see it. Robert had people, connections. There would be professionals for whom it would be just another mess of frail humanity to mop up.

She started to tell Robert he'd need to hire someone. Stopped. She wanted him to see it, wanted him to suffer. Lily had never been a fan of Robert's; she wasn't convinced that his convictions were sincere. He was too pretty, too slick, too agile of tongue for her taste. She knew the story of Dust and Robert's first meeting, knew how he had deceived Dust to get her interested in him. Lily didn't trust him. He was a politician who campaigned with impressions and promises, but once he had the prized position or possession, he changed the rules to fit his real agenda.

The stench of Robert's grief was doused in whiskey, a flambé ready to ignite. A part of Lily wanted to search for a match. How much blame should or could she put on Robert? Her brain flipped through a Rolodex of conversations with Dust as she searched for answers. Was Dust and Robert's marriage like most couples, going from boredom to passion, to anger then tenderness, to selfishness and compromise? Or had Robert sucked the soul right out of her best friend?

She had made him coffee and sandwiches, put her arms around him and felt his shuddering anguish. It was all about loss, their loss—her best friend, his wife. And yes, somewhere inside him she knew he was grieving over the damage to his campaign for the US Senate. And she hated him.

5. CHRISTINA

Christina Jones was milling around her condo dusting knickknacks, bric-a-brac, gewgaws, and tchotchkes. Each objet d'art held meaning for her. There was a clay nativity scene handmade by Dusty, her only child, in grade school. When other kids made their parents clay bowls, Dusty made Christina a lumpy manger with a baby Jesus. Cherished things, more emotionally precious than of any monetary value. There were things that had been in Christina's home when she was a child: ancient crucifixes hung in every room of the condo; a faded print of *The Last Supper* by Da Vinci; a cracked saucer where her father had rested his pipe; Hummel figurines that her mother (who everyone, including Christina, called Grandma Jeanie) had collected. There was a porcelain plate with a line drawing of Christ that her husband, Jay Jones, had given her on their first anniversary, and a wooden crèche from another anniversary, she couldn't recall which one.

And photos—photos everywhere, photos in interesting frames on the bookshelves, photos hung in a group on the wall, a photo of her baby Dusty propped up with pillows so she wouldn't tip over, and a photo of her first day of school. There was Dusty missing her two front teeth, Dusty sitting up in an apple tree, Dusty in a pumpkin patch, Dusty in a cap and gown—one from high school, another from college, and two photos from her wedding. She had a shelf devoted to pictures of her granddaughter Grace in all those precious stages of childhood.

There was a professional photo of Jay Jones inside a big wave on his surfboard. There had been scads of pictures of him in surfing magazines. He was almost famous, almost. Jay would be home, but then Christina would see this look on his face—his eyes far away, out to sea—then he'd be gone. He could have been a career navy officer with his heart longing for deep water. But no, Jay Jones was a blond beach bum, a thrill seeker who craved crashing waves. He'd come home for a while, then leave because big waves and surfing competitions were tugging at his heart in California. Home—where the Detroit River and inland lakes were disappointingly calm compared to the ocean—couldn't hold him. Gone. Maybe California girls in bikinis were calling his name too. The only way Christina's husband was ever permanently home was in a photo—Jay Jones riding a surfboard inside a big wave—on Christina's living room wall.

Once there was a stretch of three years when he called but never came home. Christina ached for Dusty, who was so young she'd hold the phone receiver in both hands, saying sweetly, *I love you, Dad. Come home soon.* Dusty was a big part of why Christina never divorced Jay Jones.

Christina continued dusting. There were the treasures she'd collected for herself: a glass box with a stained-glass butterfly on the lid; a set of nesting boxes made of straw in the shape of a butterfly; and other things she'd kept simply because she liked them. She knew it was too much. She knew it looked like she'd set up a boutique of religious and family doodads. She knew it especially on the days when she had to dust it all.

She stopped dusting, checked around the room, and caught her own reflection in a long mirror. Too much. Too many knickknacks. Too much Christina. She moved closer to the long mirror that had trapped her body. She was fat. She was determined to go on a diet every time she saw her reflection, every store window or mirror inspired a resolution. She should move this mirror into the kitchen and put it right in front of the refrigerator door. She turned away from the mirror and looked back around the living room and wondered how she'd gotten so out of control. She sighed and went back to dusting, feeling heavy, burdened by her compulsions.

An antique mahogany table with inset birds-eye maple and deeply carved legs sat in front of her living room window. It was a fussy demanding table that required her to squat down or bend uncomfortably to dust the ornate legs. As she struggled to get herself upright again, she glanced out her front window. A police car was coming slowly up the road into the condo complex.

She watched it approach. She watched it stop right in front of her place. She watched it. There was no parking on her side of the street. There were signs—NO PARKING—but he stopped right there in front of her condo and turned off the car's engine.

What did I do, she wondered? Was I speeding? Are my taillights out? But that was crazy thinking, she'd been home all day. She was a pediatric nurse and it was her day off. How could it be something about her driving? Frozen in front of her living room window, she watched the policeman open his car door. Maybe he's going to the neighbor's? Maybe it didn't have anything to do with her? But then, not looking irritated or hostile or aggressive, he was walking up her sidewalk. He seemed sad, humble, worried. He walked with dread.

DUSTY. She knew then that it was Dusty he was coming about. Christina's brain took a leap back in time. Twenty years. Twenty-five. Thirty. Had Dusty fallen off a roof, or tried dangling from a bridge just to see if she could do it? Dusty. She'd been afraid for Dusty since her baby girl was barely walking. Dusty, her silly, sweet little one, already walking at nine months old, fell off the sofa and laughed, then tried to climb back up to do it again. Shy Dusty hiding behind Christina's legs with her thumb in her mouth when strangers were around. She knew that the officer knocking at her door was here about Dusty.

He was knocking softly. She couldn't move. When he suddenly rang the doorbell, it startled her as if she'd been asleep and an alarm went off. She opened the door.

"Are you Christina Jones?" he asked, and she nodded. "Dusty Steward's mother?"

She nodded.

"May I come in? I have some bad news."

She nodded again and pushed the screen door opened.

He hadn't told her yet, this tender young cop on his terrible mission, but she knew. Her heart slid out of her body and rolled across the floor, it rushed under the sofa collecting dust bunnies and fuzz, and it hid there. This boy, probably not even thirty, had come to tell a mother something terrible. She wanted to help him—he was some mother's baby—standing there looking miserable and sad. She wanted to make it easy for him, or maybe she just didn't want to hear anything out loud.

"Come in the kitchen," she said. "I'll fix us coffee."

"Mrs. Jones," he said firmly, "I need to tell you…"

She held up her hand and slowly shook her head, stopping him before he said more. "Come in the kitchen, please, and sit with me and have coffee."

Was she making it harder on him? She didn't want to do that, but she didn't want to know what he wanted to tell her, not just yet. She turned and walked to the kitchen and he followed. She pointed at a chair and he sat. There was coffee in the pot left from breakfast, enough for two cups, but she'd make him a fresh pot. She rinsed the carafe in the sink and filled it with clean water. She got the coffee can and a filter from the cupboard. She glanced at him. He was a grown-up, a cop, not a boy. His job was dealing with the worst things that happened to people. Was he hardened to it all? Was telling parents terrible things the worst of what he had to do? She was drawing it out, and that meant he had to deal with his mission longer, but she couldn't bear for him to tell her just yet.

"Would you rather a Pepsi?" she asked.

"Coffee'd be good, Ma'am," he said. He was giving in. He would sit with her. Maybe he was due for a coffee break anyway? Maybe they didn't give him a timeframe for telling a parent something terrible. Maybe they'd let him sit a minute. He wasn't rushing her, so she knew. He wasn't telling her she should hurry to the hospital, so she knew her daughter was dead. She'd lost babies, so many she stopped counting. Rhythm method babies, conceived when Jay Jones came home from California to be her husband for two weeks, or sometimes a month, before he got restless and headed back to Malibu and the Pacific surf to ride waves and work with roofing crews. She had babies who died before they were formed, babies who weren't strong enough to hold on inside her body until they could be born whole and pink and gooey. Dusty was the only one who made it. She had her precious Dusty and then she had birth control pills. Why have more babies or lose more babies when she was married to a man who wasn't a husband or a father? Dusty was strong and daring and wild. She made it. She was born. She lived.

Dusty, her sweet, thoughtful daughter, had called Thursday afternoon while Christina was at work. She said, "Mom, I know you're busy. I just wanted to tell you that I love you." Christina was so touched, her daughter had just called out of the blue to say she loved her. She was at work and couldn't help bragging. No, not bragging, it was sharing, when she told one of the other nurses that her daughter had called just to say she loved her.

Christina took mugs and small plates from her cupboard. She had a package of cookies that she opened. She shook her head, as though it were a rug full of dust she was shaking out the back door. She shouldn't bring cookies into her house since there was only one eater. But now there was the policeman, so she could be glad for the sweets. She arranged a few on each of the two plates.

"Do you like cream and sugar?"

"Black is fine, Ma'am," he said, with a gentle patience.

She liked cream. She shouldn't have cream. The coffee was brewing, dripping with a hiss and dribble sound into the carafe. She stood staring at the pot. If she sat down, he'd say it. He'd tell her.

She heard herself panting, breathing louder than the coffee's dripping.

He pushed his chair back quickly and was standing next to her. He put his hand on her shoulder, led her to a chair and said, "Sit, please."

She sat. A pain swirled through her whole body hurting her feet and knees and hips and waist and chest and neck and the top of her head. Her hair ached. He was on one knee in front of her, as if to propose, holding her wrist and counting. Taking her pulse. Then he nodded to himself. She was fine.

He was not just a policeman. He may have signed up to catch the bad guys. But mostly, especially just now, he was a public servant. He was taking care of her. If Dusty weren't married to a state senator, would they have sent this young man to console and inform her mother? She thought not.

"Are you ready to hear this?" he asked, still on one knee in front of her.

She shook her head, but then she said, "Go ahead. Yes, tell me."

"There's no easy way to say this, Ma'am," he said, and now he was stalling. He took a deep breath and went on, "Your daughter shot herself."

"Shot?" she asked, and shook her head, confused. "Shot? That can't be." She heard herself mumbling, as if talking to herself, as if she was alone, "Dusty hated guns. She told Robert she didn't want guns in the house. She was afraid that Grace might find them and get hurt."

"I'm sorry, Ma'am."

"It was an accident," she said. "I always expected her to have a terrible accident. She was a climber, you know. She used to climb onto the garage roof, and just sit up there, smiling down at me. She went mountain climbing in the Rockies when she was still in college. She went skydiving. She bungee jumped. She did that line thing where you're high above the trees," she hesitated searching for a word, "Zipper lining? No, zip lining."

"No, Ma'am, It wasn't an accident. I'm sorry to tell you it was..." he hesitated, "intentional."

She was quiet then. She sat there on the chair where he'd put her and looked at her hands. The public servant boy cop stood up and turned to the coffee pot. He poured coffee into one of the cups she'd set out and placed it in front of her. Maybe he was thinking of his own mother, thinking that if he was ever shot, he would hope that someone would take a moment and sit with her. He poured himself a cup, seemed to savor its smell. He sat down across from her. Waited.

He gave her time to digest this news and gather her questions. They sat silent as seconds and then minutes passed by, idly sipping coffee as though nothing else was happening in the world.

"Alright," she said, fortified. "You can tell me what happened."

He told her what he was trained to tell her, but more, what he told her was what she guessed he'd want his own mother to know. As gently as he could, he told her about the locked bathroom door and all the rest. He laid it out before her like a road map on the table for her grief to follow.

"Are you sure she's gone?" she asked him, and he nodded. "How could she be gone? It wasn't an accident? It was always going to be some accident."

There was a tissue box on the table. She pulled out several and squeezed them in her hands until her knuckles turned white. Dusty called her the day before. When she called and said I love you, she was telling Christina good-bye.

The policeman told her that he'd gotten her name and address from Dusty's neighbor.

"Oh, Fred," she said. It was comforting to hold onto a name she knew. She was happy to trade the visual of her daughter's death for Fred's kind face and smooth bald head. "Dusty likes Fred. He's a good friend to her." She looked distressed. "Was, was a good friend."

The cop sipped his coffee and kept watching her, ready to react at any moment.

She looked away from him. "Why did she do it?" she asked, throwing words at the wall that she knew he couldn't answer. "Why would she do this? Was there a note?"

"No, Maam. No note that we could find," the cop said. "I'm sorry."

No note. No answers. Questions. No words. There was nothing to help her understand why. Why?

The last time she saw Dusty, she was complaining about her weight. "I'm as round as a Buddha," she said. "All I want to do is shovel food into my mouth."

"You're tall, dear," Christina had told her, "you don't look an ounce over what you should be. Women are supposed to have a belly, we're supposed to be soft, rounded." Christina patted her own stomach. "You're beautiful. Women are supposed to have bellies, we have babies."

Christina was herself sixty pounds overweight. She didn't like the weight. Hated it, to be blunt. The weight made everything harder. It was hard getting up from a chair. A walk through the grocery store left her breathless. Her knees ached and her feet hurt.

She'd put on weight after Jay Jones came home from Malibu for good. He was her husband, so she welcomed him back and pretended to be happy about it. She ate cookies and smiled. Dusty was so happy. Her dad was there when she graduated from college. Dusty's dad, father of the bride, walked her down the aisle. At last she had her dad home for good and always. Good? It wasn't much good and it was a very short always.

The young cop said, "We notified Senator Steward's campaign people. They're contacting him. Mr. Williams, the neighbor, said there's a daughter in middle school?"

"Yes, Grace," she said. Suddenly her tissue-filled hands flew up and covered her face. "Oh, Grace! Oh my God. Grace."

"Ma'am, we're concerned that the girl will arrive home and find the situation. Is there someone you could call? Are you up to getting her? It would be better if someone she's close to could tell her."

She nodded. Then, so hushed that the cop would know she wasn't speaking to him, more like whispering to the space between molecules of quiet in the room, she asked, "How could she do this to Grace?"

6. GRACE

Grace Steward had just pushed out of the heavy front doors of her middle school when she saw Christina's car. Her grandmother stood at the curb, peering around at kids and looking frantic.

"Gotta go. I'll text you later," she called out as she dashed off.

One night a few weeks ago, she'd been sitting in the corner of the living room on the squishy chair, her favorite place in their house. When the louvered French doors into the room were opened, which they always were, they hid the squishy chair from the view of anyone in the hallway. The bookcase wall was on the other side of the chair, setting her up in her own little private cocoon. She had her knees up and a large book propped up so she could text her friends without her mother knowing. Her mother would think she was studying. But snap! Her mother knew she was texting; the glow from her phone was lighting up her face. "Surreptitious Texting," her mother called it, and made her look up *surreptitious*. She liked the mouth feel of the word. It sounded interesting, better than all the other synonyms: sneaky texting, secretive texting, or clandestine texting, and way better than underhanded texting. What was the point of texting if it wasn't surreptitious? She was a surreptitious texter and proud of it.

She hurried down the school steps before her friend noticed that her grandmother looked like an embarrassing mess. Her grandmother had picked her up from school before, but she usually looked at least somewhat not embarrassing.

Grace had a big fight with her mother that morning. She didn't see the point of Bitchly making such a big deal about how long it took her to get dressed. She wanted to compose the perfect outfit. She was in the eighth grade, by now she should get to select her own clothes, for God's sake. So what if she didn't have time for breakfast?

She had some cool colored ribbons she wanted to braid into her hair. One good thing, she got her mother's red hair. She liked it. It made her special. She wore a touch of lipstick, not too bright or it would draw too much attention to her mouth and the braces, although when she was with friends who also had braces she was sort of proud of them. They were almost like an accessory that sparkled.

Today she'd decided she'd quit gymnastics and she'd sign up for basketball. That should make Bitchly Mother happy. Bitchly was always worried about her falling off the balance bars and becoming a paraplegic or just stupid from a squished brain. She knew that her mother had climbed trees and the garage roof when she was a kid. So how come she could do those things herself, but then she'd be crazy worried when Grace did a flip on the balance beam? She didn't make any sense.

When she got to her grandmother, Christina grabbed her and mashed her in a hug so tight that Grace could barely breathe. Right there on the sidewalk in front of the whole school! Boys were walking by saying rude remarks. OMG!

"Please. Please. Can we go?" Grace begged. People were staring at them.

Christina released her and opened the car's back door.

"Grandma, I'm tall enough, remember. I can sit in the front now." Grace had been riding in the front seat for at least a month. Her grandmother was losing it. Maybe she was getting Alzheimer's or something?

Christina shut the back door, opened the passenger door, then went around the car. When she got into the driver's seat she just sat there with her eyes shut. She was trembling. Something was wrong with her.

"Grandma, are you sick?" Grace patted Christina's shoulder. "Are you okay? Grandma? Grandma? What's going on?"

Christina opened her eyes, did some deep breaths, and turned on the car. Grace quickly buckled her seat belt and said, "Buckle up, Grandma."

Grace was surprised that they weren't headed toward her house, but Grandma had her lips pinched together and wasn't talking. She decided it was safer to let her concentrate on driving, so she didn't ask where they were going. It wasn't long before she realized that they were going over the river and through the woods—not really, but Grace knew this was the way to Grandma's condo.

After Christina parked the car, they went inside without speaking. Grace felt very afraid. Something was definitely wrong.

Inside the condo, she was smothered in another hug, then Christina released her and told her to come sit next to her on the couch. She did as she was told.

"I have some terrible news," Grandma started and then stopped. She just sat there not saying anything.

"Please, please, just spill it. You're scaring me!" Grace felt tears filling up her eyes; she was glad she hadn't snuck on any mascara at school. "What's happened? What's happened? Who died?"

Christina looked startled at the question and said, "Oh, Grace, I don't want to have to tell you this. I don't. It's too terrible. Your mother. Your mother," Christina's voice trailed off and tears ran down her cheeks.

"What?"

"I'm so sorry, Grace, your mother's gone."

"Gone? Where did she go?" She watched Grandma's mouth drop, her body sag, *gone* wasn't the right word. "You mean dead?"

Christina nodded. Grace felt punched, like someone had socked her hard in the stomach. That couldn't be right. "What? Was she in an accident?"

"No," Christina's voice became so quiet, Grace could barely hear her. "Your mother, your, your...she committed suicide."

"No, she didn't," Grace said softly and shook her head. Then louder, "No, she didn't." Then she was shouting, "No, she did not do that." She shot up from the couch, ran to the bathroom, and slammed the door shut. She was confused; she didn't know what to do. Her mother wouldn't do that, but Grandma was acting like it was real.

Grandma's bathroom had an old-fashioned mirror that was the door of a cabinet where she kept her pills and lipstick. The old part of Grace's own house had a mirror in the bathroom just like this. She opened the cabinet door. One at a time, she took out the pill bottles and carefully read the labels, sounding out the words in her mind. Metoprolol succ(toprol)er. Lisinopril. Atorvastatin. Omeprazole. Levothyroxine. *Damn, Grandma must be in bad shape, so many pills.* She wasn't sure what any of it was for. Her mother killed herself. She wouldn't believe it. Couldn't. *Did she take pills?* Grace put all the pill bottles back. She shut the cabinet and looked in the mirror.

There was her mother looking back at her, her mother when she was thirteen, like in the pictures Grandma had on the living room bookshelves. She was her mother. If her mother was dead, then she was dead too. *You are not dead, Mom,* she told her mother. She smiled at her young mother just to reassure her. The braces flashed and she was Grace. Her mother never had braces. Her mother didn't have perfect teeth like she would eventually have.

There was a soft knock on the door. The knob turned and her grandmother was standing in the doorway.

"Grace, are you okay?"

"No," Grace said, and pointed at the mirror. "She's in the mirror, Grandma."

Christina came up beside Grace and gazed into the mirror.

"She's very beautiful, isn't she," Christina said.

"I suppose."

"Anytime you miss her, you can look in the mirror and you'll have some of her back. I have some of her every time I see you."

Christina led her to the kitchen table. They were still standing when Grace said in barely a whisper, "I did it, Grandma. It's my fault she killed herself."

"Your fault?" Christina wrapped her arm around Grace and pulled her closer. "It's not your fault, Grace."

"Yes, it is. I said bad things to her this morning. I called her bad names."

No matter what anyone said, Grace knew she'd killed her mother. This morning she'd created a new word, the meanest word she could think up and shot her mother with it. Fucking-bitchwhorecunt. She hated the "c" word, as she figured all females did, and yet she was so mad, she threw the cunt bomb at her mother. She'd sworn before, but never directly at her mom. Well, no, take that back, there was another time when she'd said it, but she said it under her breath as she was walking away from her. This morning she'd screamed it, and over what? Her mother was nagging at her for taking too long getting ready for school. This time she knew she heard her. She killed her. She hurt her mother so bad that she killed herself.

Christina pressed her hands on Grace's cheeks and kissed her on the nose. "Grace, you're thirteen," she said. "It's your job to be obnoxious. This is when you start separating from your mom and dad." Grandma gulped then.

They both got stopped up on the *separating from your mom* part. Christina took a breath, and said. "I'll tell you a secret. Your mother called me some bad names when she was your age."

"What ones," Grace asked, looking hopeful.

"Oh, Grace. Words so terrible they're banned on cable TV. They're banned on the premium channels where you can say just about anything."

"Why did she do it?"

"Oh, I don't remember. That was so long ago."

"No, Grandma, why did she kill herself?"

Her grandmother just shook her head and tears ran down her cheeks.

7. ROSE

When Rose Abbott Martinez got off the phone with her sister Lily on Friday night, she sat on a chair looking at nothing. How could this be? When she was growing up, Dust was her next door neighbor but she felt like a big sister to Rose, just as much an older sister to her as Lily was. Dust shot herself? How could that be possible?

Rose always thought that Dust and Lily balanced each other. In spite of not being related in any way, they were like twins from a split egg. Dust was the good twin, brutally shy around people she didn't know, and she was kind. The good twin was always generous and sweet to Rose. The other half of the monozygotic set was outgoing, irascible and scared of her own shadow. That one was her sister Lily. She remembered some mean kids calling her older sister a Lily Livered Coward.

Lily was what Rose figured most older sisters were: protective and loving one minute, and put upon and impatient the next. It was easy to look at Dust and Lily objectively when they were all grown, but when she was little, she was jealous of them. There were no little girls her age on their block. No little boys either. Everyone was either older or a baby. There was no one for Rose, so she struggled on her short legs to catch up with the big girls. They were three years older than Rose, and full grown Lily and Dust were both three inches taller than her. When Rose was little, they called her Bud or Rose Bud like she wasn't a fully opened Rose yet. Often when Lily didn't want Rose to play with them, it was Dust who thought of a way to include her: *let's be a family, Rose will be our little girl; let's play school and Rose can be our student.*

Rose found it hard to think about Dust without also thinking about Lily. The house they grew up in had two small bedrooms at the back of the main floor. She and Lily shared one and their parents had the other. The walls were thin and when she couldn't sleep, she'd listen to her father's snores. Before her mother vanished, she could hear every word of argument or intimacy between their parents.

Their house was the mirror image of Dust and Christina's house next door.

When Dust was around seven, her grandfather passed away and Christina's mother came to live with them. Grandma Jeanie had bad knees and it hurt her to climb stairs, so Dust was moved to the attic room. Dust's attic bedroom was already finished when Christina bought the house. It was plastered and had molding around the windows. Christina took the three girls to the paint store, where, in spite of the salesperson giving them a dirty look, they gathered every paint chip color they liked, which was most of the colors on the display rack. Then, back at home, they analyzed each color. Dust got final pick. The next day they went back to the store and bought the paint. Christina let the girls, even Rose, who was probably around four then, help her paint Dust's new room aqua.

After Dust got the attic bedroom at her house, Lily had whined and cried and begged for the attic bedroom in their house, so their dad had worked weekends putting in insulation and paneling. When Rose was five and Lily was eight, Lily got to move out of their tiny bedroom up to the attic room. Rose was jealous. She should've gotten to move up to that sloped-ceilinged cave of a room, too. Lily's new room was only partially paneled in a fake knotty pine; it never did get any trim around the windows. They couldn't keep up with the Jones. She remembered Lily allowing her to come upstairs to wave at Dust, who waved back from her bedroom window next door.

How could Dust be gone? All night, Rose lay in bed, numb with disbelief. Why would Dust commit suicide?

Saturday morning she woke up and smelled the coffee. Carlos was already up. He was pacing the kitchen when she came downstairs in her scrubs. Her next reaction was fury. Damn it, Carlos! Damn it! She wanted to scream at him, fly at him, beat him with her fists.

Carlos did it. It was his fault. Dust was dead and it was Carlos's fault. He had humiliated her.

***

In July, Robert threw a big party for Dust's thirty-seventh birthday, but Rose knew as she watched Robert that it was another campaign party for him. There were people there that Rose didn't know, someone whispered *donors*. It was Dust's birthday party and it appeared that she'd never met the donors before either. Robert never missed a chance to sell himself and maybe he wanted to show off the grand new addition-in-progress? It wasn't finished so he could appear humble, like some bare-chested buff guy saying, *oh, please excuse me, I'll put my shirt back on in a minute*. Meanwhile, you get to admire the abs, the washboard. The bare bones of Robert's addition were spectacular. Huge. Your imagination could go crazy with ideas of how this space would look finished.

The floor in the new space was just plywood underlayment then, but that was good for a party, spills wouldn't matter. The walls had drywall, but the taping hadn't been done. The old brick wall of the back of the original house was a nice touch. It gave the new room the feel of an old loft space done up contemporary like one you might see in a decorating magazine.

The island at the kitchen end of the open space hadn't been installed yet. Rose overheard Robert telling someone that the granite for the island had a flaw and was being replaced. Doors on sawhorses became a long buffet table topped with red and white checked tablecloths. It was loaded with chicken and ribs, cold spaghetti with salsa, heaps of fresh fruit and vegetables, cheeses, and a huge mound of shrimp. Robert had hired a chef to prepare the food. Since it was Dust's birthday she shouldn't have to cook. The chef and his assistant went in and out of the sliding glass doors to the deck, dealing with the grill. A waitress came around with trays filled with interesting hors d'oeuvres, while music pulsed in the background.

It was supposed to be a barbecue. There were tables with umbrellas out on the new deck, but no one wanted to be outside in the hundred and five degree heat. Everyone congregated in the new family room and kitchen or roamed through the old house. Rose roamed. She went upstairs and glanced in at the future new master suite. Like the kitchen/family room, it also was drywalled and not yet taped. A couple of guests she didn't know were surveying the space and remarked on the size.

Rose came back downstairs and found Grace texting, curled up on a chair in the living room. When she said hi, Grace made a grunt sound that basically meant, *I heard you, I know you're there, now go away.* Rose left Grace and headed back to the dining room. It was still just like it had always been, heavy, old oak furniture that Dust had found at a garage sale, except now the dining room table didn't have a jigsaw puzzle in progress. Rose wondered if Robert had dismantled a puzzle before the party. Dust loved puzzles: boxes that came apart, crossword puzzles, Rubik's cubes, and jigsaw puzzles. Dust told Rose that one of her favorite things was the *New York Times* crossword puzzle. She'd get up before everyone else, make coffee, then run out to the front sidewalk and pick up the blue plastic bag with the *Times*. She'd sit in the quiet old kitchen considering words until everyone got up. Dust's favorite puzzling spot was gone now that the kitchen had become a mudroom. The old kitchen table and three chairs had been replaced with closets for coats and boots.

The dining room had a bay window where Dust kept a collection of natural things, a branch with pinecones from a tree in California, chipped hunks of rock she'd gathered on a trip to Utah, the bleached skull of a beaver that she bought from an Arapaho in Colorado.

When Rose came into the dining room, Fred Williams and his wife Margaret were looking out the bay window admiring Fred's garden next door. Rose wondered if they were wishing they were home instead of at this party. She chatted with them for a while and suggested they come out to the addition with her and get some food.

With the Williamses tagging along behind her, she entered the big new space and saw her husband flirting with Dust. Carlos with his Latin lover hips arcing and swaying in and out to the music, his wide male shoulders leaning in on Dust; the whole stance that she knew well and never found amusing, but it was especially disturbing when it was Dust he was hitting on. Rose watched Carlos take his index finger and brush Dust's bangs aside. He gazed at her for a moment, whispered something, and smiled before he took his hand away from her face.

Carlos wasn't especially good looking. His skin had some bad pockmarks left over from his adolescence that were clustered across his left cheek like they'd been applied with a makeup brush. He was barely as tall as Lily or Dust. But Carlos had charisma. He was hot, and when he smiled, a deep dimple appeared on his right cheek.

She watched him helping Dust arrange bowls of fruit and tortilla chips. Robert was nearby arguing politics with someone. Many people were there—neighbors, family, friends, donors—plenty of people to talk to, but damn Carlos was dogging Dust, wafting his pheromones in her direction, and flashing that damn dimple over and over.

As he was heading toward the bathroom, Rose moved in on him, pulled him aside, and said, "Cool it, Buddy."

He held up his hands with his palms open facing the ceiling, as if to show her they were empty, like a boy showing his mom that he hadn't taken a cookie. He shrugged, then said, "What? What?"

"She's vulnerable. You're leading her on. What if she thinks you're serious?"

"Dust? You're talking about Dust? She's not vulnerable," he said. "She's smart, and I am not flirting. We've just been talking, Rosie. Gimme a break already."

"And so what deep things were you talking about? How much you like her perfume, that yellow ribbon braided into her hair?"

"Rosie, are you being jealous?"

He wrapped his arm around her waist and pulled her close to him, stuck out his bottom lip and blew upward, ruffling his wife's bangs.

"We were talking about trees," he said. "The big redwoods. Did you know some of those trees in California are more than two thousand years old? Three hundred and eighty feet tall, that'd be thirty-eight stories. When one of those giant trees came down in a storm, the trunk on its side was more than two stories high. Two stories high laying on its side, Rosie. Just picture that. People came and left bouquets for that tree. It had been alive since before Christ."

"So now you're interested in trees? Give me a break, Carlos."

"Listen, Rose, I get the impression that no one gives her a chance to talk about things she cares about. So, yeah, I'm interested in trees." He turned and walked away. The next time she saw him, he was arguing with Robert about fracking for gas in Michigan.

At nine o'clock, the power went out. No lights. No AC. They brought out candles but within fifteen minutes it was so stifling, it was hard to breathe. Everyone went home.

***

Rose blamed Carlos for Dust's suicide. He was a damn flirt. He told her a couple of weeks ago that Dust had called him at the clinic and wanted to meet him for lunch. He told Rose that he thought she just wanted to talk. He bowed out, said he had too many pimples and had to work through lunch every day. That was true. His dermatology practice was swamped; patients were waiting an hour past appointment times just to get in to see him. He grabbed a sandwich he packed at home and ate lunch at his desk for a quick ten minutes.

Now he was roaming around their house shaking his head and mumbling, "Oh God. Oh God."

He had humiliated Dust, Rose thought. Dust thought he was interested. She probably felt ashamed for calling and asking him to lunch. Rose didn't fault Dust. Carlos affected women like that. She knew that, because she was one of them.

"I'm going to work," she told him.

She didn't kiss him good-bye like she did every day of the three years they'd been married. This weekend she was working the Saturday and Sunday afternoon shifts at the nursing home. She saw dead people all the time, but they were old, and for the most part she assumed that they'd lived good lives.

Dust was way too young to die.

Rose would go in early and sit with Grandma Jeannie, Dust's ninety-year-old grandmother. Jeanie didn't remember her or anyone else, but she was sweet and Rose knew that she'd feel comforted being with her. When she was a little girl—when Dust and Lily left her behind, and her own mother was sleeping on the couch or in her bed in the daytime—Grandma Jeanie would say, "Now, Rose, don't you worry about those big girls running off. We'll have a lovely tea party, just the two of us." And later when Rose and Lily's mother disappeared, it was Grandma Jeanie that held Rose on her lap and kissed her cheeks and told her everything would be okay.

Rose had followed Christina into nursing. Christina's interest was in little children and babies and Rose's was in geriatrics. They choose opposite ends of the spectrum of life. She considered herself lucky. She was an insecure person. She was aware of her neediness, aware of her tendency to think that everyone who loved her loved someone else more. Her mother had ignored her, her father was overworked and stressed out all the time, and Lily had Dust. If she hadn't had Grandma Jeanie in her life, who would she be?

Just when Rose finished her nursing degree, Grandma Jeanie became lost and confused—dementia stealing parts of her brain. When Rose got her first job at Sunset Village, she found a place there for her neighbor who had always been like a grandmother to her. She could switch positions and watch over and protect the woman who had always protected and comforted her.

8. CARLOS

Carlos Martinez, DO, was concerned last winter, February to be specific, when Dust came into his clinic for a checkup. Her skin was pale, almost translucent, typical for a natural redhead. He remembered swearing when he saw her. He didn't normally rant and rage at his patients or his friends and she was both, but still heard himself, "Holy mother of...shit, Dust. What the hell? You know better." He lost it. He heard himself sound like a condescending patriarch.

"I was afraid to come, afraid you'd yell at me, and you're yelling, Carlos. Don't yell, just fix it."

He sighed, shook his head. "You know how you take some shrimp and they're all gray and you toss them on a barbecue. You know the color the outsides turn? Well, that's you. You're cooked."

"Are you saying I looked like raw shrimp before Robert and I went to Mexico?"

"No," Carlos said, "I'm saying I can't uncook you."

He told her what lotion to slather on her skin, told her to drink plenty of water to hydrate, told her that with her fair skin she should always wear an SPF 70 sunscreen whenever she went outside.

"And get a hat. Make sure it has a big brim that blocks the sun. Some fabric is ineffective as a sunblock," he said. "We have a catalog here in the office or you can go online. There are companies with sun-blocking hats that you should check out."

He carefully checked her face, her peeling nose, and the white ovals where her sunglasses saved her eyes. There was a small area at her hairline that he questioned. His normal practice was to watch moles and leave them alone unless they changed or bled. This one warranted a biopsy. The incidence of people with skin cancer was alarming and every year it got worse. When the biopsy results were in, he called her and told her they found some precancerous cells. He had her talk to his receptionist to set up some regular appointments.

When she came in for a follow-up in September, the mole had changed. Another biopsy. Then when she came into his clinic for the results of the biopsy just a couple of weeks ago, she brought him a gift, *The Wild Trees* by Richard Preston, and said, "My current favorite book. I wish I could go climb a redwood. This is a present for cleaning up my head."

He thanked her and placed the book on the counter in the examination room, immediately deciding that it was a book he wouldn't take home. Why taunt Rose's insecurities? His little, dark-haired wife, with her bright colored clothes—red and fuchsia, and her very loud volume—laughing and talking, wasn't conscious of how much she wanted to be noticed. He wondered if other people realized how fragile she was. He wouldn't add to Rose's jealousy and insecurity. He'd keep Dust's book in his desk in the clinic, and read it on the days that he ate a sandwich he brought from home.

That day on Dust's last visit, he told her that it was a basal cell carcinoma. He wanted her to see a skin cancer specialist. He carefully detailed for her how they would use Mohs micrographic surgery, removing one layer of skin at a time. After each layer was removed, they'd do a biopsy right there, and they'd continue scraping layers and checking each one until the biopsy showed no cancer.

She asked him not to mention it to anyone. Robert was gone for weeks at a time on the other side of the state campaigning. She didn't want anyone worrying about her, and since he knew just about everyone that she knew, she said, "Please, Carlos, please. Not even

Rose, Rose would tell Lily, and I don't want Lily or my mother to worry about me."

Of course, he wouldn't say anything. He was a doctor. She didn't have to worry.

When he heard about her suicide, he'd called the cancer center, asked how her appointment had gone. They said she'd canceled.

It was treatable, treatable, but she never showed up.

PART TWO—SURVIVING

9. LILY

When Lily left Robert with his peanut butter and jelly sandwiches and coffee, she was confused about where she was going. She should go over to Christina's and visit her and Grace. She could go home, but no one would be there. Her seventeen-year-old twin sons had commitments like swim team and part-time jobs, and interests like sweet, young girls and shooting hoops in a friend's driveway. Her husband Jagger would be working. His passion was old Mustangs and Corvettes. He couldn't keep his hands off them. At his vintage car restoration company, Cummings Garage, he generously tutored folks on the details involved in bringing life back to an aging car. He gave away details of detailing, knowing that most of the people who came in for free advice would be back begging to get on his schedule, would want him and his crew to take over the work. His clients had big visions for their old cars—all bumped out, tuned, spit polished, and chromed inside and out—into cherry condition so they could parade up and down during the annual Woodward Dream Cruise. Jagger was the best resource for getting there. Jagger Cummings was a grease monkey.

Lily could go see her lover Evan Zowarski at his studio. He'd distract her. Evan was a paint monkey with a studio in a warehouse in Detroit, where he painted huge canvases and restored her body on an old mattress. One man had oil and grease under his fingernails, the other had oil paint under his nails.

When Christina's call came last night, Lily's twin sons and Jagger were home—something that was rare. Usually someone had to be somewhere else during dinner. She was grateful it wasn't one of those nights. When she relayed the news, both of her sons jumped up from their places at the dining room table and sandwiched her in a hug. Her identical babies were over six feet tall, and she became little and protected inside their hug. They released her and she glanced over at her husband Jagger. Jagger, whose mother named him hoping he'd be a rock star, but thin-lipped Jagger couldn't carry a tune and wasn't interested in instruments unless they were on the dashboard of a car. Her husband sat in his chair looking like someone had just sucker punched him.

Barely audibly, she heard him whisper, "Oh, fuck."

He held his head in his hands, his shoulders sagged, and his head bent down over his dinner plate. It startled her. Jagger rarely swore, especially in front of the boys, and if a loud "fuck" should shoot out of her mouth when their sons were around, he gave her a look that plastered her outburst with guilt. His reaction was weird, but who knows how anyone will react to shocking news? He'd known Dust since he was fourteen.

When Lily left Robert with his coffee and sandwiches, she realized after a few turns that she was on auto pilot—heading home, not to her home with Jagger and their sons, but home to Daddy, her father Ben Abbott. He still lived in the house where she grew up next door to Dust's old house. She drove down the block of modest tract houses built for returning soldiers after World War II. For several blocks the houses were all the same: living room, kitchen with eating space at one end, two bedrooms downstairs, one bathroom, and an attic bedroom. They were all frame. Most were white. A few were in colors. Some had rectangles of artificial stone around their front doors.

The phone in her pocket started ringing. Dust's phone. She'd forgotten that she had it. She pulled the car over to the curb; Lily was good at following the rules—she never texted when driving or even talked on her cell, and she always wore her seat belt. She was fairly careful about not speeding. All those things involving the safety of others and herself, she was good at those. About some things, like Evan Zowarski, well, that was another story. She unlatched her seat belt and dug the phone out of her pocket. She'd intended to give the phone to Robert.

She checked the phone—a junk call, air-duct cleaning. Dust didn't need her ducts cleaned. She pressed delete and it was gone, then she remembered the text she'd gotten from Dust yesterday. She searched the phone until she found the message that Dust had sent her just before, before...

I love U. Be. Had she texted Robert, or her daughter Grace, or her mother Christina? Lily searched through the sent messages. The only message sent was to Lily. Why? Maybe she'd sent them messages and then deleted them. That didn't seem likely. She hadn't deleted or even finished the message to Lily. Had she accidentally pushed send? Why had she only texted Lily? She was saying good-bye, but not to anyone else? Not Christina? Not even Grace? Lily knew that Dust loved her daughter. Maybe she couldn't think of what to say to her? What would you say to your child before you blew your head off? She could have said she loved her. She said she loved Lily. She searched through messages received; found her own response to Dust. It was there, unread.

I love you too. Be? Be what?

She'd give Dust's phone to Robert, but first she deleted the message Dust had sent her and her own reply. They were already hurt enough, they shouldn't see a message that didn't include them.

She put the phone on the passenger seat, put her seat belt back on, and drove past four houses to Daddy's house, parked in the driveway, turned the car off and unlatched the seat belt again. Careful. Always careful. As she walked up the porch stairs of her father's house, she could hear a crowd yelling inside—college football. She opened the front door and walked directly into the living room where Ben Abbott was sitting on his old brown tweed recliner, watching a game. Normally she'd ask him who was playing, or she'd study the screen until she figured it out for herself. Although she never had any emotional investment in who was playing, winning or losing, she'd ask simply to be social and to show some interest in what mattered to him.

He saw her, clicked off the remote, and got up. He wrapped his arms around her. He didn't ask if she was okay; he knew she wasn't. He just held her.

"I'm so sorry," he whispered. "I'm so sorry." He was a lanky man; she was built like him. Her sister Rose was built like their mother—shorter, softer, rounder.

"Come on, Honey," he said abruptly, and turned her toward the kitchen. "Let me fix you some coffee. Or would you rather have a beer?"

"Yes, beer," she said.

"I have cookies," he said.

"Okay, then coffee."

"I have pretzels and bar cheese."

Ah, this was Daddy. Don't get too emotional, let's eat, or let's go for a ride to the ice cream store. Basically, let's try not to look too hard at what's troubling us.

"Okay, then beer."

"Oh, wait. I have a bumpy cake."

"Okay, milk," she said, and started laughing. She laughed until her sides hurt. Then she cried and he held her.

"Thanks, Daddy," she said. He always found a way to make her laugh. Many times in her life she didn't want a joke, she didn't want to evade whatever issue was bothering her, but humor was the way her father coped. It was how he handled anything that made him uncomfortable, sometimes it was wholly inappropriate, but sometimes, like now, she was grateful for it.

"Bumpy cake?" she asked. "You got a bumpy cake?" Sander's bumpy cake was her favorite—one square layer of dark chocolate cake with white icing piped into thick rows, then dark chocolate icing was poured over the white icing moguls. She'd called him after talking to Dust's mother the night before, and he probably ran out to the store as soon as they got off the phone, figuring she'd be over and would need cheering up. Could cake and humor cure everything? Anything?

"I have ham and cheese and rye bread," he said, nudging the game one more move.

"If Dust had had you for a dad, maybe she'd still be around."

He frowned at her. Shook his head. "So how many psychology classes have you taken?"

She knew he was scolding her, but chose to answer straight.

"One abnormal psychology and one child development class," she said.

Lily was taking night classes once a week at the community college. She was thirty-seven in a class with students fresh out of high school—better late than never. This semester she was taking American Literature, currently reading Steinbeck's *Grapes of Wrath*: dustbowl, human tragedy brought on by greed, overplanted wheat, mother nature rebelling, devastated land, and devastated people turned into refugees trying to find a new home. She'd been taking one class at a time for a few years. Maybe she'd have a degree by the time she was fifty.

"Listen, Lily, Christina was a good mom to Dusty. Lots of people have one parent and are perfectly happy and never consider taking their own life."

Lily knew the *lots of people* he was referring to were his daughters, and she regretted her comment. Her mother had abandoned them, had run away from home, had disappeared into the night with her clothes and her car and was never heard from again, when Lily was eight and Rose was five. Daddy had to deal with raising his two girls alone. As his girls matured, Daddy was the one who was sent to the store for emergency items like sanitary napkins. "Feminities," he called them. They gave him their shopping lists for Hollywood Market or Meijer's. "Why are there so many choices of those damn things, anyway?" he complained.

When Jay Jones, Dust's father, was living the life of a professional surfer in California, the three little girls came up with all sorts of schemes to get their parents together, but Christina never divorced Jay. She loved her husband. He popped home now and then—all tan and blond bearing gifts of dolls and perfume. By the time Dust was in her senior year of college, her father's skin was like leather and his abs sagged. He'd graduated from beach stud to creepy old guy, then Jay Jones returned home. He was home in time for his daughter's college graduation and he was there to escort Dust up the aisle for her wedding—where he gave her away to another blond, good-looking man.

Lily ate bumpy cake with a glass of milk sitting at the kitchen table with her father. They hadn't said a word, but that wasn't unusual or uncomfortable. He was a quiet man. He was there and that's all she needed. She didn't need small talk; there were no solutions or useful platitudes for her grief.

She cleared their plates and glasses, resting them gently in the sink and said, "Daddy, go ahead back and watch your football game. I'm fine. I want to go sit upstairs for a while. Okay?"

He seemed relieved, but still said, "Are you sure?"

She nodded.

"Okay, yeah. Well, okay then," he said, and went back to his recliner.

As she started up the stairs, she heard the sounds of thousands of people shouting in a stadium. At the top step she stopped and looked around. Her attic bedroom was about the same as the last time she'd come up here and that was years ago. The knotty pine paneling had never been finished. There were a few sections missing at the stairway end of the room. They had run out of money, and no one, Lily included, cared. Besides it made for easy access to the storage space under the sloping roof. Ben Abbott had cardboard boxes stacked against the wall filled with treasures he was storing—a broken chair he might fix someday and a tipsy lamp that needed rewiring.

She remembered the smell of new wood when Daddy was remodeling up here.

When Robert's new addition on Dust's house was just studs, filling the air with the sweet scent of fresh cut wood, Dust had said, "Do you know how many trees died for this addition? Do you know how much energy it'll take to heat and cool all this space? All this space for just the three of us." She picked up a box of nails and said, "Sometimes I feel so angry I could spit these."

Old wood lost the sweet smell. The air in Lily's old attic bedroom was stagnant, still, with a smell of ancient dust. Dust. Dead air. Why did they call it dead air? Dust was dead.

Lily opened the window at the far end of her childhood room, hoping some live air would blow in. She looked out at the house next door, and at Dust's old bedroom window directly across from hers. Years ago her father had rigged a pulley between their bedroom windows. They used clothespins that pinched and attached notes that they sent back and forth. No one had worried that they could fall out of the windows then; well, Lily had worried about it. Of course, they were older, maybe twelve by pulley time, so were unlikely to tumble to the ground. The pulley was long gone. Strangers lived in Dust's house. After Christina's mother, Grandma Jeanie, had to go into the nursing home, Christina had moved into a condo.

Once Dust had knotted a rope and climbed down from her bedroom window, just to see if she could do it. Lily stood at the bottom and held the rope, worried silly that Dust would fall and smash them both to bits. Dust was fearless. They were so different. Dust wasn't afraid of anything physical. Fearless. Reckless. Impulsive. Lily was the opposite; afraid of so many things it embarrassed her. She'd never been on an airplane. She avoided boats, deep water, high places, tunnels, caves, and escalators.

A few years ago at Christmas, she was so rushed that she thought that instead of waiting for the elevator, she'd simply walk up to the escalator like a normal person and step on. How bad could it be? Just then, as she walked toward the escalator a mother and little boy were getting off the down escalator and he let out a piercing cry. The escalator had sucked off his rubber boot. Ate it. Lily thought it was an omen and headed to the elevators. She also had a weird thing with Jell-O. She couldn't look at or smell Jell-O. It made her queasy and faint feeling.

Lily patted the lavender comforter on her old bed and a stale cloud rose up. She carefully folded the comforter back and put it on the floor hoping the dust hadn't permeated through it to the sheet below. It seemed okay, so she stretched out on it and immediately started sneezing. When her sneezing stopped, she stayed motionless—straight and rigid on her old bed. She put her forearm over her closed eyes blocking out the light, but the scene in Dust's bathroom slid into the dark space and she opened her eyes again.

Her father had said, "Lots of people have one parent and are perfectly happy, and never consider taking their own life." He thought his own girls were safe from such thoughts, but he was wrong. Lily had considered suicide. It was before Rose and Carlos got married, so more than three years ago. She couldn't finger what was wrong—why she was so unhappy. She knew she was depressed. When she was with other people, she listened to herself chatting and talking and laughing, as though she was listening to someone on the radio, but it was herself. She functioned like a normal person just as Dust had been doing. No one ever guessed that Lily wanted to die. She'd considered putting her head in the oven and turning on the gas, but the oven needed cleaning, and what if she blew up the whole house. She wanted out, but she didn't want to take anyone with her. Sleeping pills? She searched online for information. Pills were an option, but when she slept she had nightmares.

Bad dreams had intruded on her sleep since she was a kid, but around the time when she considered suicide, the nightmares had become a nightly event. It had been a miniseries of bad dreams, beginning with a nightmare of rusty orange water coming into a dark, cold room and touching her bare feet. She woke up terrified. In each consecutive night's dream, the water got deeper. It was up to her ankles. The next night it was up to her knees. The next night it was up to her hips. The next night it was up to her neck. Each night she woke up with a start or a shout that woke Jagger.

Finally one night, she dreamed she was in a boat with her mother. It was a sunny day—so bright the reflections on the water made it hard to make out her mother's features, probably because she couldn't remember exactly what her mother looked like. Her father had thrown out or hidden all the pictures of her mother. She was telling her mother a joke, and when she laughed at her own joke, she tossed back her head and flipped right out of the back of the boat into the water. Under the water, she could see the bottom of the boat. Her mother rowed away. She forgot her. Lily drowned.

She was dead.

She woke up sobbing.

Jagger said, "Another nightmare?"

"I drowned," she said. "I'm dead." It was true. She was dead.

Jagger got up and went to the bathroom. When he came back, he had a glass of water for her. Why would you give a person who just drowned a glass of water? She was angry with him, but she also knew that she wasn't dead and more important she didn't want to be dead anymore. She wanted to live her life. Squeeze every bit of juice out of it. Live. Dying in the dream was so real that all thoughts of suicide were done.

She started taking night classes at the community college. She was going to be alive. She was going to learn things. Then one night during a break in her geology class, she met Evan Zowarski at the coffee vending machine. He was an art instructor at the college and she learned a few more things.

She never told Dust any of this. If she'd talked about her experience, would Dust have been able to talk about how she was feeling? If she'd told Dust that she'd seriously considered suicide, would Dust have talked about her own plans? Could talking about it have saved Dust's life? She used to share everything with Dust. Why not this? Shame? Ashamed that she was so vulnerable? Ashamed of her depression? Ashamed of her behavior? She lay on the bed furious at herself. Fury at her mistake—not the affair, not the unfaithfulness to Jagger—the mistake of not telling her best friend all of it, especially that she'd been so unhappy at one time that she'd wanted to die.

Now, too late, she wanted to tell Dust that things get better, things change. She wanted to tell the bravest person she ever knew to be brave. Live.

When Dust talked about her unhappiness over the addition to the house, what had Lily done? She didn't pay much attention. Barely listened, waiting for her turn to whine about her job dealing with some upset client at the insurance agency, or something that was going on with the twins. Her brain was elsewhere, often at Evan's studio. When Dust told her things that meant something to her, Lily wasn't there. Had she ever tried to see things from Dust's point of view? She could only think how lucky Dust was and that she should quit complaining. Most people would love to have that new addition on their house. She was never interested in gardening herself so when Dust's organic garden was destroyed to make room for the addition, Lily said wearily, "Every Saturday morning we're at the farmers market. When things are ripe in your garden, they have the same things ripe at the market. Get over it." She blew her off.

And yet Lily was the one who got Dust's only text message. "I love you. Be"

"Be," Dust had texted her. Be. Be ashamed. Be unworthy.

There on her childhood bed, Lily had a memory of her mother. Vague. Not clear or concise. She was sleeping. It was dark in her room with just the light from the bare bulb over the stairs, and her mother was shaking her, "Wake up. Lily, wake up, it's time to party." Her mother was so pretty. Her lips were so red. Her smell was a confusion of perfume and wine. She couldn't picture anything beyond a sense of herself thinking the words, *pretty* and *red lips*. Her mother was shaking her, "Wake up. Wake up. I want you to come with me." Her mother helped her change her clothes. Dopey Lily with sleep in her eyes felt the pulling and tugging off of pajamas and then pulling and tugging on of a T-shirt and jeans.

The memory stopped abruptly and Lily started to cry. She wanted more. More memories. Grief overwhelmed her and she wasn't sure if she was grieving for Dust or her mother or both. Dust's death had poked a mean little finger into an old wound, had picked at a scab she'd long forgotten that she had. Why did her mother leave her? Why did Dust die?

10. ROBERT

They wasted no time. His wife died on Friday, and by Sunday afternoon Robert had gotten calls from several major donors to his campaign who wanted to express their condolences, or more likely, they wanted to know if he was staying in the race. They were polite, even kind, but he knew they were checking on the bottom line. The last call was from a billionaire oilman who cut directly to the race for the senate seat.

"My condolences, Robert," he said, then before Robert could respond, he went on, "You know we want to take the senate back. Your wife created a real mess. Yes, sir, a real mess. People are gonna wonder what kinda man you are, what terrible things you did to drive your wife to do what she did."

Stunned, Robert questioned his own hearing. "What?"

"Clean it up, Robert. Whatever you have to do, just get this here mess cleaned up."

The only thing likable about this man was his money, and the amount of money he was spending on this campaign was exceptionally likable.

"Listen," Robert said. "Cut me some slack. My wife just died."

"What do you think voters are gonna think?" the older man said.

"At this moment, I don't care what they think," Robert said.

"You gosh durn well better care about what the voters think," the oilman's voice boomed. Then after an audible breath, he went on, "You want to stay in the race, Son, I'll back you. You could have a fine career ahead of you. I mean, a couple terms in the senate and then you could move up to the top. You do get my meaning? You've got the looks, the charm, and the smarts. But first you gotta get that senate seat. That means you get this here mess cleaned up fast."

"How do I do that?"

"You're a smart man, you'll figure it out," the billionaire said.

Robert was a smart man—he knew the White House was being dangled like a chew toy for a puppy. He was ambitious, but also smart enough to know that to this man he was a commodity, something to be used to enhance his wallet—investing in the future.

It was a good thing that it was a phone call, Robert thought, picturing his fist slamming into the man's face. In spite of the money, in spite of the dangle, he wanted to hit this man. He couldn't remember ever hitting anyone in his life.

It was also good that no one had invented the Smell-a-Phone, he was so rancid he could barely breathe around himself, a difficult situation, since there was no escaping his own body. He needed to shower, shave, and roll on some deodorant. He needed to get out of his rumpled navy jacket. He hadn't taken his suit jacket off when he came home Friday, then he'd slept in it on the couch for two nights. Shock and grief had poured out of his pores. His clothes smelled so bad he'd be embarrassed to take them to the cleaners.

Dust would do it.

How could he forget so fast? For one second she was still alive, ready to deal with his stinking laundry. He kept forgetting that she was gone.

Everyone—well, the cop and Chuck—said he shouldn't go upstairs until someone cleaned up, so it must be bad. Lily couldn't do it. He needed a shower. He could use the old bathroom, but he'd still have to get his clothes from the new closet in their bedroom, and he'd still have to pass by the new bathroom.

He went upstairs. Dread made his shoeless feet weighty. He was exhausted. Every joint, every muscle in his body ached, probably from sleeping sitting up on the couch. He examined the broken door jam to the master suite, touched the splintered wood. He looked in at the disarray in the room—dirty clothes scattered around, the white carpet needing a vacuuming—and it was irrelevant.

He walked across the bedroom toward the closet with his left hand held up to the side of his face, as a shield blocking the view of the bathroom. Inside the closet he stripped down and stood there naked. In this beautiful closet with its bins and shelves, Dust had hung three old pillowcases on hooks on the wall. They were now cloth laundry bags labeled with a black Sharpie marker: DARK, LIGHT and HOT (meaning use hot water, not sexy clothes). He put his underwear in the hot bag, although his jockey shorts and socks were dark blue. Was that right? Maybe they should go in the darks? He was confused. Normally he just dropped his clothes on the closet floor and she sorted them. It was her job. His shirt and suit would go to the cleaners, so he did his usual and dropped them on the floor. He smelled his tie, and found a sprinkling of stains. Scotch? He tossed it on the dry cleaning pile.

The closet was only half filled with clothes. Why did he think they'd ever need such a huge closet? Need or want? He *wanted* this big closet. The architect told him that no matter how much space you have, it always gets filled up. He had more clothes than Dust, and together they barely made a dent in the space. He went over to her side, pushed hangers aside and touched at her things. Other than shoes and underwear, she bought most of her clothes at church rummage sales or resale shops. *Reduce, Reuse, Recycle, yada, yada, yada.* But honestly, she always looked good to him, soft and pretty and the feel of her skin was like…he glanced down and saw himself getting hard. *For God's sake, she's gone. Stop it.*

A pink cashmere sweater that she bought years ago at Christ Church Cranbrook's rummage sale was folded on one of her shelves. She was disappointed when the Episcopal Church in Bloomfield

Hills went out of the rummage business. She'd worn the sweater recently. He picked it up. Pressed it into his face. Inhaled. With his face imbedded in her sweater, he couldn't smell himself. There was just her scent, and he started to cry again. He sat down on the new valet chair with its back shaped like a hanger for a suit jacket, and held the sweater up in front of him, wishing she were inside it, wishing he could touch her, wrap her up in his arms, and hold her. He would tell her he was sorry, sorry for destroying her garden, sorry for all the cruel things he'd said to her.

Sorry. Sorry. Sorry.

He sat there holding the sweater until he started smelling his own body again.

He left the closet still holding her sweater. A serious nap would help; his head was splitting from trying to drown himself in whiskey, which he retrieved after Lily left. He wanted to get into their bed and fall asleep smelling her sweater, but again his own foulness overwhelmed him. He left her sweater on the bed and went toward the new bathroom.

Deal with it, Robert. Man up, he heard his great uncle Rob's voice as he neared the bathroom door.

It was his mother's idea to name him after his dad's über rich uncle Robert Steward. Although his parents called him Bobby when he was little, his uncle always called him Robert, and when Old Rob did that, his mother switched to calling him Robert too. His father still called him Bobby. His sister called him Row-butt or Robot.

Robert's dad was the sweetest person he ever knew. He drove a cab, then a SMART bus in Detroit, and finally a potato chip delivery truck. He heard once that more potato chips were consumed in Detroit than anywhere else on earth. He also heard that Michigan ranked fifth on a list of the fattest populations in the country. There was probably a connection. Robert figured any warmth in his personality came from his father. His mother was a good woman, not at all a cold person, but she had a calculating mercenary side. He suspected that he'd inherited some of that too. His mother made sure that her husband's millionaire uncle knew his great nephew. She didn't have to work too hard at that; Uncle Rob had lost his only son to a drug and drinking problem, and he welcomed his little nephew into his life.

Once his great uncle retired, Robert spent most of his summers hanging out with Old Rob. Robert loved his uncle. He also lusted for a house like his great uncle's mansion in Grosse Pointe. He remembered getting lost inside the house and feeling a thrill instead of fear. He'd call out, *hello, hello, hello*, and his voice echoed like he was yodeling in the Alps. Eventually his great uncle paid for Robert's law degree at the University of Michigan and nudged him, no, it was more like shoved him, into politics. Uncle Rob had said, "Live up to our name, Robert. You're a Steward. So be a steward of the people. Be part of the government and protect the interests of business, and then you'll be protecting everyone."

Dust told him he should be a steward of the earth.

"Deal with it, Robert. Man up," he imagined his great uncle saying to him. "Deal with this. You're a big boy."

Still naked, Robert went to the bathroom door. He stood staring into the room. He stepped into the room and knelt down near the blood as though it was a shrine to his departed wife. Sacred. No one else should touch it but him. The hard tile hurt his knees, but he ignored the pain. He ran his finger over the edge of the slick black stain, and it came up unmarked—the blood was dry.

He knew her blood: the color, the smell, and the consistency. Women were messy. Bloody. The first time he made love to her, there was red evidence of her virginity on the sheets in his co-op bedroom in college. He remembered how he was afraid of hurting her. Several years later when Grace was born, he was there to cut their baby's umbilical cord. Grace was tiny and blotchy red with blood. He held Dust's hand while she pushed the bloody afterbirth from her body. Then there were all the menstrual periods that came before she expected them and left maroon stains on their bedding. Sometimes they made love when she was having a period; that was messy and he didn't care. Afterward his penis and pubic hair would be sloppy red with her blood and white with his semen. Just days after they bought this old house with its shallow basement, she went down the steep stairs and forgot to duck. She cracked her head on the basement ceiling joist. He thought he'd never seen so much blood. He was wrong. This was more, way more, but it didn't repel him, this was part of his wife. She was the only woman he'd ever loved, and the blood was all he had left of her.

***

Last April the contractor was digging up the back yard for the addition's foundation and a Bobcat was swallowing up her vegetable garden and spitting it into a pile. The vegetable garden was just dirt then, nothing was planted yet. She didn't look at him; she just stared out the kitchen window at the Bobcat. Then she told him she wanted a divorce. Robert was stunned. She didn't get her way about the addition, so she wanted to divorce him? She loved him. She loved him. He knew that. They loved each other. But he was a stupid, prideful man. He could have said, "We love each other. Despite all our differences, we belong together. We're like the country we both love—red states and blue states. United we stand, divided we fall."

Instead he'd shouted at her that he would never divorce her and if she tried he would make sure she never saw Grace again. He was a lawyer and she wouldn't have a chance. She shouted back that her mother had refused to divorce her father. Her mother wasted the best years of her life in a shitty marriage to a man who was never there. Dust said she wouldn't suppress everything that she valued to stay married. Robert shouted again, "I'll never divorce you and you'll lose Grace."

She ran out of the house, got in her car, and drove away. When she came back hours later she had groceries. Without speaking, he helped her unload her cloth bags filled with food. Neither of them said a word. Later, when she was standing at the kitchen sink chopping organic carrots and avoiding looking at the hole in the back yard, he came up behind her and wrapped his arms around her, nuzzled her neck, and told her he couldn't divorce her because his heart would break without her.

She didn't stab him with the paring knife, and she never mentioned divorce again.

Was that when the light went out of her? Was that when she changed, when she became resigned and distant? If he'd let her go, he wondered, would she be alive? It was too late for Sting's wisdom—*if you love someone, set her free.*

He thought again of the billionaire donor saying, "Clean it up." Robert knew he meant the political fallout from Dust's suicide, but the scene in the bathroom was fallout too. Lily had left her bucket with the spray bleach, paper towels, black plastic trash bags and rubber gloves. He ignored the rubber gloves. He filled the bucket with water using the long, stainless steel handheld spray attachment in the shower. The water ran cold; it always took a two-gallon bucket full of water before it got hot. He soaked paper towels in the cold water and spread them on the dry blood. Dust would want him to use rags. Paper towels mean some tree had given its life to wipe up a floor. Jesus. Then he'd have to wash the rags in some biodegradable laundry detergent.

***

He was in his last year of college studying law when he met Dust. There was a rally about global warming. Across the crowd he saw this tall, red-haired girl. He'd maneuvered his way through the crowd until he was standing next to her. He came to the rally out of curiosity—his great uncle Rob had devoted hours to raging against Al Gore and global warming —and here was this girl, ardent and pure, engaged in saving the planet. He didn't believe in love at first sight, but standing next to her his heart felt swollen and big inside his chest. He wasn't sure what he thought about climate change, but he wanted her. He wanted her to feel her heart thump faster when she looked at him. He wanted to win her. He found someone with a box of flyers and offered to help hand them out. Then he moved back to where she stood and handed her a flyer. She smiled at him. Her eyes were green. Two of her bottom teeth crossed over each other, which somehow made him even more infatuated.

He never told Uncle Rob that the girl he loved was an environmentalist, and it took several years before she realized that her cause—the thing that made her tick, the thing that mattered most to her—was irrelevant to him. No, worse than irrelevant, it was something that he had to disparage for the sake of his career.

***

He wiped up her blood with paper towels, irrelevant paper towels. Would they be considered hazardous waste, he wondered, as he picked up sopping paper towels dripping with rehydrated blood and plopped them into the trash bag. He used more paper towels to wipe up the residue on the floor. Then he started cleaning the walls. He tried not to think about what he was cleaning when he found bits of bone and her hair. The bullet was imbedded in the new aqua glass tile.

Suddenly he was angry. *How could you do this to me? How? How? Why?* He punched the wall with his fist. The bones in his hand mashed his skin against the hard tile wall and then his knuckles were bleeding. He let them bleed for a bit then rinsed his hand in the sink and wrapped it up with another paper towel.

"No, hell no, I'm not going to feel guilty for using a damn paper towel. This is your fault, Dust. How could you do this to me? How?"

Then her voice in his head said familiar words, *Robert, it's not always about you.*

And he yelled back at her, "It IS about me! It's about me and Grace and Lily and your mother! You didn't just do this to you. You did this to all of us!" Dust shot herself, and when she did that, everyone around her was left wounded. She could have been using an assault weapon, an AK-47 or something, splattering pain over all of them.

His knuckles hurt. His hand would probably turn purple, then an ugly green and yellow. So now if he went out in public with banged-up knuckles, would people think he was a brute? Would they think he was a wife beater when he was, in fact, a wall beater? Everything mattered when you were running for office: every word you said, every fart you let, if you rolled up your sleeves, if you wore dry-cleaned jeans that had sharp creases, how often you went to church, how many times you said God in a speech. If you were like Charlie Crist, the Republican governor who had the temerity to hug the Democratic President of the United States, your career could be over. If your wife was a lefty environmentalist, who never campaigned with you because she was shy with strangers and worse, disagreed with your politics, that could also be the end of your political career.

The stains wouldn't come out of the grout. Maybe he should try Lily's spray bleach and a toothbrush? He went across the room still filled with fury and reached for his blue toothbrush. Stopped. Put it back. Took her purple one from the cup on the counter. She wouldn't need it—that thought quelled his anger and the tears were running again. When he finished scouring the grout lines with her toothbrush and picking up pieces of broken door, the room was still damaged—beaten up with scars from a fight.

Besides the bucket Lily brought with her cleaning supplies, there was a second bucket inside the shower. They always put the long, stainless steel handheld spray attachment down into the bucket and ran the water until it got hot. Then they used the bucket water to flush the toilet—saving water and the gas that heated the water. Of course, this was not his idea. That stupid bucket stared at him, expecting him to fill it as he waited for the water to warm up for his shower.

"Fuck you," he said, and kicked the bucket.

Cold water splashed his skin, and his big toe wished he hadn't done that. The bucket banged and thudded around, and then fell over on its side. The water ran down the drain until it got hot, wasting away, and he didn't give a shit.

The architect had suggested environmental crap like on-demand hot water heaters, wood that's harvested from forests in a sustainable manner, low VOC paints, solar for hot water, photovoltaic panels to produce electricity, and LEED-rated green products like bamboo flooring. But since Dust didn't want to be involved in any of the planning for the addition, he'd only gone for thermal windows. Since he didn't spend the money on environmental upgrades, the house could be bigger. The only thing Dust requested was that they leave the old house intact. He would have preferred to open up the whole back of the main floor, creating a big, open area that encompassed the old dining room and kitchen but she wanted that old brick wall to stand.

When the water ran hot, he stepped into the shower. Even with a shattered door the bathroom was getting so steamed that he felt like he was standing inside a cloud. His great uncle Rob was somewhere in the steam saying, *I told you so. I told you it would be a mistake to marry a fish-eater.* Fish-eater—a slur about Catholics from back in the days when the Pope dictated they eat fish on Fridays. He loved many things about his great uncle, but the old man was blatantly prejudiced against just about anyone who wasn't Presbyterian of Scottish descent. More than blacks or gays or Hispanics, Old Rob hated Irish Catholics. Maybe it came from a rivalry between the Scots and the Irish, like the rivalry between the University of Michigan and Ohio State?

When they were seniors at U of M, he'd told Dust that old Rob threatened to stop funding his education if he married a Catholic. She told him she could easily join the league of lapsed Catholics. Except for the mantra of the beads, she wasn't interested in religion. When she was growing up she went to the Catholic Church with her mother, and after they married, she went to the Presbyterian Church. Dust had brought her rosary into the bathroom with her, both of his guns and the rosary—Guns N Rosary—heavy metal, heavy religion. An incongruity. Had he wrung her religion from her? Or was she sincere when she told him that holding the beads was like saying "om" in a yoga class?

The loofah sponge was hanging there waiting for him to scrub her back. Her back wasn't there so he scrubbed himself. He scrubbed away his smell and stood there with hot water hitting his head. To spite her he'd stand there until the hot water tank ran cold. He stood in the shower letting gallons of hot water pour over him. They had a huge hot water tank so he stood there for a long, long time. When the cold water hit, exhaustion left him, but by then his anger had swollen up big and mean and vindictive. He dried himself with one of the towels meant for show on the mahogany shelves. He dressed in jeans and a sweatshirt, then he vacuumed all the black sock fuzz in his beautiful bedroom and picked up the clutter of her dirty clothes, and dumped them all into the HOT bag in the closet.

Then, still angry, he called Chuck, his campaign manager.

11. LILY

On Sunday, Lily woke up with a deep ache in her chest as grief filled her, crowding her heart. It hurt. She was in physical pain. Why would a broken heart feel swollen? She felt sick—like fluids were pressing in on her lungs. Pain engulfed her as she searched her drawers and closet for clothes in the dark. Lifting things up and putting them back. Unsure. Thoughts were fragments, broken circuits in her brain. Wear this, no this, no that. Yesterday's clothes were in a heap on the chair. Wear those, but there was something wrong with them, she wasn't sure what it was. She went back to the closet and touched fabric, then back to her bed and curled up in the blankets, closed her eyes, and she was asleep still searching for clothes. There were things she had to arrange for a funeral, but she couldn't find her clothes. Should they be black? But if she was just arranging a funeral, she wouldn't need to be dressed in black, would she? She couldn't remember just what she was supposed to be doing, and she couldn't find her clothes. No wonder they said you shouldn't make any major decisions after the loss of a loved one. She couldn't even decide what to wear.

She was standing in front of a long mirror, feeling lost and confused. A woman came into her room and held her. She knew the woman, but was unsure exactly who the woman was. The woman said. "Why didn't you call me?" But how could she call her if she didn't know her name? The woman morphed from Dust to Christina to someone unknown. Was it her mother? The woman said, "You know you can count on me. I'll always help you, you know that." And then Lily realized she was alone talking to herself in the mirror.

She was moving her lips and saying to herself, "You know you can count on me."

Daylight poked at her eyelids. Awake. Had she ever gotten up or was all of it a dream? What did it mean? Jagger was sleeping beside her. She got out of bed and quietly showered and dressed in yesterday's clothes. It didn't matter what she wore. Her chest still felt crowded—aching still—just as it had in the dream.

There was noise downstairs. She went down to the kitchen. The twins were up. Amazing. On weekends the boys might sleep until noon, but they were up and banging around the kitchen. They wanted to make everyone breakfast—pancakes and bacon. They were sweet guys trying to make happy music from the funeral dirge that pervaded the house. They were valiantly trying to turn Chopin's "Funeral March" into "If You're Happy and You Know it Clap Your Hands."

The kitchen would become a disaster area, treacherous from splattered bacon grease, and disgusting with dribbles of pancake batter all over the counters, down the cupboard doors, and onto the floor. They'd do their good deed, then go sprawl in the living room to watch TV, and she'd be left with a mess to clean up.

She wasn't happy and she knew it. The pain in her chest wasn't letting up. She didn't want to eat pancakes. She didn't want to eat anything. She wanted to go to bed and cover her head and just disappear. But she wouldn't do that. She'd eat their pancakes with raw dough on the inside and she'd try not to gag when she ate limp, fatty bacon. She'd smile and thank them for being so thoughtful. She'd clean the kitchen when they were all finished, and she'd pretend to be grateful. She was their mother.

Irritable—she'd slept fitfully since Friday—Lily paced the house and left her teenaged sons, Henry and Andrew, to their cooking. She went upstairs. Jagger was up. He was fresh from a shower: clean, naked, gathering underwear and socks. He had his back to her when she came into their room. He had lovely wide shoulders and narrow hips and perfect perky round butt cheeks. She liked his back. But when he turned around, she saw that he was not clean, his face was emotionally grimy, and she wanted to scrub that look off his face.

"Why did she do it?" Jagger asked, as he put on his socks. He sounded angry, accusing her. "Why did she go and do that?"

"That?" Lily shouted, "Stop skidding around it. She shot herself! She put one of Robert's fucking, goddamned guns to her head and pulled the fucking trigger. She shot her brains out, and splattered them all over the fucking bathroom wall. I saw her brains stuck on the wall, Jagger. I never wanted to see her brains."

Though tears blurred her vision, Lily saw or felt the anger in him. He was planning to stay home today, and she didn't know what the point was. It was Sunday, but Sunday hadn't been a stay at home and relax day for him in years. She was crabby. He was crabby. She wanted to shout at him, Just go work on a car or something. Just leave, obviously you don't want to be here.

"Why are you angry at me?" she said. Even as the she heard her own words, she recognized that she was the one who sounded angrier and wondered if she was projecting her anger and making it his.

"I don't know why she did it," she said, "I don't know why. And I wish to hell you'd stop acting like I did something. I didn't do it." She wasn't sure about that, hearing her voice falter. Maybe she did do it, but what had she done?

"I'm sorry," he said, pulling on his jeans. "I know you didn't do it. I'm just upset. What was she thinking? She was always brave and sensible and beautiful. I don't understand it. I just can't wrap my head around it. Things get better. Why couldn't she just give it time?" he hesitated then, like he was choosing his words carefully, "Whatever was bothering her...whatever it was...she could have been patient and let time heal whatever was bothering her. Time heals all things, or all wounds, isn't that a quote from somewhere?"

"Yes," she said, "from somewhere, but I don't believe it. Time has no power to heal anything. It just goes by." Time hadn't healed the wounds she had from her mother leaving her. Dust dying had drudged up all that old pain and time would never heal this new wound. "Time is impotent."

"What's that supposed to mean?" he said. "I am not impotent."

"Oh, for Christ's sake, Jagger. I said time is impotent. I wasn't talking about you. I was talking about time. I know you're not impotent. You're just not interested in sex right now. That's what you're always telling me, anyway."

The boys were shouting up from the kitchen, "Breakfast's ready. Come and get it."

"Or maybe it's just me," she said, as they left their bedroom. "Maybe something's wrong with me."

"You're right, as usual," he said, as he followed her downstairs. "It's you."

The boys had set the dining room table with placemats and silverware. No one made coffee and there was no juice, just pancakes and bacon. She went to the kitchen and got the butter and syrup. As much as she didn't want it, the breakfast was sweet—sweet and other than no coffee, perfect—and she was warmed by her love for her sons. The bacon was crisp; the smell of it filled the house. The pancakes didn't ooze wet batter.

The twins had done good.

The boys were ecstatic—yumming and humming and lolling their heads around with their eyes closed like Stevie Wonder singing, "I Just Called to Say I Love You"—over each bite of their perfect culinary achievement. Jagger was overtired; he probably hadn't been sleeping well either. He was chewing with his mouth opened, which he seemed to do unconsciously when he was tired. She hated the echoing sound of the food rolling around inside his open trap.

As they ate their breakfast, the testosterone around the table didn't speak to her or each other. Testosterone doesn't speak; it shouts at spectator sports and carries heavy auto parts: batteries and dirty tires. Testosterone is goal-oriented: it shoots the basketball, gets the job done, eats the pancakes. Testosterone is expedient. When the estrogen in the house spoke to the testosterone in the house, the testosterone was usually deaf. Deaf and mute. The estrogen talked and talked. The testosterone shoveled large hunks of food into the three mouths and didn't nod or hear.

Each bite of the sticky sweet food that she hadn't wanted to eat was bringing some calm, lulling her, drugging her into a sugar high.

"Wow," she said, "you guys could go on Top Chef. This is delicious." Occasionally one or both of them would sit with her and watch the cooking competition on TV.

The boys glowed with pride. Testosterone listens to compliments. It frequently amazed her, when she happened to think about it, how powerful words were. With one sentence you could make another person feel good about himself, or you could make him shrivel just as visibly as if you'd thrown a bucket of ice water at him. Then again, the painful question, with one sentence could she have made Dust want to live? The pain in her chest was still there; did it feel crowded or empty? She wasn't sure.

When they finished eating, Henry said, "We sorta made a mess. We'll clean the kitchen, Mom."

Andrew gave him an, *are you crazy look*, then said, "Yeah, Mom. Henry will clean the kitchen." After he got a laugh, he added, "We'll both clean up. You can just relax."

"Maybe your dad and I will go for a walk," she said. She knew the boys would argue over who would do what, and she wasn't in the mood to listen to them.

Jagger was startled, but said, "Yeah, whatever."

After they had their jackets on and were walking down their block, he said, "Starbucks?"

"I didn't want to mention that there was nothing to drink, they were being so sweet, but yeah, Starbucks would be great."

It was a mile to the Starbucks on Main Street. When they got to the busy intersection at Woodward Avenue, she put her index finger into his palm. He squeezed it and they walked across the street. She was perfectly capable of crossing a street on her own, but she wanted to hold his hand for the crossing. She always did that when they crossed a big street. Why? Was she five? But still they walked like they used to walk with him holding her finger. After they had crossed the street, he let her finger go and put his hands in his pockets. They walked the rest of the way in silence.

By the time they got to Starbucks, she felt lighter. The pain in her chest had evaporated. What was it? Guilt crowding her lungs? Sorrow leaving a hole inside her? Whatever it was, she decided that walking was good for a broken heart. They found an empty table in Starbucks, and sat facing each other with their coffee.

"Why did she do it?" he asked, as though she had the answer. "Damn, and why now?"

Now? Where was he coming from? Should Dust have waited a year, or done it last year. Why did *now* make a difference to him? Why was now any more inconvenient than any other time? She shook her head. He thought she was responding to his question, but she was questioning him. Dust was the victim and he acted like she was the perpetrator. But it was true. Dust was both.

"Remember her birthday party last summer when the remodeling wasn't finished yet?" he said. "She was beautiful."

Lily nodded. She remembered. "I loved her," she said.

He looked like he might cry, right there in Starbucks. "I loved her too," he said.

12. ROSE

By Sunday night, Lily's sister Rose still wasn't speaking to her husband Carlos. Avoiding being home, she'd volunteered to work a double shift at the nursing home when one of the other nurses called in sick. Back home she kept herself busy all evening, and when Carlos came into a room, she left. He was being shunned like a leper, an untouchable, a wearer of a scarlet letter, an Amish who had strayed from the church. When it was time for bed, she was grateful for their king-sized bed, she didn't have to be near him. Normally she slept naked, but she put on flannel pajamas.

Why did she choose a man who was a flirt? Rosie, who always struggled with jealousy, had picked the perfect man to feed her vulnerabilities, picked him as if he were in a line up and she'd pointed her finger and said, *Him. He'll make me feel the most insecure, he'll feed my jealousy, and so that's the man I want.* Was it like an addiction? Crave the thing that will feed your addiction? Indulge, knowing you'll end up in your own private skid row gutter.

In their darkened room he scooted over close to her in their bed. She pushed him away. They struggled—him toward, her away—until she was at the edge of the bed. Her options: fall off, get up and go sleep on the couch, or cling to the edge. The bed was comfortable, which made the decision for her.

"Stop it, Rosie," he said. "Stop it. I feel guilty enough already without you punishing me."

"You led her on," Rose said. "Carlos, you led her on."

"Okay, okay," he said, and grabbed both her hands to stop her from swatting at him like he was a swarm of gnats. "I admit it. I flirt with women. I like women. I enjoy being around women. But, Rosie, I married you," he said. "And yes, she was flirting with me too. It didn't mean anything to me, and it didn't mean anything to her."

"She called and asked you to lunch," Rose reminded him. Dust never called and asked *her* to lunch. Jealousy, there was always something or someone to make her feel slighted.

"I know. But it wasn't about sex. Anyway, I don't think it was. I think she just wanted to talk. I should have taken the time and met her."

"What!" Rose sat upright in bed. "You should have met her?"

"Well, then we'd know, wouldn't we? If she had a crush, I could have gently, without humiliating her, let her know that I care for her, but also let her know that Rose Abbott Martinez is my one and only love."

Rose settled back down under the comforter next to him.

"But, Rose, that wasn't it at all," he said. "I guess I can tell you this now. She asked me not to tell you. She didn't want her mother or Lily to know, or any of you to worry about her. When I saw her last spring, I found a suspicious area on her forehead. Then a few weeks ago, I did a biopsy and it was a basel cell carcinoma. I sent her to the cancer clinic. It was treatable, Rose. Treatable. And she never showed up at the clinic."

"Skin cancer, Carlos? Skin cancer? Her father died from a melanoma on his head. Didn't she tell you?"

"Melanoma? Why didn't I know that? We take a patient history. I don't remember anything like that." He flopped back on the bed. "Oh my God. I was worried that I hadn't reassured her enough about the basal cell. Oh my God."

"It was terrible what her dad went through. He was gone surfing in California for years. He was even in some of those surfer movies where the guy is inside of a big wave. And when he wasn't surfing, he did roofing to make money. That's a lot of sun exposure.

When he came home, he had a funny patch on top of his head. Christina made him get it checked."

"I didn't know any of that."

"You wouldn't have unless she told you. She was twenty-two when she got married, so that was fifteen years ago, long before you and I met. She was devastated by his death. I mean she'd spent her life with a father who popped in and out and was unreliable. One day he'd show up, then a week or maybe even a month later, she'd come home from school and he'd be gone again. Finally he came home for her college graduation. He told her that he was home for good and always. Those words exactly. 'Good and always.' She was so happy. But, when she finally had her father around full time, he had cancer. Dust wanted her father to walk her down the aisle when she married Robert, so they rushed plans for their wedding. And he did it. Jay Jones bucked up and walked her down the aisle. I think she was holding him up as they walked. After the wedding, they put off the honeymoon so she could spend the last few weeks of her father's life with him. It was brutal. Dust spent all her time with him then, taking him for chemo, nursing him while Christina was a work, and cleaning up when he was vomiting from the chemo. It was terrible. She barely got to know her father and then he was gone."

"Could that be it? Rose, do you think she could have been scared of having to go through what her father did?" Carlos said. "But I assured her that this cancer was not the end of the world. It wasn't something that would kill her."

"In a way, maybe it did?" Rose whispered.

13. LILY

On Monday morning, Lily woke up tired again. Her dreams had been exhausting, filled with searching: searching parking lots for her lost car, finding it, and then discovering that she'd lost her purse, finding her purse, then shoving tissues around searching for the car keys.

She went to work as usual, as though nothing terrible had happened on Friday afternoon. The bad thing was inside her and she promised herself that she wouldn't let it out while she was at work.

Lily loved her job at the insurance agency, especially today, when other people's problems would keep her from thinking of her own. Her desk was a few feet away from the storefront's big window and she could watch the world pass by on Woodward Avenue with four lanes heading north, a treed median, and four more lanes heading south to Detroit. Cars passed by at forty-five miles an hour, or at least that was the posted speed limit. She'd been working at the insurance agency since the boys started first grade. Twelve years. When anyone asked her title, she said, "I'm customer service, sales, housekeeping, lender, office closer, consoler, fixer, and banking depositor." But mainly her job was to build relationships with the clients, make them glad that their insurance policies covered the car that crashed, the stove that caught fire, a stone that created cracks like daddy longlegs on the windshield, and whatever disaster or inconvenience came into their lives.

Insurance didn't cover the disaster that came into Lily's life.

Not long after the coffee had been dripping into the pot, Lily's boss, Amanda Powell, the agent whose name was on the red awning across the storefront, arrived.

"Hey," Amanda said, with a gentle tone, as she was taking off her coat. "Dusty Steward was your friend, wasn't she?" Amanda's tone was soft, the tone they both understood helps people when the worst things happen.

"I'm so sorry, Lily. Are you sure you want to be here today? If you need some time, I could cover things. I could get our part-timer to come in for a few days."

Amanda was one of the many reasons Lily liked her job. She was always professional, kind, firm, or whatever the moment called for.

"It's better for me to be here," Lily said. "It's good to be distracted. Besides, I have that CE class at Troy Collision this afternoon." Every two years, she was required to earn twenty-four continuing education credits. Between her job and her classes at the community college, the twins, taking care of the house, buying food and cooking meals, laundry, Jagger and Evan, her life was full.

Amanda went into her office and left Lily staring out the front window. She liked her job. She liked the clients who came through the front door. Dust had told her that she should start thinking about another career. Violent weather changes were coming, not coming, they had already arrived. There had already been the droughts in the Midwest that caused farmers to lose crops—insured crops. Fires in the west had destroyed hundreds of expensive homes—insured homes. Dust said that insurance companies would start to fold, that weather disasters would come so fast and ferocious that the insurance business would implode.

But Lily loved her job. How many people can honestly say that?

14. FRED

Fred Williams was trying to distract himself by playing a game of Mahjong on the iPad. How could he distract himself from thinking about Dust when he was playing with the iPad that she'd given him? A few days before she died, she came next door and handed it to him. She told him she was getting a new one, the latest version, and wondered if he'd like to have her old one. She lied.

Of course he wanted it, but it was expensive.

"Are you sure?" he said.

"Yes, yes. I'm sure, Fred," she said, with a big smile, that in his memory was so happy, so genuine, that it was hard for him to think that she was planning her suicide. But of course, she was. She was giving him something that mattered to her, giving away her things.

When he offered to pay for it, she said, "No, no, it's a gift," And that was a relief. Margaret, his dear, frugal wife, and the only wage earner in the house, would have a fit if he spent money on a toy.

Dust sat beside him on his sofa for more than an hour showing him how to open the apps. He had a computer, they had Wi-Fi in the house, and he'd been an engineer, so he caught on quickly. She gave him an index card with her passwords. She showed him how to open books that she'd purchased, mainly books about trees and environmental books by Bill McKibben.

At the time, he thought that she was giving him the iPad because she was still feeling guilty about Robert's addition shading his back yard. He'd asked her outright.

She said, "No, I feel terrible about the shade in your garden, but no, I'm getting a new iPad."

She lied. Lied and died.

After she died, Fred realized that she'd given him—had trusted him with—what was almost like her diary. The details of her life were in it. The books she liked and her calendar. She told him to feel free to go to the Apple Store at Somerset Mall and have them reconfigure it, or whatever they would need to do to make it his and get rid of all her junk. She told him to feel free to erase her from the iPad. She didn't tell him that she wanted him to, or that he should— so he didn't. He'd thought about doing it, and now was glad that he hadn't. She didn't tell him that she was planning to erase herself.

He wondered, since she'd given him her iPad days ago, if that was a part of sealing her fate. If you've given away your favorite things, could you change your mind? Was it like planning a move to another state? The people where you work gave you a big going-away party or maybe took you out for lunch. You've given friends and family your possessions. You've got the car loaded up. What if you change your mind? What if you don't want to leave after all? How do you go back? Had she locked herself into this awful decision when she gave away her things?

Fred was watching the morning news while he played a game on Dust's iPad. No, he *listened* to the news, while he matched the Mahjong tiles. He didn't need to see the talking faces.

The newscaster said, "Elsewhere in the news, Senator Steward's campaign has released information that his wife was severely bipolar. She was being treated for many years, and had been hospitalized in Mexico last winter, before her suicide on Friday morning. The senator is in mourning, but will not be withdrawing from the race for the US Senate seat. A memorial will be held at a future date."

"What?" Fred said to the TV. Then he said it again, louder, "What?"

Dust had never mentioned being bipolar. He thought that she was open and comfortable with him, but she never mentioned anything like that. He didn't believe it. Robert was saving his ass, making it seem like her death had nothing to do with any flaw in him. His campaign people were saying that something was wrong with her, therefore, Robert wasn't culpable or responsible in any way. The candidate was married to a very sick woman.

The newscaster said that she was being treated for bipolar disorder, which would mean she was seeing a psychiatrist. Fred opened Dust's calendar app, every little square was filled through October 1, the day before she gave him the iPad. She wrote down what she was going to do and what she'd done. He searched back through the calendar but wanted more detail, so he opened the daily calendar pages and searched each day.

It was almost like she kept it as a journal. There were entries like "Visited Grandma Jeannie. She sang to me. Remembers every word of ancient songs but she doesn't know who I am." She noted the hours she was there.

Fred began his search with Friday, October 5. It was blank. She might have written a suicide note here, but she didn't, because Fred already had the iPad. He worked his way back through blank days to the last entry. There was a dermatology appointment on October 1. She wrote, "Canceled," but didn't delete it. There were several appointments with the dermatologist. Dr. Carlos Martinez was a friend of the family; Fred met him at Dust's birthday party in July. He noticed that she wrote, "Canceled," but didn't delete appointments throughout the calendar pages. If she'd been seeing a psychiatrist, it would be in her calendar. He found an appointment with a Dr. Patrillo; he cross-referenced the doctor in her address book, then called the number and discovered that Dr. Patrillo was an ob/gyn doctor. Then he went through the rest of her address book searching for a shrink.

There was no appointment with and no listing for a psychiatrist anywhere in her iPad.

They said she'd been in a mental hospital in Mexico for two weeks last year. He remembered her being gone in February on what she referred to as their second honeymoon. Grace had stayed with her grandmother. Dust had been happy about going and happy when she came home. A fair-skinned redhead, she came home sunburned with new freckles all over her face. She complained about her skin peeling and itching. He could see it. Her nose was pink, no, closer to a painful red with dry, white peeling edges of skin. He remembered asking her if her nose hurt. She replied, "Only when the air hits it." He remembered it because she laughed after. She had a good, full-bodied laugh. The next day she came over for coffee and, as a joke, had a bandage on her nose. It was a kid's bandage that she'd had for Grace when she was little. Dora the Explorer was glued on her nose. How could he forget that?

If she was in a mental ward at a hospital, they must have had a balcony with chaise lounges where she got her sunburn. But there wouldn't be such a thing—suicidal patients would jump off the ledges. Maybe they had a swimming pool where suicidal patients could put rocks in their pockets and jump in.

Fred gave a bitter snort and shook his head, disgusted with the whole lot of them—Robert and his lying cohorts.

Fury built inside him. Lies. They had cooked this up; Fred was sure of it. He said out loud, "Burn in hell, Robert." He wanted to tell the world on them. They're lying! He wanted to run next door and beat on Robert's door. He wanted to confront Robert. Poke his finger in Robert's chest. Shout, "Liar!" He wanted to show him the evidence. The iPad knew the truth. She never saw a psychiatrist. He pictured himself waving it in the air and yelling, "I know you're lying!" He pictured himself in front of one of those hungry-for-blood-and-scandal TV cameras telling the world, telling the voters, that Robert Steward was a liar. But then another thought came into his head, Robert probably didn't know she'd given him her iPad. Robert could say that Fred had used the key she gave him and had come into the house and stole it. He had no way to prove that it was a gift. He was a black man, and among his survival instincts was a healthy dose of paranoia. He wouldn't talk to Robert.

Perhaps it was to justify his reluctance to confront Robert that Fred started thinking about Grace. What would it do to her if her father was labeled as a liar. She already lost her mother. And the fact was that people don't commit suicide if they're fine mentally. Dust must have been depressed, but maybe it wasn't actual depression, maybe she just felt hopeless, defeated. Maybe it was the only way she could see to solve the problems in her life. She wanted to save the planet, but even in her own house, she was ignored and ridiculed. The Be Green truck came whether she wanted it to or not, the addition was built, and her garden was destroyed. She got worn down.

They said a memorial was planned for "some future date." Obviously, they were letting this tragedy cool down until after the election.

Fred wanted a smoke.

15. LILY

A year ago in October, Lily (the oldest student in her evening geology class at Oakland Community College) was heading home with her brain busily digesting information about rocks. Her head was crammed with facts about the earth's tectonic plates: continental crusts made of granitic rocks, quartz, and feldspar; oceanic crusts made of heavier basaltic rock. The earth's floating tectonic plates were constantly shifting and moving. An oceanic plate could sink under a lighter continental plate and eventually disappear. The thought of it made her feel a bit unsteady on her feet. Wobbly. She thought of her father's infatuation with Carole King and a song he played over and over about the earth moving under her feet.

She wasn't in a hurry. As usual, Jagger was working late and the boys were with friends, so she stopped at the vending machine to get a paper cup filled with nasty coffee to drink on the short drive home. The machine ate all her quarters, but no cup dropped down. She pushed buttons. Nothing happened. She kicked the machine. Shook it. Bumped it with her hip. Nothing happened.

Behind her, a deep male voice said, "You can get five years in jail for assaulting a vending machine."

He was cute, shaggy-haired, with laughing eyes.

"Are you the coffee cop?" Lily asked.

He laughed, and said, "You're quick. I like that."

"If you're the coffee cop, do you give quarters back?"

"Nope. But I'll buy you a cup of coffee, or a beer, if you'd like."

She gazed around the room, feigning shock, and asked, "They have a beer vending machine?"

"Not here, Goose. We can drink elsewhere."

So they walked up the street to Elsewhere, where students and teachers hung out after class, where huddled young adults were being inculcated with the wisdom of their elders around old pine picnic tables. Goose and the Coffee Cop found stools at a puddled laminate counter. He ordered beer and she ordered coffee. They talked. They laughed. He introduced himself, "Evan Zowarski, professor of painting and art history." He shook her hand, and didn't let go of it.

She felt her oceanic tectonic plate sliding under his continental tectonic plate.

She was a goner.

***

A year had passed. Evan was her friend and her lover. Lily was playing hooky from her Tuesday night literature class, where she'd miss a discussion of Steinbeck's *Grapes of Wrath*.

Hooky. She desperately needed hooky tonight. She was playing hooky from her class and playing hooky from being Jagger's wife. She didn't like missing her class, but as far as Jagger was concerned, she was surprised that she didn't feel guilty about that truancy.

When she called Evan's studio, unsure if he'd be there, she had her fingers crossed. When he answered, her fingers relaxed. After she told him about Dust, the phone line was quiet for what felt like a full minute. She wasn't sure if she had lost the connection.

"Evan? Evan, are you still there?"

"Lily," he said, "I'm so sorry. But what are you doing on the phone? We should talk in person. Come on down here. I was going to head home, but I'll wait. Come down here."

***

As she walked down the long corridor of the industrial building in Detroit, she saw Evan standing outside his studio door waiting for her, and she felt lighter. Whatever this relationship was or wasn't, she knew that being here was the right thing to do at this moment in her life. Evan would listen to her, or at least look like he was listening to her.

When she reached him, he took her hand and lead her inside his studio, then put his arms around her, and held her. He soothed her hair, then held her face in both of his hands and kissed her.

The windows faced north (the best light for painting) but they were so dirty it didn't matter which way they faced and besides, it was dark out. Around Evan Zowarski's large studio, paintings were stacked against the walls. The bottom right corner of each finished painting was signed Zoo—the Z written with a Zorro swash.

He had a fresh pot of coffee, brewed while he waited for her to arrive. He sat her down at his old oak table and poured her a cup.

"Okay, talk about it," he said, as he sat down across from her with his own paint splattered and smudged cup.

"I don't understand why she did it, and I do understand. But I thought, all our lives, I thought she was the strong one, resilient. I was the one more likely to do it, not with a gun, for sure, but I was the one more likely to throw in the towel. Not Dust."

"So how does that make you feel?" He was watching her face, intent, like some psychiatrist on a TV show, only without a notepad. She hadn't responded, and he asked again, "How does that make you feel?"

"Angry."

"Angry at her, or angry at you?"

"Everyone," she said.

Evan got up, went across the room and came back with a pad of newsprint paper and a box of pastels. She wondered if he was planning to draw a picture of her in pain, and was even more irritated. She thought he would just talk to her, not use her as a model of misery.

"Here," he said and pushed the pad of paper toward her.

"Here, what?"

"Take a pastel and make a mark."

"I'm not an artist, Evan. Why do you want me to do that? I can't draw."

"You don't need to draw anything. Make a mark."

"Why?"

"Just do it, Lily."

"Which color?"

"Pick whichever you're drawn to."

She took a red pastel from the box and drew a careful line on the paper.

"Are you angry?" he asked.

"Yes, damn it. What's the point of this."

"Who are you angry at right now?"

"You!"

"Make angry marks," he said, his voice calm and quietly firm. "Stand up and attack the paper. Mark it."

She pushed her chair back and stood. Clutched the red pastel and slashed the paper with hard red lines, again and again. The pastel crumbled and broke. She stopped then, guilty for breaking his toy.

"Keep going. Take another color, who else are you angry with?"

"My mother," she said, and surprised herself.

"Scream at her without words. Tell her how she hurt you."

She chose black, and with the pastel held in her fist like a dagger, she stabbed at the paper. Again and again, stabbing her pain into the soft pad of newsprint.

She stopped. Looked at him. He nodded approval.

"Who else?" he asked.

"Dust."

She took an aqua pastel from the box.

"Show her how angry you are. She's the paper and you want to hit her hard. Let her know what a terrible thing she's done to you."

Messaging Dust, at first she scribbled violently, but then her strokes became gentle, then letters—x's and o's, kisses and hugs. Tears dripped on the paper. She was suddenly exhausted. Used up.

"Do you feel any better?" he asked.

She thought about it, felt her fingers gritty with chalk dust. Did she feel better? She smiled at him, and walked around the table, put her dirty hands on his face, all over his face, and said, "Thank you. I needed that."

16. ROBERT

It was a month before the election, but Robert wouldn't campaign anymore. He wouldn't chat in diners or expound behind a podium. He wouldn't sip coffee in constituent's living room. What would it look like? A man whose wife committed suicide out glad-handing—rah, rah? It just wouldn't look right. It would be shameful. His commercials were playing on the radio and TV; no one needed to see him live and in person. His heart wasn't in it. He imagined some heckler shouting out something cruel and him crying, standing at a podium with his face splotchy with tears. Nope, he was staying home.

A few people from the campaign had dropped by Sunday night. Someone brought him little plants in a big jar—a terrarium. Bouquets of roses and lilies had been delivered. If he had a best friend, he'd probably come over and hang out with him—watch football, drink beer, and avoid talking about death. But his best friend had shot herself last Friday.

It was Monday. Was it three days? Four days? He occupied himself with counting days on his fingers. Three days—three long, interminable, painful days.

When the doorbell rang, he ignored it. The old iron doorknocker thunked impatiently, and he pretended deafness but the knocker was persistent. He peeked out the side window, and saw a strange car parked on the side street. The knocker banged again, resonating through the house. He gave in and opened the door, and there, standing on his porch, was his second best friend in the world—his sister Elizabeth, better known to him as Lizard.

"I told you I was coming up, Bobby. I guess you didn't believe me," she said. "Remember, didn't I tell you on the phone? I said, 'I'm comin' up there,'" Elizabeth said, and wrapped her arms around him.

"Liz," he said, and gratitude rushed over him. "God, it's good to see you."

She was Lizard and he was Row-butt or Robot. He wished she'd call him Row-butt again, then the world would be back to normal. She was being gentle with BobbyHoneyBabyBrother, but Elizabeth was a year younger than Robert, his baby sister.

He thought he wanted to be alone, but now knew that he didn't. He took her suitcase, brought it in off the porch and shut the front door. "But, Liz, you know you shouldn't be here. You've got an election of your own to deal with down thar in Taxes." He always said Taxes instead of Texas, only because his fake accent bugged her.

She swatted him—like he knew she would—and they both laughed.

"I am so happy to see you," he said, and felt like he was gushing too much. "How're the kids? How's Bubba?"

"The kids are fine," she said. "And I'm just gonna ignore the Bubba bit. Rodney is fine too. God, Bobby, I'm married to a skinny Englishman, quit calling him Bubba."

"How's your polling going?" he asked. If they talked politics, he was much less apt to start blubbering.

"Actually," Liz said, "it's pretty good. Bobby, just think of it. I could become Austin's tenth district Democratic Congresswoman Elizabeth Steward Taylor. Sound's good, huh?" she said. "You probably don't like that Democratic part, right? Sorry, Bobby. Anywho, I'm banking on the name recognition Elizabeth Taylor will buy me." She stopped then and looked at his face, "Oh, hey, Bobby,

I'm sorry. I'm going on and on and not giving you a chance. Tell me how you're doing?"

"Election-wise?" he said. "It's hard to say. Bad in some polls, good in others."

"No, Bobby, not the election. How's your...your self? How you holding up, Baby Brother?"

He shook his head, felt his lip tremble, but didn't want to speak. He took her hand and led her back through the house to the family room. As they went through the doorway of the old dining room, she let out a gasp.

"Holy crap, Bobby!" she said, looking around the addition. "Holy crap, this place is huge."

Since Dust died, he'd talked to his sister daily. Between them they had decided that they shouldn't try to contact their parents. What could they do about anything anyway? They couldn't bring Dust back to him. Their folks were on their dream trip, two months in France, Spain, and Italy and then a cruise in the Mediterranean Sea. The big trip and his father's retirement were all courtesy of Old Rob's last will and testament.

Old Rob hadn't helped his sister Elizabeth pay for her law degree; Old Rob thought education was wasted on women. He was from another era. Robert's parents had both worked and helped her with college tuition, and she'd had student loans up the wazoo. She wasn't mentioned in the will, so Robert had shared some of his inheritance with her. *See that, I'm a good guy,* he told himself, whenever he felt bruised and beaten, which certainly was how he was feeling since Dust shot a bullet through his self-esteem.

Liz sat on one of the stools at the kitchen island and gazed around, twirling on the stool like a kid. "This is the wide open sort of space they like in Texas—land of big houses and women with big hair."

"So, can you be successful with your little hair?" he asked. "Don't you have to tease it up or something? You look too Northern to me."

"Austin's different."

"Austin's weird," he said.

"Is Grace still at Christina's?"

"Yeah, I think she's afraid of the house," he said. "It has ghosts. A bad thing happened here. She's not ready to come home yet, and I think she's mad at me."

They hung around the house all afternoon. Liz put some pieces in Dust's jigsaw puzzle on the dining room table. The table and all the puzzle pieces were dusty, obviously untouched for weeks. A puzzle piece picked up left a dark impression where it had been before the room went without being cleaned. Was the dusty table and untouched puzzle a visual sign of his wife's depression?

Robert put his sister's luggage in a bedroom, and then gave her a tour of the new master suite. She raved about how beautiful it was—oohing and aahing. He was glad he'd vacuumed on Sunday afternoon. Then she followed him into the bathroom. She stood still in the doorway, and then turned away sobbing.

They ate a casserole someone had dropped off and watched TV. The evening news came on with reports that Senator Steward's wife had been seeing a psychiatrist for years for bipolar disorder, and that she'd been hospitalized in Mexico.

"Bobby, why didn't I know that?" Liz said. "How she must have suffered, and you, Baby Brother, it's a painful thing. I know people who are bipolar and truly it's so difficult. Medication helps, but then they miss the euphoria of the highs and don't take their pills. Lithium, I think. And the lows, oh crap, the lows. I have a friend who becomes bedridden with depression for days. Was Dust that extreme? And poor Gracie, does she show any signs of mood swings?"

She was talking so fast he could barely get a word in, but then that was her normal speech pattern. Maybe it came from their childhood when Uncle Rob ignored her, so she had to get everything out in a hurry, before the old man just turned and walked away from her. Robert had seen him do that many times, and it always made him feel bad.

"Stop. Stop, Liz," Robert said. "Don't you know by now that during political campaigns you only get the truth when it's caught on a hidden camera?"

"So? What do you mean?"

She looked at him, confused, then her eyes widened. "Oh crap. Oh crap. Wait a minute. Are you saying that the news reports aren't true?"

"Yes."

"You mean, yes, not true? And the psychiatrist that was on TV? Oh crap, Bobby."

"I told my campaign manager to tell the press she was depressed, but no, depressed wasn't enough for Chuck. He had to turn it into something else, something that would leave me innocent." His voice cracked then, "I'm not innocent, Liz. Maybe she was depressed or maybe she just felt hopeless. Everything she believed in, I smacked down. I did it." He was remembering how Old Rob had constantly dismissed Liz, like whatever she said had no value. Had he treated his wife like Old Rob treated his sister?

"Oh crap," she whispered again.

"I don't know what to do about it," he said. "I'm responsible for whatever my campaign says. The campaign wrote checks to that quack doctor. If I tell the truth, I'm dead. Disgraced. Any ideas?"

She just shook her head, and said, "Oh crap."

On Tuesday, she went with him to make cremation arrangements for Dust's body, then that night they took Grace out to dinner. Grace was polite and affectionate with Liz. The girl could actually act civilized. But she never looked at him, never met his eyes. She hugged Liz and brushed him off like a cockroach. She acted like if she even looked at him her eyes might fall out of her head or she'd go blind. Liz saw it, and he was mortified.

He had his sister's company for two days, two good days, and then she was off in her rental car, heading back to the airport and back to Taxes.

17. GRACE

By Thursday, Grace had been back in school for two days. Both she and Grandma decided that it was going be tough, but they were tough women. They'd go back to school and work. When Grace came in the school doors, it felt like a safe place. Kids going back to a school where there had been a shooting, like at Columbine High School in Colorado, had to be scared going back into those buildings. The scary thing in Grace's life happened in her own house. She hadn't been back there yet. Grandma had collected the clothes she needed. Grace was afraid of her house.

Kids were talking about her mother. She knew that because they'd be standing in the hallways between classes huddled in groups—leaning in, gossiping. Now she knew that her mother hadn't taken pills; she shot herself. Neither Grandma nor Dad told her, she saw it on the news before Grandma could change the channel. Her mother's picture had been on TV, and she looked like her, so even the kids who never spoke to her before gave her sad looks or just stared at her, or avoided her altogether. Maybe people always did that and she just hadn't noticed before. She was suddenly conspicuous, or maybe just self-conscious.

The newscasters said that her mother was bipolar, manic-depressive, so the kids in the halls seemed afraid of her, like being a maniac was catching. Oh yes, these people were so stupid they never looked things up, even though they all carried the Internet around in their pockets. Grace overheard *maniac* whispered as she passed kids in the halls. Everyone thought that she was going to be crazy too.

Maybe she'd come to school with a gun and shoot people; everyone knew that her dad had guns in the house.

Grace looked up bipolar disorder on her laptop. Then she carefully studied all the websites as though she had to write a paper for a class. People in a manic state have high energy levels. They make impulsive decisions, talk fast, and move in a hurry. It made her think of the white rabbit in *Alice in Wonderland*, rushing about, singing, "I'm late. I'm late," and not even knowing where he was going. That rabbit was definitely manic. Sometimes people in a manic state had delusions; believing they could read minds, buy whatever they wanted, win at gambling, or cure illnesses like they had psychic powers. Sometimes they showed inappropriate behavior like dressing outrageously or they did sexual things that weren't in their best interest. The chemistry inside their own brains could make them act stoned or drunk.

Her mother could be very happy, like last June when Grace brought home her report card and her mother twirled her around the kitchen, congratulating her for getting all A's. Her mother knew how hard she worked to get those good grades. Grandma told her that Mom used to be bursting with joy when she was a child, especially if frogs or tree climbing were involved. But that was nothing like what the websites described as manic.

One website had a test so you could see if you had the symptoms. She answered the questions for her mother and then for herself. Neither of them was manic. The other part of the bipolar disorder was depression. When she looked up the symptoms of depression, she found her mother there.

Her mother was so irritating during the last few weeks before she died. When Grace tried to tell her something that she thought was very important, it was like her mother wasn't home inside her own head. Grace recalled times when she'd get frazzled and say, "Mom, Mom, pay attention. You're not listening to me." Then her mother would seem startled, like she'd been asleep and Grace had just woken her up. She'd say, "What? What is it, Grace?" And Grace, feeling irritated, would walk away, saying, "Never mind."

She wished she hadn't done that; she wished she was smarter; wished that she'd read this list with signs of depression then instead of now. Her mother wasn't sleeping well at night. Sometimes Grace would wake up hearing the stairs creak and knew her mother was wandering around the house. She'd see her sitting in the living room staring into space, not reading or watching TV or doing anything, or she'd be curled up on the loveseat with a pillow over her head, like she had a bad headache.

Grace knew her mother was upset about the house remodeling, but that had been going on for months, long before she went into this depressed fog. Grace tried to remember, was it when the house was finally finished that her mother went from normal to depressed? For months she'd grumbled and had a few shit-fits, but she had also laughed a lot and worked on the jigsaw puzzle in the dining room with Grace. But then, just a few weeks ago, she didn't feel like working on the puzzle; she didn't feel like doing anything anymore. She let her hair get stringy and dirty and the house was a mess. Her mother was depressed. Then on that awful morning, Grace swore at her mother like she was some piece of junk or garbage. Grace pushed her right over the edge.

Grace was mad at herself, mad at other kids, mad at the teachers, sometimes even mad at her mother, but most of all she was mad at her dad. She hadn't gone back to her own home yet; she asked her dad if she could stay at her grandmother's for a while longer. She didn't tell him, but she was furious with him. After Grandma told her it was normal for a thirteen-year-old to say mean things to her mother, she thought of all the mean things her dad had said to her mom. He said she was worthless. "Worth nothing." He said it right to her face the night before she shot herself. Her dad was way older than thirteen. He should be past that stage of being nasty to someone you love.

So now it was a balancing act for her, like being on the balance bar in gymnastics, careful not to lean too far in one direction. She was angry with him and had decided that her mother's death was all his fault—especially during those moments when she didn't want it to be her fault—but she couldn't say it or show it. What if she hurt him so much that he killed himself too? Then she'd have no parents and she would be responsible for his death. She might feel so bad that she'd kill herself too, and then Grandma would be alone. Grandma would be so sad with her daughter and granddaughter both dead that she'd kill herself too. There would be no one left. All her anger at her father had to be smushed down inside her so everyone could stay living.

Her mother didn't leave a note for Grace or her dad, and it made perfect sense to Grace. Why would she leave such mean people a note?

**

Grace's mind wandered. She couldn't concentrate and was having trouble in her classes. She'd probably never get all A's again in her whole life. She overheard one teacher telling another that she was surprised that Grace was back in school so soon. Teachers were being extra kind to her; they weren't calling on her with hard questions, or any questions for that matter. She figured most of them were mind readers anyway, and they knew if they asked her to stand up and speak, she'd probably cry, then stupid kids would laugh and sensitive kids would cry too. Everyone would be upset in one way or another. She could stay home from school and that would probably be understandable to everyone, even the principal. Maybe it would even be a relief to everyone if she weren't around making them uncomfortable. Grandma went back to work at the hospital and after their first day back Grandma told her she was having all the same problems. People were avoiding her. People just didn't know what to do or how to act around her.

Kids that Grace thought were her good friends were suddenly busy. One girl that she thought was a close friend said, "Sorry about your mom," then rushed off saying she was late for "mumble, mumble." Maybe she was late for mumble, or maybe she was just uncomfortable. Another girl's parents suddenly took her on vacation, and another was sick with laryngitis or something, so she couldn't even talk on the phone. Maybe her friends were being honest, it could all be real and true, but it felt like no one wanted to be her friend anymore just when she needed one the most. Maybe her friends and their parents were afraid; Grace's environment was unstable and there were guns in her house. If she was a parent, she wouldn't let her child hang out with her either.

She was thinking that whatever anyone else was doing had something to do with her—she was, after all, the center of the whole universe. Ha. That was a laugh.

What was true and real was that her mom was dead. Maybe her friends weren't rejecting her? Maybe she was rejecting them? Surreptitious Texter wasn't communicating. There was a message from her friend Julia, the one home sick with laryngitis. *So sorry about your mom*, Julia texted. Grace didn't respond. It was so confusing. She was hurt because people were avoiding her, but when they paid attention, she couldn't deal with that either. Why was she so weird?

Her English class ended and she walked down the hall on her way to the cafeteria for lunch. People looked away from her as she walked past. They all looked at the lockers as though something interesting was happening with a wall full of metal boxes. Oh, would you look at that, those lockers have vents at the top, probably so the stinky gym socks you keep in there won't smell up the whole school. Grace was mad at lockers and socks too.

In the cafeteria, she picked up a tray and got her lunch, then looked around for a place to sit. A boy behind her said, "Grace, come sit with me. That is, if you want to."

Max Mellon. She knew Max from grade school. They had been in classes together for most of their lives. Max had on skinny jeans, and the ends of his hair were bleached white blond. He used to get beat up all the time when he was little. She wondered if kids were still mean to him. Maybe he needed someone to be nice to him too?

"Okay, sure," she said, and smiled at Max.

"I think you're very brave, Grace," he said. "I heard about your mom. I'm sorry that happened."

She nodded, afraid that if she said, *me too,* she'd start to cry and drive him away.

While they ate lunch, Max did most of the talking. They were in the same Spanish class.

"El burgereno mucho delicioso," Max said, and they both laughed. He pulled a slice of pickle from his burger, and held it up, and exclaimed, "Pickle-o."

She laughed.

"No, Max," she said, "a piccolo is a wind instrument."

"No, baked beanos are wind instruments."

She was having fun, but the bell would ring any minute and it would be over.

"Want to come over to my house after school?" he said. "I've got a Wii. We could play some games."

Grace felt lighter. It was like she'd been carrying a pile of books on her head, trying to walk erect like a fashion model. Max lifted off the books. Her shoulders stopped aching and even her neck felt better. "Yeah, okay," she said. She would text Grandma at work and see if she could pick her up at Max's house later.

18. LILY

The next time Lily visited Evan's studio, she brought him a new pad of newsprint and a fresh box of pastels.

"You didn't have to do that," he said.

"How did you know that taking my anger out on your art supplies would make me feel better?"

And it did help, the anger had dissipated, somewhat anyway, but the sorrow was still there.

"I've worked with kids with issues. Art therapy. It does help. Maybe you should keep that stuff yourself and use it whenever you feel upset."

"How would I explain a sudden interest in drawing to my family?"

"Why would you have to?"

Excellent question. Why?

Evan sat down on the mattress in his studio and reached out his hand, inviting Lily to join him. He was staring across the room studying his latest masterpiece. The huge painting filled most of the west wall of his studio. Tree trunks, a whole forest of them, red and pink and beige and brown with rays of light shining down in white streams. He'd been working fast since the last time she was here and had covered yards of canvas with paint. She could tell that this was the under painting. The paint was thin and almost transparent in places. She'd learned a lot from Evan over the past year.

"Trees," she said. "I like them."

He laughed. "Actually, I thought they were penises."

She got up and moved closer to the painting. Were they tree trunks growing out of rocks, or penises shooting up out of testicles? Skinny penises and fat penises were rising high off the canvas. The heads of the penises were somewhere above and beyond the painting surface. She laughed.

"Seriously? Penises? What does your wife think of you painting six foot tall penises?"

"My wife?" he said, and looked startled. "It's none of her business what I paint. Besides, maybe they are trees. It's for the viewer to decide."

She sat back down on the mattress beside him. "Dust believed that trees could save the planet," Lily said.

He turned away from the painting and stared at her for several moments. "She was right. Trees can save the planet, but they need government to help. Governments. Plural. And people doing the right things, like not chopping down trees or emitting toxins into the air."

Some months ago, Evan had given her an intense dissertation on how he struggled to find a safe way to paint with oils without damaging his brain or destroying the ozone, but he still wanted the juicy feel of the paint moving under his brush. None of the commercial options felt right. Obviously, he hadn't found an answer yet. The air in the studio was toxic, which she didn't mention. Maybe good intentions weren't enough; maybe change meant some sacrifice. Lily noticed that her own internal voice had started sounding like Dust. She was being haunted. Maybe her brain was possessed. She didn't believe in reincarnation, but...

"I miss her. I miss Dust," she said.

"I'm sorry about your friend," Evan said, and put his arm around her. He kissed her. He had nice lips—soft, not too wet, not too dry.

"I have something that can make you forget for a while," he whispered.

"Would it be a tree?"

"Yep, a woody, working on being a tree."

"How long can it make me forget?" she asked.

"Oh, maybe half an hour."

"Sold," she said.

They stripped quickly. She stretched out long and languid on his ratty mattress, waiting for him to play her like he played the accordion he kept in his studio. The man was free. He painted what he wanted to paint. He took lovers without guilt. He played the uncool accordion like an enthusiastic musician squeezing out a polka at a Polish wedding. He tinkled his fingers delicately over her breasts as though she had buttons and keys that made sound. He played a stanza of silent music down her belly and into her pubic hair, finding her moist and open, ready for a song. He fluttered two-fingered notes, playing her clitoris like a mandolin and she quivered. She held his tree, stroked it, and then reached for the box of condoms he kept beside the mattress. She opened a packet and dressed him for their party. Then he was inside her, moving slowly, concentrating on her face, watching her.

"Where are you, Lily?" he said. "Where are you right now?"

"I'm here."

"No, you're not here. Tell me where you are." He continued to glide smoothly and slowly inside her.

"I'm ten years old in Dust's attic bedroom. She's telling me that she saw her parents in bed covered up to their necks, but she could see that her father was on top of her mother. So we decided to try it. I was supposed to be the dad. I went to the far end of her room and knocked on the wall. She said, 'Fathers don't knock when they come home. They just walk in and say, hello, Honey, I'm home.' So I went back and did it over. 'Honey, I'm home,' I said. Then I went over to her bed and laid on top of her."

Interest piqued, Evan's movements intensified.

"Did you rub against each other?" he asked, "Did you have an orgasm?"

Lily laughed. "No, we were fully clothed, we took turns being the dad on top, and we just laid there squashing each other. We had no idea that there was more to it. I think we decided it was boring."

Swiftly, expertly, he rolled them both over and she was on top. "Now it's your turn to be the dad," he said, and laughed. "Being on the bottom is passive, you can daydream and just be a receptacle. On top you have to be The Force. Be here. Be in this moment. Be The Force, Lily. Be The Force."

She was The Force. They were in *Star Wars* and she was The Force. She slid herself up and down on his tree, or maybe now it was his sword or glowing light saber.

He was wrong, her body moved up and down, but she wasn't there. She was with Dust again. They were thirteen taking a walk down their block one autumn night. They were on a mission. They wanted to scope out the house of the new boy the next block over on Rembrandt Avenue, the cute new boy with the weird name. They'd just walk casually past his house, see if they could catch him in a lighted window inside, but the boy was outside hidden in the dark shadows on his front porch. He'd heard them giggling and saw them standing still in front of his house. They were exposed, embarrassed. He came down off the porch and asked where they were going. Of course, they didn't admit that they were stalkers. Gallant, he said he'd walk them home, keep them safe from danger; after all, he was fourteen, a whole year older than them. So he walked between them, and when they got to their houses, he said goodnight on the front sidewalk. Lily remembered how thrilled she was. She couldn't wait to tell Dust that the boy held her hand all the way home. It was so romantic, and then hilarious since Dust had the same story to tell.

Evan was groaning, cranked up, not caring anymore where her thoughts were going. She contracted and then relaxed her pelvic muscles helping him along, making it better for him. When he came, he shouted her name, "Oh, Lily. Oh, Lily." She knew there were other women besides his wife and was always impressed that he never got the names mixed up.

No orgasm for Lily, her heart couldn't be distracted, and it didn't help that her husband had shown up in her youthful memory—Jagger walking with Dust and Lily and holding both their hands. Jagger was a perfectly nice guy. He was her husband. Why was she doing this?

She washed up in the shallow sink where Evan cleaned his paintbrushes. They used a condom, but she worried about carrying his scent home to her husband. She dried herself on the towel she'd brought Evan after their first meeting. The towel and washcloth matched her linens at home, so periodically she could take them home and wash them. The other choice was cleaning up with his paint rags, but then she risked red oil paint or turpentine-scented body parts.

He was naked and obviously in no hurry to dress. He poured her a cup of coffee from his paint splattered Mr. Coffee machine while she finished getting into her jeans and sweater.

He kissed her as he handed her the coffee.

"Lily," he said, "where are you now."

"You know how much I like you, Evan."

"Oh, oh."

"I think I have to go back to being a good wife again. I'm feeling so bad about Dust. Maybe if I'm a better person, I won't feel so bad. I'm so guilty. I didn't know what she was going to do. She was my best friend and I didn't have any idea she would..." her voice faded, "Maybe I need to start living in some way where I don't have to feel guilty about anything. Do you think that's possible?"

"No."

"I could try," she said. She was thinking that maybe if she started treating Jagger like someone she loved again, then maybe that would cause the love to grow back.

"Lily, you're not going to tell your husband about us, are you?"

"No, don't worry. What good would that do?"

He sipped his coffee, then said, "I guess you have to decide what's best for you."

He put down the cup and reached out, pulled her close, and whispered, "I'll miss you. If you change your mind, you can come back anytime."

She left her towel and washcloth with him. He might think it a hopeful sign that she'd return, but she was thinking that when he had another lover, she would want a towel too. As she walked down the wide corridor of the industrial building, she could hear accordion music coming from his studio. It sounded sad.

19. CHRISTINA

On a scale of one to ten,
how would you describe your pain?
Ten.
Unrelentingly ten.

Christina was an open wound, oozing anger, sorrow, guilt, and regrets. Everything she'd done as a mother was up for questioning. Maybe she should have taken Dusty and moved to California to live with Jay? Dusty would have had a full-time father, but would Jay have been a *good* father full-time? Christina had one child, but she had three dependents—her parents needed her back then. Her father was always ill and her mother couldn't manage on her own. Maybe she could have taken them to California, too? No, they wouldn't have moved. There were doctors her father trusted, doctors that he wouldn't and shouldn't leave. And the fact was that Jay Jones never asked her to move. He preferred his freedom over his family.

She should have divorced Jay, since it was obvious that Jay had never been interested in a real marriage. Catholic was how Christina saw herself. Now she looked back and felt that she had been trapped by her religion, or maybe she'd used religion as a tool—a reason—for doing what she would have done anyway. Maybe being a good Catholic was her subterfuge. She'd kept to her standards of being a good person by caring for others, being a faithful wife, and being a good neighbor. She took care of her parents, the neighbor's girls like they were her own, and the fragile little ones at Children's Hospital.

She'd done all the things that a good Christian woman was supposed to do. She used to like being who she was—a good woman.

But now it all felt wrong. Had she been smug about her godliness? Smug. She didn't want to think that God would punish her for that, but it did cross her mind. Everything in her life was now questionable. She held up a microscope and found fault lines as deep as craters in everything about her and her life.

What had she shown Dusty about marriage? When Jay Jones came home for a week or a month, Christina had been (especially in the early years, Dust's formative years) so in love, so lonely, and so willing to be anyone her husband wanted her to be, so willing to defer to whatever made him happy, all with hopes that he'd stay home for good. In later years when he showed up on her doorstep she'd be sweet and loving, even when she was madder than hell. Dusty never saw a balanced give-and-take marriage, she saw her mother give and her father do exactly what he wanted to do. They had been terrible role models.

Christina thought about Dusty's love of nature, and how she had observed seasons and weather and bugs and plants—all on her own, she found meaning beyond romance. Dusty had centered her interest in the world outdoors, on a place with more checks and balances than in her family life. Then a man, who looked scarily like Jay Jones, had swept her off her feet. Dusty had smothered all her own dreams to please the man who looked like her father, and Robert took advantage of it. Perhaps she was being unfair to Robert, Christina wondered. Maybe Robert was just being Robert, and dominating her daughter was instinctive. And what about that beautiful new addition? To some people it might appear like Robert was giving, and Dusty was unappreciative. But Robert was taking. He wanted what he wanted, and he would have what he wanted regardless of the cost. Her son-in-law dismissed every value that was important to her daughter.

Dominating. Making the choices. She saw for the first time how the Church had influenced her choices. The Church she loved had decided for her; she had to stay married to Jay Jones. Was abiding by the Church's rules an easy way to do what she wanted to do? The Church took responsibility out of her hands. The Church was the decider. If she followed the rules, everything would be fine. But it wasn't. Nothing was fine. Her daughter was dead.

Father O'Donnelly had come to see her. He held her hands and told her that her daughter was no longer suffering, that she was at God's side. She told the priest about a time when she was a young woman and an acquaintance of hers, a woman in her twenties, had committed suicide. The priests had refused to say a mass; they said suicide was a mortal sin. Father O'Donnelly told her that the Church had evolved, and now someone who commits suicide is considered mentally ill. They aren't sinners but sick. The Church doesn't turn its back on the ill—at least not anymore.

Her daughter had stopped being a Catholic. There would be no mass for her. Christina had to defer to Robert's wishes. Lily had come over, had taken her hand and laid the rosary in her palm. She told her that Dusty had it in the bathroom with her. What did that mean? Was rubbing the beads merely a stress-relieving habit? Christina held the pink rosary in her hands. Was Dusty looking for God? If she was seeking a God that would pay attention to her—a God that would reassure her and tell her that life gets better, worse, then better again—she hadn't found Him.

They had all seen the news reports. "Dusty was severely bipolar, under a psychiatrist's care," or had been. A psychiatrist, a doctor from some clinic Christina had never heard of, came on the news saying he'd treated Dusty for many years. Christina had known people who were bipolar, had seen the frantic mood swings, the racing euphoria, and the crushing depression. As far as she knew, bipolar disorder tended to run in families. No one in either her or

Jay Jones's family displayed any of the symptoms you'd expect. Nothing about Dusty seemed bipolar to her.

But then what did Christina know? When your children become adults, you are only privy to the things they choose to tell you. These entities—who formed inside your body, whose ears you cleaned, whose snot you squeezed away with your bare fingers, whose poopy bottoms you gently wiped until they were pristine—grew up and it never crossed their minds to tell you when they were in trouble. They moved beyond you into some netherworld of their own dark secrets and bright pleasures.

Ben Abbott, Lily and Rose's father, had been her friend for nearly forty years. It was normal for him to call her every few weeks. But now he'd started calling daily, and some days he just showed up at her door with some sweet confection they'd share. He brought fattening treats and gentle hugs for her and Grace. He was a good man. Years ago, after his wife Wanda had been gone for a while, Ben had tried to woo her. He would have been a good husband and a good father to Dusty. But Christina was afraid, afraid of God, afraid of doing the wrong thing. But being afraid of doing that wrong thing, had she done another wrong thing?

Her daughter killed herself. Everything was up for questioning.

Rose had been to see her. She'd arrived in her pink scrubs, coming from the nursing home where Christina's mother lived. Rose cared about her—watched her and worried over her and Grace. These young women, Lily and Rose, and their father, Ben, loved her. She was grateful for them.

Work was hard. Now that her own grown-up baby girl was dead, caring for the young lives at Children's Hospital was painful. She was so distracted, she was afraid of making a mistake with the children in her care. The doctors, the nurse practitioners, and the other nurses were suddenly watching everything she did. She'd begun thinking about retiring. She was just old enough to get social security. It was probably time to make room for some younger person to have her job.

On busy days there often wasn't time for an actual lunch hour, so she'd eat a yogurt in the lunchroom. But on quiet days, she spent her free time roaming though the Detroit Medical Center, where pale blue underground tunnels connected Children's Hospital and Receiving Hospital. In Receiving, she could lose herself in the art. Courtyards housed huge sculptures, hallways were filled with fine paintings, African art and beadwork, Pewebic Pottery tile mosaics, and fiber pieces by Robert Kidd. Her favorite was an abstract painting by Louise Nobili. All of it distracted her as she looked at form and color and left her pain somewhere else.

She walked the halls and was aware of walking, aware of her feet moving in a straight line. After Dusty's suicide, Christina's first thought was that Dusty was unhappy about her weight. That was almost funny since it wasn't Dusty who had that problem, it was Christina. A year ago her daughter had suggested that they join a health club. She told Christina that she was too shy to go alone, and so they had joined a club with a wonderful track that they walked together round and round. They giggled about the young men who flexed their muscles when cute girls—or sometimes cute guys— walked past them. Now Christina acknowledged that her daughter was only slightly overweight, maybe five pounds. Dusty didn't need her mother to exercise with her. Dusty was getting her mother out to help her lose weight. Her gentle-hearted daughter never said a word about Christina being too fat, but she got her out exercising.

Christina knew it would be too painful to walk the track at the health club, so in the meantime, she'd get some exercise and some peace by walking the Detroit Medical Center's halls, surrounded by the art. She wondered if she'd ever be able to go back and walk that track at the health club again. Dusty had given her a lifetime membership; she wanted her mother to get healthier. She wanted

Christina to have life, even when she may have started thinking about taking her own.

The day before she died, she called Christina at work and said, "Mom, I know you're busy. I just wanted to tell you that I love you." Christina held onto those words, treasures that she rubbed in her memory, shining them like valuable silver spoons, keeping them from getting lost or tarnished.

20. LILY

Lily had decided that she was going to change. She was determined to be different—better, braver, nicer, and kinder. The world was going to get a sweeter, gentler Lily. Lily's house would be The Sparkling House—beds made, carpets vacuumed, counters wiped, mirrors de-splattered, clothes ironed or at least put away. Lily's body would be The Sparkling Body—bubbled and creamed, plucked and shaved, curled and combed, flossed, clipped, and polished. She put away her baggy-assed sweats.

It occurred to her that she was turning into a supplicant: a 1950's wife—a June Cleaver without the pearls, a humiliated secretary on *Mad Men*. She brushed that thought aside. Was it so bad to put her husband first? Couldn't she be a good feminist and a good wife at the same time? She was paying attention to Jagger—listening, responding intelligently and lovingly: *how was your day, honey; oh wow, there's still someone with an Edsel; can I get you a beer; sure I'll watch the Lions game with you.* It was exhausting, but she was determined.

Sometimes she watched herself—detached and appalled—as she followed her husband around, as eager and needy as a lap dog waiting for her master to pet her head. She could have been panting and drooling with her tongue hanging out, alert at his knee, waiting eagerly for him to toss her a bone. She was knowingly turning herself into Jagger's bitch.

As she polished furniture and her body, her brain was racing. Dust's death was a new and painful wound that filled her every minute, but sneaky thoughts of her mother kept snarling around in her head. Does the death of one person that you love stir up all the other losses you ever had? What happened to her mother? Where was she? Did she die? Why was she there one day and then never heard from again? Why did Dust shoot herself? Why did her mother leave her? Where did she go? If her mother died then why wasn't there a funeral? If there was a funeral, did her father protect his girls by keeping them home from it? Why did her car and all her clothes disappear too? She hadn't thought about her mother in years, and now she was haunted. Memories. *Daddy, when's Mommy coming home? Where's Mommy? Doesn't my Mommy miss me?* She was eight again, crying herself to sleep, thinking she did something bad that made her mother leave them. Where the hell was her mother?

When Henry came home from school, she hugged him so hard he yipped. "I will never ever leave you," she said to her seventeen-year-old son.

He looked at her like she was crazy, and said, "Huh?"

Then she laughed at herself and him too, just what a teenage boy wants, a mother who will never leave him.

"Yep, Henry," she said, "when you go away to college, I'll get a room next door to yours in the dorm."

Without any enthusiasm, he said, "Yay."

21. GRACE

Before noon on Saturday, Max's mom dropped Grace off at Christina's condo. No one was home—a very good thing. She hurried into her bedroom and was examining herself in the mirror over the dresser, checking to see if she felt any different. Did she still look like herself and like her mother? She heard a key turning in the front door. Grace quickly hid in her bedroom closet and closed the door. She wasn't ready to face her grandmother yet.

***

Max's mom drove her home after having a major shit-fit at her son and at Grace too. But she mostly ranted at Max. "How could you? How could you? My gracious, what will Grace's family say?"

Mrs. Mellon caught them in the basement laundry room. Grace had her T-shirt off so it wouldn't get stained. It's important not to wreck your clothes. She wasn't naked. She had the AA bra on. Her grandmother said it was a training bra. Why were they called training bras anyway? Was the bra getting your boobs ready for the Olympics or something? She had a towel wrapped around her top so all that anyone—including Max—would see was her bra straps. They had just finished. The windup timer had pinged. What if Mrs. Mellon had come down to the basement right in the middle? But it was done and she was glad they did it. Actually, Max did it. He had some experience. He had his own set of rubber gloves that were better than the gloves that came stuck to the directions in the package. Mrs. Mellon let Max rinse Grace's hair in the laundry tub, while she held an old washcloth over her eyes so none of the black dye would blind her. Then he rubbed the conditioner that came in the packet with the hair color into her hair. Grace had to stand there dripping while they timed the conditioner, then Max rinsed her again. Mrs. Mellon also let Max blow dry Grace's hair.

"Well, for pity's sakes," Mrs. Mellon said, "you can't go out in the cold with your hair all wet."

Grace was crying on the ride home and Mrs. Mellon said, "Grace, you're pretty no matter what color your hair is. It looks nice. But, oh gracious, your family's gonna hate me."

Grace wasn't crying because of her hair color, she was crying because it was her fault that Max was in trouble, and because their great Saturday plans were screwed. They were going to color her hair and then go to the movies, then go to Leo's Coney on Main. Grandma didn't expect her home until six. The movie plan was out now, and maybe—a much worse thing—maybe no one would let her and Max hang out together anymore.

Mrs. Mellon was mumbling something about how Grace's family would never forgive her. Grace didn't want Mrs. Mellon to be in trouble either. Mrs. Mellon planned to come in and talk to Christina and beg her forgiveness. When Grace pointed out that Grandma's car was nowhere to be seen around the condo, that obviously she must be shopping or something, Mrs. Mellon's whole body seemed to relax and the look on her face was, *Whew!*

***

Grace had been standing in the closet since she heard a key turn in the front door. She figured it'd be a while before she would want to face Grandma, so she sat down on a pile of her dirty clothes on the closet floor. They made a soft cushion for her butt.

Her closet backed up to the eating end of the kitchen so she could hear Grandma opening and closing cupboard doors and the refrigerator. She guessed she was putting groceries away. The longer she sat there, Grace knew, the harder it would be for her to come out of the closet.

Ha! Max was already out of the so-called closet. She and Max had talked about kissing people and told each other who they'd like to kiss at school. Both of them wanted to kiss boys, but neither of them had. It was good to have a friend that you could be honest with about such things. Another good thing was that both of Max's parents loved him no matter who he was. They loved him. They treated him like a good person, except today when his mother had the shit-fit.

Grace and Max had been planning the hair coloring all week. He'd done his own hair, tipping the ends with bleaching solution from a kit. He did a good job. She liked what he looked like.

"Do you want to be a hairdresser?" she asked him.

"Grace, that's a stereotype," he said, with his hands on his hips, doing an exaggerated swishy motion. "Just because I'm gay doesn't mean I want to be a hairdresser. I'd like to be a firefighter, or maybe a paramedic. I'd like to save people."

He had saved her. She knew that.

It was taking a long time for her mother's suicide to become yesterday's news. Everyone was still tippy-toeing around her, being too nice or too leery of her. Either way, she felt conspicuous. Everyone kept seeing her mother in her and she wanted to be invisible. Every time she looked in a mirror, there was her mother. It had become too painful to even see herself. She'd decided that it was her hair. Max knew this. He was easy to talk to. He'd be the perfect person to save people.

The principal had talked to her parent—she couldn't say *parents* now—about her getting counseling, so after school her dad picked her up and took her to see a woman doctor who was very kind to her and told Grace she'd feel better if she could talk about her feelings. But that wasn't the same as having a friend. Friends never said, "Well, our times up for today." Well, maybe they did if they were late for dinner or something.

She was hunkered down in her bedroom closet feeling the strands of her newly black hair when the doorbell rang. She heard shuffling feet and people talking. Oh geez, now she was really stuck in the closet. The doorbell rang again and there were more voices. What was this? Grandma was having a party while Grace was supposed to be at the movies? The bell rang again. There was a mumbling of voices and then the herd of people was moving to the kitchen. She heard chairs being scraped across the floor and then it was quiet. They must be sitting around the kitchen table

Now she could make out some of the voices. Ben Abbott. She knew Ben's voice since he'd been coming over a lot. She was hoping that her grandmother and Ben would have a romance—that might brighten up Grandma's life. She'd seen a commercial with old people holding hands walking in a park—Grandma and Ben could be like that. She told Grandma that one time after Ben left, and Christina laughed, and said, "You know, your mother was always trying to fix me up with Ben. Dusty, Lily, and Rose were always conniving to get us together."

Ben's daughters, Lily and Rose, were in the kitchen too, and Rose's husband Carlos was there. Carlos had a deep voice with a buttery accent—when he talked it sounded like music.

She wasn't sure of the other man's voice until someone said, "Fred," then she knew it was her next door neighbor, Mr. Williams.

Fred was saying something about her mom's iPad. Grace had her ear pressed against the closet wall, but still couldn't make out every word, especially when several people were talking at the same time. She heard, "Robert lied." She made out something about cancer. Then she heard someone say, "We should have our own memorial for her right here and now." It sounded like Lily. They were talking about having a memorial for her mother and Grace wasn't there. Well, she was there, but they didn't know it. She forgot about her hair and rushed to the kitchen so she wouldn't miss anything.

Later, when she recalled the moment when she popped into the kitchen, scaring the shit out of everyone, she'd laugh so hard her eyes would get tears. She didn't say boo or anything, but just suddenly appeared, a black haired girl that no one recognized for a minute. A few people jumped because they were startled. There were a few "Oh, my God's," and an "Oh, Sweet Jesus," that was from Fred.

Then they all just stared at her.

"It's me!" she shouted. "It's me, Grace. Don't be scared, it's just me. If you're having a memorial for my mom, I want to be included."

Grandma was the first to laugh. They had to get rid of the tension somehow or other, so then everyone laughed.

"Where did you come from?" Grandma asked.

"Do you mean like being born or where I came from just now?"

That got some laughs. If you make people laugh, they don't yell at you for having black hair.

"Were you already here when I came in the house?" Grandma asked.

"I was hiding in the closet," she held out her black hair, "I was afraid you'd be upset."

Grandma waggled her index finger at Grace with a "come here" motion. Grace moved over to her and Christina wrapped her arm around her and stroked her hair.

"Why black?" she asked.

"I'm in mourning," Grace said.

22. FRED

Grace did scare Fred—gave him that extra bump of a heartbeat. Not the kind that can kill you, more the kind that makes you laugh afterward. But she overheard him talking smack about her father, heard him calling her father a liar. Not good.

Fred had some rules of conduct for himself. He didn't gossip—you don't say things about people behind their backs that you wouldn't say head on—at least he tried not to do that sort of thing. Sometimes it was hard to stick to. Now Grace had heard him calling her father a liar—this motherless young girl was hearing that her father was a liar. He was overwhelmed with regret. He should've stayed home. He shouldn't have called Lily, or told her what he found on the iPad (or rather, what he hadn't found). He shouldn't have agreed to come here to talk with everyone. He'd spent his life avoiding trouble, and here he was causing trouble. A philosophy he held—let sleeping dogs lie. But did that apply to letting liars lie as well? Stupid philosophy. He was causing Dust's daughter more heartache. Philosophize that.

"I'm real sorry, Grace," he said.

Grace walked around her grandmother and stood beside him. She reached down and picked up her mother's iPad. "My mom gave you this?" she asked.

He nodded.

"That's good. You were her friend. I'm glad she gave it to you."

"I'm real sorry, Grace," he said again. "I think you should keep it, not me." It pained him to say that.

She seemed tempted, but then seemed to shake it off. "She wanted you to have it. We should stick to what she wanted."

He nodded.

"I heard you say my dad lied."

"I'm real sorry, Grace. I'm real sorry," he said. Redundant—his brain was caught on a replay circuit. He hated hearing himself as much as he needed, yes sir, *needed* to continue apologizing. No child wants to hear bad things about their parents even when they know it's true. It chaws away at little pieces of their heart. Even children who have been neglected or brutalized by their parents don't like other people to say bad things about their folks. They'll defend the person who whipped them. Why was that? You don't bite the hand that feeds you? Or was it an innate knowing that whatever they are is part of you too?

He wished with all his being for a cigarette.

"Grace," he said, "your dad's not a bad man. Something probably went wrong with lines of communication or something. I don't think your dad made up those stories about your mom. The campaign people probably came up with the stories. I sure didn't mean to imply that he was lying."

Okay, so now Fred was lying.

"Don't feel bad for saying it," Grace said. "I already knew that what they've been saying about my mother is lies. I looked up bipolar. She wasn't bipolar, at least not that I could tell." She patted his shoulder, trying to make him feel better; a there, there pat that he imagined came from times in her life when her mother consoled her.

"And she wasn't in a mental hospital in Mexico either," Grace said. "I know for sure that she and Dad went to Mexico on a romantic vacation. They were there for Valentine's Day. She texted me every day and sent me a postcard every day. Most of the postcards came after they were already back home. And she came home with a bad sunburn." Grace turned to Christina, and said,

"Remember that, Grandma? Her face was all peely. She came home and was very happy, but when Dad got back to his remodeling plans and meetings with his architect, she just seemed to get unhappier and unhappier."

Christina nodded.

"I heard someone say something about cancer," Grace said, "but I couldn't make it out very well through the closet wall. What was it about cancer?"

Then Carlos told her about the cancer he'd found on Dust's forehead.

She nodded, slowly, knowingly, and said, "Hmm," like a scientist taking in some new facts.

Fred understood now about the pink hat Dust always wore, and then she stopped because, sweet Jesus, what was the point of worrying about skin cancer if you were planning to die anyway.

Rose said, "And your mom's father died of melanoma. That's a bad type of skin cancer. Dust didn't have that, but maybe she was scared of getting it. I think she felt hopeless, like everything was piling in on her."

"The last time she came to see me, just a couple weeks ago," Carlos said, "I had the biopsy results, and set her up to see a skin cancer specialist. She made an appointment, but then canceled it."

"I wish I'd known that," Christina said. "Maybe I could have reassured her. I know you did your best, Carlos, especially seeing that she didn't tell you about her father's cancer. She was so upset when Jay was sick. She was newly married to Robert, but she was at our house every day with Jay. She was devastated. I remember when he died, she kept saying, 'But I was just getting to know him. It's not fair.' I tried to comfort her."

Lily said, "She wasn't afraid of much, nothing physically, but I can see how getting cancer would scare her. She went to pieces when her dad died. It was fast and terrible. I can see her not wanting to go through that."

With everyone talking about cancer, Fred lost his craving for a smoke.

Grace dashed out of the room, and everyone glanced around at each other concerned that the talk was too hard for her to deal with, but a moment later she was back carrying the desk chair from the living room. She placed it at the corner of the table between Fred and Christina and plopped herself down on it.

"If we're going to have a memorial for her, let's all hold hands," she said, and took Fred's hand and her grandmother's. "I've never been to a memorial. Do we all just say nice things about her?"

Fred could see that Christina wanted to free her hand and just squash her grandchild in a big hug. He could see her holding back.

"Yes, that's how it's done. Usually it's at a church, sometimes at a funeral parlor," Christina said, "but I don't see why we can't just do it right here at the kitchen table."

"Good." Grace was beaming.

"Can I start?" Fred said, and checked around the table. He was eager to redeem himself after the "liar" bit. Everyone nodded.

"Okay, well then, here goes. Back when I first got laid off from my job, it was your mom that pulled me out of quite a depression. I'd be moping around, kickin' dirt, so to speak. She must have seen me out there in my yard, and she'd come out and tell me she had some problem she needed help with, like the garbage disposal wouldn't work. Turns out the fuse had blown."

Grace laughed, and said, "Yeah, in our old kitchen if the toaster was running or even the coffeepot was on, when you turned on the garbage disposal it would blow a fuse." She laughed more and asked, "Did she ever have you come over because the hair dryer wouldn't work?"

Fred said, "As a matter of fact, yes, she did."

Grace hooted with laughter, she threw her head back and laughed hard. Everyone was laughing. It was downright uplifting. Fred had noticed this happening at every funeral he'd ever been to. The human spirit just didn't seem capable of continuous sadness. There was always someone who told some story that made everyone chuckle. Comic relief, that's what they needed.

"In our old bathroom there's a heater on the ceiling, and if you turned that on, and then turned on the hair dryer at the same time, it'd blow a fuse."

"Well, she sure had me snookered for a while," Fred said. "She had me runnin' over at least once a day to save her from some disaster. I'm real familiar with the fuse box in your house, Grace. Every time I'd come over, after I'd fix the fuse, we'd sit in her kitchen drinking coffee and chatting up a storm. She helped me through a hard time."

They had stopped holding hands, and Christina brought out more cookies and cheese and crackers. She poured more coffee and got a glass of milk for Grace.

"Okay, okay, can I go next?" Lily asked, and was waving both her arms in the air with excitement. "When the twins were born, Dust was just home from her freshman year in college and she moved in with Jagger and me. She spent her whole summer vacation helping me with the babies. Jagger was working at the Vinsetta Garage, which you all might know is now a restaurant. You have to wait in line forever to get in, but it's fun. Oops, sorry, got diverted there. Anyway, Jagger was working a lot. How I'd manage two tiny," she bowled her two hands with her fingertips touching, to demonstrate their size, "I mean really tiny babies, all by myself was unimaginable. Christina came over a lot when she wasn't working."

Lily stopped and nodded to Christina, "I've always been so grateful to both of you for that."

"I helped too," Rose threw in, looking hurt.

Lily nodded at Rose, and went on, "Those babies, Andrew and Henry, looked and acted so much alike that we couldn't tell who was who. We called them Andry and Hendrew. We still do," she faltered, looked distressed and went on, "umm, well, I do."

"Anyway," Lily continued, "I've always been grateful to her for that summer. She could have been working somewhere, making some spending money for school the next year. And I know she gave up a trip to Utah with her ecology class, just so she could help me."

Fred saw her eyes watering up and he quickly stared at a plate of cookies. Crying can be contagious. He reached for a chocolate chip.

"She loved your boys," Christina said.

"She did," Lily said, and sighed. "When one baby woke up crying in the middle of the night, he'd wake up the other one. She slept on the nasty lumpy old couch in our furnished apartment. I'm surprised that she didn't have permanent back damage. For the first few days the babies were home, she'd take the night shift with Jagger, feeding and changing the boys so I could recover from having them. They'd be up half the night, whispering and humming to the twins so I could sleep. Once I woke up and went out to the living room and they were sitting next to each other on the couch, each holding a tiny baby. He was asleep with his head on her shoulder. I remember how sweetly she smiled at me, and she mouthed, 'Go back to sleep.' In the morning Jagger would drag himself off to work, and Dust would be up early helping me. We napped together in the double bed while the babies slept, and sometimes when I'd wake up, she'd be gone down to the apartment's laundry room washing diapers and using her own quarters in the machines."

"I'm afraid we'll all forget her," Grace said. "I'm afraid that after a while we won't even think about her anymore."

"I won't forget her," Ben said, and startled everyone by speaking. He was one quiet dude, Fred thought.

"She was always one of my girls too," Ben said. "I confess, when Jay Jones came home before her wedding, I was disappointed. Maybe I shouldn't say that, Christina. I'm sorry, but I was kinda hoping she'd ask me to walk her down the aisle."

"Oh, really, Daddy?" Lily said. "That's so sweet."

"She always shared," Rose said. "She shared you, Christina, and she shared Grandma Jeanie. If you were my mom, I would have been jealous of you paying attention to the little girls next door. But she was never like that. We were all her family."

"She loved trees," Carlos said. "She was passionate about trees."

Fred noticed a frown pass over Rose's face when Carlos spoke, so he added to Carlos's comment, "Yep, she sure did love nature. What's been happening with the erratic weather seemed to cause her real pain, actual physical pain. It was like she was the earth, and all this stuff, the high heat, the drought, the fires—all of it was physically assaulting her. She once told me that the planet would survive. It would be different, but it would survive. The people would be wiped out. First, all the islands and low coastal areas would flood, and the plains would turn to scorching deserts. Billions of people would die. She wanted us to pay attention—do something about it, get on it. We need to conserve our resources, and be conscious of our carbon emissions—all of that. But everyone has gotten greedy. It's a gimme more, more, more world." Then, before he said anything about Robert's addition, he stopped. It was bad enough that he called Grace's father a liar.

Lily said, "Every Saturday morning at nine o'clock, we met at the farmers market. We did that for years. When the twins were little I'd bring them. She kept track of one and I'd chase the other. Then, Grace, when you were a tiny baby, she'd come with you swaddled up against her chest. She always brought extra cloth bags, guessing that

I'd leave mine at home, which was usually the case. I couldn't afford organic and she said that just buying local was helpful. Then trucks weren't driving three thousand miles to bring me the same lettuce that a local farmer was growing."

She was choking up, Fred thought, and looked down into his lap. He heard her say, with a hurt in her voice that ripped at his heart. "I'll miss meeting her at the market."

"Lily, if you're strong enough to go to the farmers market," Christina said, "then I'll go to the gym. Dusty gave me a lifetime membership, you know. Did you know that? She wanted me to get healthy."

Lily touched Christina's hand. "We can do it. She'd be proud of us. I want her to be proud of me."

"I miss finding her notes," Grace said. "She'd write messages on Post-it notes and hide them in my clothes. One time, when I went to put my shoe on, I felt a crinkle in the toe and I reached in and pulled out a note that said, 'P.U.' She'd put notes in my pockets and I'd be at school and reach for a tissue and find a note that said, '*I heart you.*' You know how they do those bumper stickers that have a drawn heart instead of writing out love." She was fighting tears, but went on. "Sometimes the notes would be folded in half so the sticky part wouldn't stick to my clothes. And some times she'd curl them, so I could wear them on my fingers like paper coats. She liked sticky notes. When I was having trouble with some spelling, we wrote each word on a note. Then she'd walk around the house with a word stuck on her cheek, or on her back or on her arm. She was a very fun mother."

Fred could see the pleasure Grace was getting from talking about Dust, her whole body had taken on a calm—a sadness, but a calm too.

"So where do you think she is right now?" Grace asked, as casually as if she was asking where her blue sweater was, and dunked a cookie in her milk.

"Well," Christina said, "of course, she's in heaven. Listen to what everyone says about her. She was a good person. Yes, she's in heaven."

Fred was very aware of the cross on the kitchen wall. In the living room, he'd noticed a small marble sculpture of the Virgin Mary on the bookshelf, and a manger scene made of wood. There was a portrait of a long-haired, blond Christ in an oak frame, another painting of shepherds on a hill with a star blazing in the night sky, and a plate on a stand—white with a black line drawing of Jesus reaching down to a cluster of small children. Christina's religion screamed at you from the tabletops, shelves, and walls. He took it all in, absorbing it, getting to know Dust's mother better. He hoped Christina's religion was bringing her comfort.

"I think she's here," Lily said, and pointed to her own head. "I'll always have her right here in my memory." Then she patted her chest and added, "And here."

Grace looked at him, so Fred patted his hand over his heart as Lily had. Gone, he thought. She's just gone. Gone forever. Not coming back. But he certainly couldn't and wouldn't say that to Grace. What he believed in, he kept to himself. He wanted Robert to burn in hell, but that was just a phrase. Fred didn't believe in hell. It was just silly. Horned men with pitch forks and flames flashing around—it was movie stuff. He didn't believe in heaven either. Didn't believe in angels or any gods. Didn't believe that lighting candles could save a soul. When he said, "Sweet Jesus," that was part of his camouflage, a pithy phrase culled up from memories of his grandmother. Jesus was a prophet, a real man who cared for the poor and sick. But rising from the dead or walking on water, the Bible writers were embellishing a good man into a superhero.

What Fred believed in was nature: earth, atmosphere, rain, snow, trees, plants, lakes, and mountains. Nature. Maybe you could say it was bipolar with its dark-burdened sky, or its calm glory, or lashing cruel violence. Since he didn't believe that there was any god watching over everyone, he believed that folks had a responsibility to watch over each other. He didn't spread his views on religion. Why throw rocks at other people's beliefs if they gave them comfort? One of the few people he ever talked about his beliefs with was Dust; they were closet atheists. When she shot herself, she didn't think she was going some place better. He knew that. She was ending. Period. His knowing that—remembering their talks about how folks had to watch out for each other—made his failure to protect her all the worse.

"I think her spirit is here in this room with us," Carlos said. "She's hearing how much we all cared for her."

"I like thinking that my mother's here with me." Grace said.

Suddenly, Lily turned to her father and said, "Where's *my* mother?" Her voice carried an agony of loss, and she seemed surprised at her own words.

Fred saw a look pass between Ben and Christina. Eyebrows went up. Startled. He wondered what that was about. He saw Christina nod at Ben.

"New Mexico," Ben said. "Taos."

"What!" both Lily and Rose shouted at the same time.

"You knew where she was and you didn't tell us?" Rose said.

"You never asked," he replied. "Well, when she was first gone, you asked all the time. And I told you I didn't know, because I didn't. But after a few years passed, I heard from Wanda. Christina and I both hear from her every few years."

It seemed that Dust's memorial had taken a turn, Fred thought. He scooted his chair back, getting ready to leave, but Christina said, "I think we should end with a silent prayer for Dust."

So they held each other's hands, and bowed their heads. Fred closed his eyes and he imagined a glowing white light surrounding each one of these people who loved his dear Dust. The light wasn't God calling someone to heaven; the light in his imagination was love.

23. ROSE

Rose was faking prayer; her eyes wouldn't stay shut. With her head bent to match the other bent heads at the table, she looked over at her sister Lily. Lily had her head down but was staring back at Rose. They mouthed to each other, *Oh my God! Can it be true?* Talking without sound. How could they pretend to pray or even think about anything—when their mother was in Taos, of all places? Carlos had family in Santa Fe; Rose had been to New Mexico every year since she and Carlos met. He had family there. They had been to Taos several times. Now *she* had family there!

The silent prayer ended. Then, just as they were all lifting up their bowed heads, a male voice sang out in the living room. A Gregorian chant ringtone. Timely, Rose thought.

"Phone," Grace said. "Should I answer, Grandma?" but she was already up and rushing to answer.

A moment later she was back with the receiver in her hand. "It's Mrs. Mellon, Max's mom," she said, then, with her hand over the mouth piece, she whispered, "Please don't be mad at her, Grandma," Grace said, "I wanted to have black hair. She didn't even know we were doing it, anyways, not until we were almost done."

Christina took the phone and there was some conversation, but Rose wasn't paying attention. She was in Taos with Carlos, walking the streets, roaming in the art galleries. Maybe she walked right by her mother and didn't know it? Maybe her mother served them lunch in the Bent Street Deli and Cafe, or dinner at Doc Martin's? There was that charming bookstore Moby Dickens; could her mother have been there?

Her thoughts returned from their trip to the Southwest, and she listened to bits of conversation. Somehow it had been decided that Grace could still go to the movies with Max. Fred had volunteered to drive her back to the Mellon's house to pick up Max and then he'd drop them off at the Emagine Theater.

There was hustle and bustle, and everyone was up and hugging and kissing—even Fred and Carlos hugged. Then Grace and Fred were gone and it was quiet.

Christina said, "We should talk," and herded them all back toward the kitchen.

24. CHRISTINA

It was Ben's memories that his daughters needed, but Christina could see how he was struggling. He spent a long time just staring into his coffee cup, maybe hoping that words would jump out of the brown liquid and form in his mouth. The girls waited and watched...and waited.

Finally, Christina said, "Your mother was a tormented soul."

"I don't know about her soul," Ben said. "She was a drunk."

"Wanda had serious problems," she said. Though she hadn't intended it, her tone was almost scolding Ben. *Don't villainize your daughters' mother,* she wanted to whisper to him. She wanted the memories softened, cushioned, to protect these women from any more ugliness. Yet there was a time when she herself would have put Wanda in a guillotine and dropped the blade. But nearly thirty years had passed and in the passing, Christina had softened and become more compassionate about human frailties and addictions.

"Do you remember anything about your mother?" she asked, and looked from Rose to Lily. Like telling young children where babies come from, it seemed wise to begin by asking them what they already knew.

"I don't remember much," Rose said. "Most of my childhood memories seem to be after she was gone. I don't even remember what she looked like. As far as adults in my childhood, mostly I remember you, Christina, and your mother. Grandma Jeanie was always so sweet to me. She seemed to know whenever I felt sad and she'd sing to me. She still does even though she doesn't know who I am anymore."

"I remember thinking our mother was pretty, but I can't picture what that means visually," Lily said. "I had a memory recently of her waking me up. She had red lips and smelled like wine."

"She was pretty," Ben said. "Looked a lot like Rose."

"What happened?" Rose said. "Why did she leave us?"

"You've heard how sometimes people with addiction problems hit bottom?" Christina asked.

The girls nodded and Ben said, "Your mother hit bottom over and over again."

"We were all worried," Christina said. "Ben was working the afternoon shift, and I was working afternoons at the hospital. Grandma Jeanie was doing her best to protect you girls. Your mother would often bring you both over for Grandma Jeanie to watch while she went out for the night."

"Bar hoppin'," Ben added.

"One night, Grandma Jeanie saw Wanda drive away in her car, but she hadn't brought you girls over to our house. I was home that night, and we were concerned, so I went over to your house. We always had a key. I found Rose asleep in her bed. But I couldn't find Lily."

Rose said, "You mean she just left me there in the house all alone and she took Lily?"

"She did," Ben said.

"I was nothing," Rose said, her whole body seemed to droop, and Carlos put his arm around her shoulder. "I was just forgotten and she took Lily somewhere."

"You were the lucky one," Ben said.

"I have a memory of her waking me up and getting me dressed, but I don't have any more than that," Lily said.

It was getting sticky now, Christina thought. She got up, put on another pot of coffee, and searched the cupboard for more cookies, aware that she was now the only one eating any. She opened and closed a few doors and then came back and sat down.

"What happened to me?" Lily was asking. "Where was I?"

"When I couldn't find you," Christina said, "I called your dad at work. Meanwhile Grandma Jeanie and I took Rose back to our house and put her to bed. We didn't know what ruckus might come up, so we wanted to protect Rose from whatever might happen. Then I went back to Ben's and searched every closet and everywhere I could think of. I took a flashlight and hunted around the back yard and in the garage, just in case she hadn't taken you with her."

"When I got home," Ben said, "Christina and I went off to search all the bars in the area. At first we just checked the parking lots for her car, but we didn't see her car anywhere. Then we backtracked and went inside every one. Finally, we went in a biker bar."

"A scary place," Christina said. "When we went in, all these rough looking guys and their girlfriends watched us, like we were from another planet." Christina remembered walking into that bar, she was thirty-five years old then, a cute chick—thin. She could feel the lecherous eyes scoping her out, lingering on her breasts, ogling. The place was crowded with dangerous looking men with beards and mustaches, tattoos, leather vests over bare chests, chains dangling from buttonholes. There were a few women. Christina was more afraid of them than the men. They had hard, mocking eyes, daring her to even glance at one of their men. She was terrified. She checked the women's room, forcing herself to be brave and remember their mission—Lily. Where was eight-year-old Lily?

"Wanda was nowhere in sight," Ben said. "We talked to the bartender, and he remembered her leaving with some guy. We asked if she had a kid with her, and he said, 'Man, we don't allow no kids in here.' We started to leave, but then Christina decided to check all the booths. It was crowded, but most everyone was standing around the bar. She found you way back in a dark corner sound asleep in a booth."

"My mother just left me there?" Lily said.

Christina and Ben nodded.

Ben said, "When I picked you up, your body was limp. You were unconscious."

"I got hysterical, and started screaming, "Who gave this child alcohol?" Christina said, remembering how fury had overrode her fear. She remembered one guy saying, *Must have been the kid's skank mother*, and hoped Ben didn't recall that, or at least wouldn't say it to the girls.

"We found out Wanda had been doing Jell-O shots before she left with some guy," Ben said. "So we raced you to the hospital. They pumped your stomach and put you on an IV, but you must not have had much, because it wasn't long before you were awake with a big hangover. While you were passed out, a social worker and a cop came in checking on child abuse. It was like we were criminals. We told them that we had a party and you had snuck a Jell-O shot because you thought it was a dessert. We said it was an accident. We were afraid that the state would take you girls away. Thank heavens, they believed us."

"I guess I was the lucky one," Rose said.

"Could this be why I'm so afraid of everything?" Lily asked.

Ben shook his head. "No, even as a baby you were nervous and jumpy. If the doorbell rang, even if you were awake, you'd be startled and start to cry, whereas baby Rose just seemed to be more comfortable with the bumpiness of life. I think it's just in your character to be a more cautious person than most."

"So you took me home from the hospital. Then what happened?" Lily said.

"Your dad and I sat up all night waiting for Wanda to come home," Christina said. "We put you to bed and just sat drinking coffee. We left Rose sleeping at my house."

"Your mom tripped in the front door just before dawn," Ben said. "She was semisober by then. I asked her, 'Where's Lily?' I wanted to know if she was even aware of what she'd done. She just looked at me stupidly and said, 'Well, isn't she in bed?' and then a look came over her face and she said, 'Aww, shit,' and ran upstairs to your bedroom."

"Ben and I just sat there and waited, When she came back downstairs, she said something like, 'Lily's asleep. She's fine.'"

"She got real defensive," Ben said. "I've always wondered if she had much memory of that night. So then we told her about finding you at the bar and taking you to the hospital and the stomach pumping and all that."

Christina said, "I think she was genuinely sorry and humiliated too."

"I told her to pack. Said that I didn't want her around you girls anymore." Ben sipped his coffee, then said, "I couldn't take a chance on her doing something stupid and having the state take you away and put you into foster care or something. She had to go. I've often wondered if I did the right thing. Maybe I should have tried to get her help. But I didn't trust her around you girls. Sometimes, after she was gone, I'd stay awake all night wondering if she was dead or alive."

"Should we worry about fetal alcohol syndrome?" Rose said. "I've always felt normal, but are we?"

"She never drank when she was pregnant. Maybe she had some depression after you were both born, postpartum or something. Maybe she just wanted to party and forget her responsibilities. I don't know," Ben said.

"I can remember asking where Mom was," Lily said.

"It was awful," Ben said. "Every day, one or both of you would say, where's Mommy? Is she coming home today? Will Mommy come home for my birthday? Will Mommy be our surprise Christmas present? It broke my heart. I didn't want you to know that I sent her away. I wanted to be the good guy. It went on for months, but eventually you just stopped asking. That was a relief, but somehow it felt worse because I knew you had given up."

"So how did she wind up in Taos?" Carlos asked.

"Several years passed before we heard from her. Long after you girls stopped asking about her, a letter arrived. Basically, she just sent a note with her address and said she was sorry. I didn't want to tell you that I heard from her, because I was afraid that it would just stir up your sense of loss and pain again. Then for a few years she moved all over the place, you could tell by the addresses: Illinois, North Dakota, Colorado, and then New Mexico. She's been there at the same address for a long time. Settled down I guess."

"I feel sad for her," Christina said. "I can't imagine the pain she must have suffered. She'd been a good person before she got into drinking too much. She was my friend, and I don't think she was a bad mother before, before she just sort of fell off a cliff. She did something bad and was sent into exile. I can't imagine being without my child for all those years." She didn't say children, she said child. When she heard herself say *my child*, it hit her that she would spend the rest of her life without her own daughter. "My child," she said out loud. She was suddenly sobbing and quaking in pain. She'd been holding everything in, being strong for Grace, and now it just poured out of her.

Lily wrapped her arms around her and Rose handed her tissues from across the table.

"I'm sorry," Christina said into the tissue, then wiped her eyes. "I'm sorry."

"Oh, Christina," Lily said, with tears running loose and free down her own face—infectious crying was affecting everyone at the table, "don't be sorry. Dust's gone and we all need to cry." She held up her coffee cup, and said, "Here's to tears all around, for our beloved Dust."

The others raised their coffee cups and clinked, then sipped.

25. ROBERT

Robert wished that people would stop bringing him food. Casseroles—dishes with noodles and hamburger and canned mushroom soup. The Presbyterian Church women had evidently set up a committee with a schedule for bringing him Pyrex dishes filled with cheese-slathered condolences. They brought cakes and pies and cookies and ever more casseroles. The food was a problem. Casseroles were multiplying like rabbits in his refrigerator, then his doorbell would ring and someone would be standing there with yet another dish. What he wanted to eat was Cheerios with milk in a big bowl, or hot dogs on soft buns with onions and mustard, and a beer in a frosted mug. Some of the dishes arrived in the hands of single women, or women he recognized as widows from his church. With their dishes held out before them, they were offering him more than their noodles; they were cleaned up—shiny, offering him a new future.

He wanted his old future back. He wanted Dust back so she could figure out what to do with all this food. No, that wasn't it. Irrelevant of the food situation, he just wanted her back. Every minute of every day he wanted her back. Every wakeful, tangled, sorrowful, lonely moment during the night, he wanted her back.

He called Christina and asked her what he should do with the food. He suggested she take it home for her and Grace, since Grace wasn't ready to be back home yet. An hour later, Christina was at the side door with a shopping bag filled with plastic bags and foil pans. She looked older, tired, and weary. He took the bag from her and kissed her cheek.

She ignored him as she tugged the handrail to heft herself up the three steps into the old kitchen—now a mudroom—then she lumbered through the old dining room. He opened the door that had once opened to a back porch, and followed her into the new kitchen/family room with her weight slowing her movements. She was probably well under two hundred pounds, but her heart was heavy. He didn't remember her lumbering before. She seemed to be hoisting her weight, dragging the terrible burden of her dead child. Dust told him how she worried about her mother. He knew about the gym membership. Was Christina still walking the track, or was it too emotionally painful without her daughter? Had Dust even thought about her mother and what this would do to her?

He hadn't been in public yet, except to go to the funeral home and schedule cremation for Dust's body and then again to pick up the box with her ashes. He'd only gone to the campaign office once. When he walked in, everyone applauded. It appalled him, but then he figured it was like someone who gets injured on a football field and everyone applauds when they're back up and walking. Hey, you survived, congratulations!

Christina opened the refrigerator. "Good grief, Robert. Did you tell them to stop?" Casseroles stacked on top of casseroles suffocated every bit of space.

"No," he said, "I guess I'd better, huh?"

"Yes," she said.

She seemed abrupt—angry, as she started pulling dishes out and putting them on the island. She was being efficient, but rough, almost slamming some of the casseroles on the granite countertop. He grabbed a few dishtowels and laid them out for her to put the casseroles on to cushion the blows.

She stopped and just stared at him and shook her head.

"I'm so angry," she said, and pinched her lips together before she burst forth. "How could you do it? How could you do it? Dust was not bipolar. It's all over the news that she was seeing some shrink. When was she ever institutionalized? They're saying she was in an institution in Mexico. So what mental hospital has you lying on the beach getting a sunburn? Tell me that? She came home from that trip with a sunburn. How much did you pay that quack psychiatrist? Do you even think about Grace? Your daughter, Robert. Remember her? Do you even think about what your lies are doing to your daughter? Do you even care? No. It's all about winning. You want to be a big shot, you want to be a senator of the United States of America, and everyone else be damned. You want a big fancy house. What do you care about Dust's garden? My child can't even have a decent funeral because that might interfere with your election. You want more, more, more of everything. Well, sir, it looks like that's what you've got." She waved her arm at all the food. "That's what you got. No people in this house with you, just a big ole bunch of casseroles."

He didn't say anything, just stood motionless like a boxer in the ring being pummeled, and like a boxer, he imagined himself putting his hands up to protect his face and avoid the bruises. He was throwing the fight.

She picked up the grocery bag filled with plastic wrap and containers that she'd brought with her and handed it to him. "Divide all the damn food, wrap it in foil or stick it in plastic containers, then put it in the freezer downstairs. Wash all the plates and send them back to their owners. This is your problem, Robert. Deal with it. I don't want any part of it." She hadn't taken her coat off. He followed her back through the old dining room and new mudroom. She walked down the steps and out the side door without saying good-bye. He could tell her knees hurt as she went down each step.

He was a boy again, firmly scolded, reprimanded, upbraided, and his reaction was the same as it would have been if he were ten-year-old Robert. He quickly started cutting the casseroles into meal-sized portions, then wrapped or packaged them, and took them down to the basement freezer. He fed the contents of some of the containers to the garbage disposal. Then he washed all the dishes, carefully getting all the browned food out of the corners. After washing a couple, he realized that there were names taped to the undersides, so he pulled them off and after each casserole was clean and dried, he stuck them back on. When that task was complete, he loaded all the Corning and Pyrex into some cardboard boxes he found in the basement and took the boxes out to his car.

Maybe there are people who relish being the bad guy—gang members, Mafia guys, or thugs—but Robert didn't. He drove to the church with his heavy load of guilt and clean dishes. It was too bad that the Presbyterian Church didn't have a priest. *Forgive me, father, for I have sinned.* He'd seen enough movies with priests that he knew the drill. The only person he saw in the church was the secretary, Mitzi Burg. When she saw him, she came around her desk and hugged him.

"I'm so sorry," she said. "It's such a terribly sad situation. How are you and Grace holding up?"

He shrugged and shook his head. If he spoke, he would cry. He didn't want to do that. *Forgive me, Mrs. Burg, for I have sinned.* He swallowed hard, took a breath. "Could you tell the women that I appreciate everyone's kindness, but they can stop bringing food?"

"Oh sure," she said. "By the way, Robert, I was happy to hear that you're still running for the Senate. I've told all my neighbors that I know you."

Back home, he went into their old living room. When they first bought the house, they closed the rounded archway that went into the dining room and installed bookcases. Now it was a room that could be closed off with louvered French doors near the front hall. It was Dust's favorite room, where she hid out when she wasn't speaking to him, or watched Rachel Maddow on TV while he was at the back of the house in the new family room watching football or Fox News. Windows on either side of the fireplace looked out at Fred and Margaret Williams's house next door.

A pair of comfortable loveseats faced each other. Between them, Dust had an old banged-up coffee table—junk-picked on a trash day years ago—a table you could rest your feet on, that never required a coaster put under a hot cup of coffee or a sweaty glass of iced tea. The table was rough with deep gouges where strangers had carved in their initials and Grace had done art projects. It was a cozy room. He found himself spending most of his time in her living room.

The box with her ashes was in the center of the coffee table. He hunted all over the house for candleholders and candles. He gathered silver candlesticks tarnished almost black, white china candleholders with cupids hugging the bases, crystal cups, and an ancient plaster candle stand with old wax drips down its sides. He found squat fat candles, tall tapers, and tea lights—fifteen candles, one for each year of their marriage—surrounded the box containing his wife's ashes. A sixteenth candle symbolized their year together in college. It was bent and had dripped white wax onto the tabletop. He opened the square cardboard box and untied the bread bag type of twist tie that held the plastic bag closed. He reached into the bag and pinched a bit of ash in his fingers, her ashes were pink with tiny fragments of bone like little bits of seashell.

Just weeks before she died, she told him she wanted to be cremated. She wanted her ashes sprinkled in a forest somewhere, and no funeral. Emphatic. No funeral.

He'd been taken aback. How many thirty-seven-year-olds plan their death? He should have been alerted, instead he thought it sensible to have your wishes known well in advance. You never knew what was going to happen. He should have registered how defeated she seemed. She spent hours on this loveseat staring into space. God, why hadn't he caught it? She was telling him that she was going to die, and all he said was, "Sure, if that's what you want. Cremation it is. If I go first, cremate me too."

He touched her ashes—silky but gritty. "I'm sorry," he said to her. "I'm so sorry."

Then he lit all the candles and told her all the ways he would be better. But no matter how much better he was, she wasn't coming back. He knew that, but still he needed to tell her.

They went too far. It wasn't *they* that went too far, it was his campaign manager Chuck that went too far. He couldn't remember exactly what he told Chuck to release to the press. Maybe he told him to say she was depressed. Obviously, that was true. Chuck being Chuck had to make it bigger than it was, had to fabricate a detail. Depressed wasn't enough. What was the reason for her depression? The press would push for a reason. He knew he hadn't told Chuck to say she was bipolar...or did he? He was so angry with her after cleaning up the bathroom, what exactly had he said to Chuck?

But no, it was Chuck. It had to be just Chuck. Then Chuck found a shrink willing to say—for a huge amount of money—that he'd been treating Dust for years. Suddenly the lie became engorged. Every time they made her sound sicker, he went up in the polls; they said it was a sympathetic reaction. Now they were saying she'd been institutionalized at some point. How stupid could they get? There would be records. But then, via Chuck and one of the billionaire donors, records appeared at a hospital in Mexico. Timing is almost everything—he'd taken her on vacation there last February, so they had chosen those two weeks to say she was hospitalized. He went up in the polls again, but still was well behind his rival.

Since her death, it seemed like the main topic on TV was suicide and suicide prevention. Network and cable news shows—hungry for in-depth news topics—gobbled up Dust's suicide and spit it back out in every form their research departments could find. There were bulleted charts listing ways to recognize a potential suicide—valuable information that came too late in his case.

Other shows talked about how to cope when a loved one dies. Elisabeth Kübler-Ross & David Kessler's Five Stages of Grief: denial, anger, bargaining, depression, and acceptance, were hot topics on all the media. It hadn't been two weeks yet and he'd been through all the stages. Some days he felt all the stages at once. Except acceptance, he doubted that he'd ever feel acceptance. He thought that they should add more categories in the case of suicide—like guilt and regrets.

He was ashamed of himself, and he was worried about his daughter. She didn't want to come home and he didn't blame her. The house had become a creepy place, filled with death and ghosts and sorrow. He felt trapped here, trapped with his memories and sadness. He could go stay at his parent's house, but he didn't want to. He didn't want to leave this space with her ghost. As perverse and strange as that sounded, he was afraid that if he left the house she would really be gone.

But he'd left the house to take Grace to the woman psychologist that the school recommended, and he would take her again. He would do whatever she needed. Grace was barely speaking to him, but that wasn't much different from when Dust was alive. Dust told him it was hormones and that thirteen-year-olds are a pain in the butt. Now he wasn't sure if Grace hated him or if it was body changes gone berserk. She'd been so sweet and lovable before turning into a huffy teen.

He sat in a chair in the psychologist's waiting room and wondered if he should get counseling too; he didn't know how to handle anything anymore. But then seeing a therapist would be fodder for the opposition—not only the opposition, but also his own party. Always—irrelevant of need—there was politics to be concerned with.

He sat before his shrine to Dust for a long time, then he put out the candles with a long-handled brass snuffer that had been Dust's great grandmother's, and headed to the back of the house, leaving the louvered French doors into Dust's living room open. His latest insanity—when he entered or exited any room, he was compelled to close the door. He opened doors and then shut them behind him. Was he closing something out or closing something in? The only doors he never touched were the ones to her living room; she liked them opened, so he kept them that way. He walked through the front hall and then into the old dining room. He opened the storm door into the family room and new kitchen, and after he crossed the threshold, he shut the door behind him. He didn't understand this new compulsion he had with the doors. Was it a superstition, like crossing the street when you see a black cat? A broken mirror meant seven years' bad luck. Step on a crack, break your mother's back. At least he hadn't started wearing a clove of garlic around his neck.

He looked in the refrigerator. It was better—airy, although now it was the other extreme—nearly empty. He was hungry but everything that wasn't a condiment was in the basement freezer. He was too tired or too lazy or too depressed to go get one of the packages he'd put down there earlier in the day. He'd make a peanut butter and jelly sandwich, but he wanted something warm, something more comforting, so he'd toast the bread.

In this expensive new kitchen, he'd insisted that Dust get rid of their old ratty toaster. She bought a new one. Black. Unobtrusive. But still he didn't like it cluttering up the counter. Toasters always had little bits of bread litter beneath them, making the counter messy. He wanted the new toaster in a cupboard when it wasn't being used. There were plenty of empty cupboards.

He got it out, plugged it in and toasted his bread. He made two sandwiches and sat on a stool at the island eating them off of a paper towel. He took out his cell phone.

"Hey, Lizard, it's me," he said, when his sister Elizabeth answered the phone. "Tell me something good."

"Austin wants to secede from Texas. That's good." She laughed.

He recited their usual opening lines. "And I just know that if you're there, Austin will stay weird."

He wished she were still up here, alive and in person.

Her voice went gentle. "Hey, Baby Brother, ya having a bad day, Honey?"

"There aren't any good days anymore," he said, and heard himself sounding needy and pathetic.

26. LILY

Royal Oak is a nightlife city. It's not unusual to see a limo dropping off a crowd of partyers at the restaurants and bars on Main Street and Washington. On Thursday night—cycle night—all the parking spaces on Main are filled, handlebar-to-handlebar, with Harleys, Kawasakis, and Ducatis, but on Saturdays (until one o'clock in the afternoon), the action switches to a huge, barn-like building built in 1927—the Royal Oak Farmers Market.

Lily parked in the lot next to the library, deciding that the extra walk would be good for her, or maybe the extra steps were a way of stalling. She was anxious, afraid that coming here without Dust would make her cry. She watched a toddler throw pennies in the fountain. The fountain was pleasant, but the Marshall Fredericks sculpture growing out of its center—a rigid, nude male holding up an equally rigid female—was something she chose to ignore. A man looking worn and tired, probably homeless, rested on the ledge along the path that led to the library. A woman in her Sunday-go-to-meeting clothes offered Lily a pamphlet about Jesus. Lily declined, and continued along the shady path.

Lily told everyone that she would go back to the Royal Oak Farmers Market, so that's what she was doing. Hyperalert—self-conscious in her aloneness—she merged with the crowd filing into the market. Strings of Christmas lights hung all over the ceiling. Were they always there? She studied the stained glass window—a cornucopia spilling vegetables—that filled the peak on the south-facing wall. Why had she never noticed the window or the Christmas lights before? Did loss of her companion awaken her senses? Would isolation change her awareness? Had she previously been more involved with what was at eye level—Dust's face, and waist level—tables filled with produce?

Antique dealers had permanent stalls against the outside walls. On Saturdays, Herman's bakery brought in pastries and fresh bread. Venders sold honey and maple syrup, soaps and seasonal plants, popcorn, and gluten-free baked goods. There was the farmer with organic grains—oats, dried beans, and homemade bread. Another vender sold mushrooms. Otto's sold chicken out of a white truck outside in good weather, and John Henry's sold antibiotic and hormone-free meats, cheeses, and eggs. Produce came from organic and nonorganic farms. The Market Cafe was tucked in the northeast corner of the big barn. Food could be ordered at a window in the kitchen.

Every Saturday morning for years, Lily met Dust at the farmers market. Seasons changed and it didn't matter, they still came here every Saturday morning. Summer and fall were all about abundance—abundance of food, abundance of shoppers—and a scarcity of parking places. It was slow moving through crowds of shoppers. In the winter, you noticed the vast, gray concrete floor, the quiet, and the bright pink sheets of paper proclaiming that the produce came from California or Florida. Spring brought piles of asparagus and flats of seedlings for home gardeners.

It had been two weeks and one day since Dust died. Lily had come here alone the Saturday before Dust died—the morning that Dust said she was sick but was out buying a deadbolt lock for the bathroom. It had felt lonely without her then, but it was just a blip on her radar, a momentary aloneness that was barely noticeable. Now the blip was permanent. Lily wasn't sure about being at the market without Dust.

She ordered a fried egg sandwich as usual and found a table against the wall. The same people she saw every week were there with their coffee, greeting one another as their groups gathered. A white-haired woman smiled and nodded to her. Everything felt normal. After sitting and watching market customers pass by with their cloth shopping bags, she went to the order window and got her sandwich wrapped in green-and-white checked paper. She looked at the empty chair across from her; she was waiting for Dust and Dust wasn't coming.

It was hard being here, hard knowing that Dust would never join her again. She opened the wrapper on her sandwich and just stared at it. When she looked back up she saw her sister Rose working her way through the crowd and coming toward her. Rose with her almost black hair, neat and short, little diamond studs in her ears, was dressed in jeans and a bright yellow sweater. Rose's yellow competed with the older couple who sold Charley's Mustard while dressed in mustard and yellow colored clothing.

"Nine o'clock on Saturday morning, right?" Rose said. "I thought you might need moral support, or at least some company."

Lily laughed. She was thrilled to see her sister.

"Did you bring cloth bags?" Lily said. "If not, I have extra." She pictured Dust giving her a fist bump.

Rose held up a black and green cloth bag from Westborn Market.

"Ta-da! Are you impressed?" Rose sang out and people at the tables around them looked over. Rose had good lungs, her voice carried around the dining area.

"I'm impressed." Lily reached out and took Rose's hand. "Thank you for coming. You have no idea how much this means to me."

"I do," Rose said. "And you have no idea what this means to me. I need produce. I need chicken and mushrooms and homemade soap. Maybe I even need an antique whatchamacallit."

"Want half of my sandwich?"

"Yes," Rose said. "Do I get the bigger half?"

"They're the same."

"Measure."

Lily lifted one half of her sandwich and placed it on top of the other. It was like they were kids again, Rose always concerned with getting less.

"See that little sticking-out part of the bread, the top half is bigger," Rose said.

Lily laughed and handed the top half to Rose.

They ate the sandwich halves then Rose said, "Okay, you stay here, I'll go get us some apple fritters from Herman's. My treat."

Lily watched her sister walk away among the crowd. She felt smiles all over herself. Across the aisle, she watched customers selecting vegetables at Van Houtte's huge display of colors: yellows, oranges, greens, purples, reds, and whites. It was October's abundance: peppers, eggplants, broccoli, tomatoes, and cauli-flower—all in vibrant beautiful colors. She thought it was something a painter should capture. Evan Zowarski? No, don't think about Evan.

Rose came back with a white bakery bag and placed it between them. She pulled out two fritters wrapped in dry waxed paper.

"I want the bigger one," Lily said.

"This one's thicker and that one's wider. So how can we tell which is bigger?"

"Did you notice anyone with a scale?" Lily asked. "Maybe we should weigh them."

They both laughed and ate the fritters.

As they were licking the sugar off their fingers, Rose said, "Carlos thinks we should go to Taos and see Wanda."

"Do you want to?"

"I'm not sure. She left me," Rose said.

"She left me worse, drunk in a bar with scary strangers," Lily said. It struck her as crazy and funny that they were competing over whom Wanda had neglected more. She laughed.

"Listen to us, Rose. God, we're goofy."

"Na-na-na," Rose sang, "Mom was worse to you than me."

"So are you and Carlos going to go see her?" Lily asked.

"Me and Carlos?" Rose said, and looked perplexed, "No, Lily. Carlos thinks we—meaning you and me, not him and me—should go see her."

"What?" Lily said, as dread filled her. "Well, how would we get there?"

"Lily, I know you've never flown before, but it would be good for you to conquer this one fear. We could have an adventure. Dust would be so proud of you. Carlos wants to pay for our trip. He thinks it would resolve questions and conflicts we have with our mother being gone for most of our lives."

"But," Lily said, feeling her stomach flip, "but, oh, Rose, I don't know."

"Come on, Lily. Let's do it," Rose said, and added a pleading, "Please."

"But when would we do it? Next summer?"

Rose looked at her like she was crazy. "What? Next summer? So you want to spend all those months worrying and dreading flying? I was thinking more like next week. We'll get you a prescription for Xanax. That'll make it easier. I was thinking we could make it a long weekend. Leave next Friday and come back the next Monday or Tuesday. What do ya think?"

Lily couldn't think. She felt panicky. "I don't know that I even want to see her. Why don't you and Carlos go?"

"Lily, I want you with me. Not Carlos. Not Dad. Just you. She hurt us both, and like Christina said, she's paid a big price. Maybe she's just a jerk and never missed us, and if that is the case then we'd find out, but we'd have each other. Maybe she's a wonderful person, someone that we should know. Whatever the case, we should find out. Wouldn't you like to know?"

"I'm afraid."

"Of meeting her or flying?"

"Both."

"Which more?"

"Couldn't we take a train or a bus?"

"Ah, so it's flying. Well, a bus or train would take days. I can't take that much time off from the nursing home." Rose leaned in across the table, and said softly, "Lily, I've flown dozens of times and here I am safe and sound. Well, maybe not so sound, but I know how to do it. I'll be right beside you."

"I've never been anywhere," Lily said. "I don't even have real luggage."

"You can use Carlos's carryon."

"But, Rose, it's only been two weeks since Dust died. We can't just go gallivanting off when Dust just died."

Rose put both her hands on the tabletop and leaned in. "You're right," she whispered. "What was I thinking? We can't go now. We'll miss the big funeral Robert's having for her."

"He's not having a funeral."

"Oh yeah, no funeral," Rose said. "Lily, I know you're mourning Dust. I am too. But don't you think she'd want you to go find your mother? Don't you think she'd be thrilled and proud of you for flying?"

Lily glanced over at the crowd of people gathered in front of the piles of vegetables across the aisle. The sign above them read, *Van Houtte's Farm, Home of the Giant Pumpkin.* She imagined Dust in that crowd, turning around and giving her a thumbs-up. *Do it,* Dust said. *Do it, Lily.*

"But what about voting?"

"Wow, now you are reaching. The election is November 6. If we go next weekend, we'll be back in plenty of time to vote."

Lily was quiet, trying to find another excuse not to go.

"Do you think Dust would have voted for Robert?" Rose asked.

"No, probably not," Lily said. "Rose, think of the conflict that would be. Here's this man that you love, and she did love him, and the thing he wants to do with his life has the power to smack down all the things you hold dear. You want him to be happy, but you're afraid of what he would do when he got that power. What a terrible conflict."

Then she thought of another reason not to fly.

"Rose, I shouldn't leave the boys right now, so soon after Dust's death. I shouldn't leave Christina and Grace. If I go, they might be traumatized. It wouldn't be right to go off on a vacation so soon after Dust died."

"Are you kidding me? You're kidding, right?" Rose said, and laughed. "Henry and Andrew will be fine. They know you love them. They know you'll be back. Christina and Grace will be fine. Daddy will be fine. Your boss will be fine. It'll just be a long weekend, Lily."

"Well, what if we call Wanda and she doesn't want to see us? What if she's moved again? What if she hangs up the phone when we call?"

"Then we won't go," Rose said. "Simple as that. I'll get her number from Daddy and I'll call her. Would that be alright? I'll just call her and see if she'd like us to come see her next weekend."

"Okay, yes," Lily said. "You call her. This was your idea."

Rose grabbed Lily's hands, squeezed them, and said, "Let's do it, Lily. Let's do it."

"I'm sure I could get the time off work," Lily said, and then wanted to slap her own forehead. Why did she say that? It could have been a good excuse to get out of this. Her stomach was seriously churning just thinking about flying, let alone seeing her mother.

27. GRACE

Grace used to come into her house by the side door. She'd burst in the door and hang her jacket on the hook by the basement stairs, then yell out, "Hey, Mom, it's the burglar, hide your jewels." It was a joke they had after a time when she came in on her quiet cat feet and scared her mom to death. Her mother had screamed so loud that Grace jumped.

"Don't do that, Grace," her mother said. "I thought you were a burglar."

Grace knew it would be too painful to come in the side door, hauling in all her memories. Besides, she felt formal and nervous. So far, when she'd needed things from her house, Grandma collected them for her. She hadn't been in her house since her mother died.

Grandma had dropped her off on her way to the grocery store. Grace unlocked the front door and came into the dark hallway. She was surprised to see her father sitting on one of the loveseats in her mother's living room. Ever since the addition was done, he seemed to like the back of the house—his addition—better than the living room where her mother was happiest. The whole coffee table seemed to be lit up with candles. She was still angry with him and couldn't or didn't want to look at him, so she stared at the candles. When he saw her in the dark hallway, he seemed confused, probably wondering about her black hair.

"You told my mother she was worthless, Dad," Grace said. "Worthless."

"I don't remember doing that," Robert said.

"How come it's easier to remember the bad things other people do than it is to remember the bad things that we do?" Grace said, "I remember. You were shouting at her about sock fuzz on the carpet in your new bedroom. You were loud. She was sitting in here, right where you are, and you came and stood in the doorway and shouted at her. It was the night before she died."

"Where were you exactly?" That was her father, the lawyer. She'd probably have to draw up a chart and put it on an easel for him to get it. She came a few feet into the room and pointed at the squishy chair behind the louvered doors to the hallway. He hadn't seen her that night, when he stood shouting in the doorway.

"When you left the room, she was crying," Grace said.

"Did Christina color your hair?"

"You're changing the subject." Now she was huffy. "Grandma did not color my hair. I did. I thought it would make me feel better, but it didn't. Nothing makes me feel better. Nothing."

"Hair grows. Come sit with me." He patted the loveseat cushion beside him.

"You just want me to sit with you so you'll feel better."

"Yes," he said. "I need you to sit with me for just a minute."

She gave in—not because she wanted to sit by him—she was just curious about all the candles. There were so many candles, the coffee table was like a birthday cake for someone old. But up close, counting them, there were just sixteen—making it a birthday cake (if it was a cake and not a table full of candles) for someone barely older than she was. When she sat down, he put his arm around her and snuggled her close. She considered resisting, but instead put her head on his flat chest and listened to his heart beating. Da-da. Da-da. Da-da. Da-da. Dad's heart. When she was little, sometimes she'd lay her head on his chest and listen to his heart until she fell asleep. But she was very angry with him and now angry with herself for wanting to listen to his heart. She lifted her head and sat up. He still had his hand on her shoulder.

She pointed at the cardboard box on the table.

"What's in the box?" she said. He still had his arm around her. They used to sit like this sometimes. She was trying hard to stay angry with him, but it felt cozy. And although she didn't want to acknowledge it, she missed him.

He took his arm away from her and picked up the box. He handed it to her.

"It's Mom's ashes," he said. His tone was hushed like he was in a library or a church.

She held the square cardboard box and looked puzzled, asked him, "They could fit my whole mother into this box?"

He nodded.

"May I look inside, please?" she asked.

"Yes," he said.

She opened the box flaps and saw the plastic bag. "Can I open the bag?"

"Go ahead," he said.

She opened the twist tie. She held up one finger.

"Can I touch?"

He nodded.

She delicately laid her finger on the surface and tears rolled down her face.

"I miss her so much, Dad. I just miss her and it hurts all the time."

"Me too."

"Were you having a memorial for her with the candles?"

"She made me promise not to have a funeral, so sometimes I sit here and talk to her," he said.

"You should straighten up that one candle, it's dripping on the table. What do you say to her? Do you think she can hear you?"

"I like the candle dripping. And when I talk to her, I mostly tell her that I miss her."

Grace watched a drip run down the side of a white candle and thought it looked like a tear. Did he see it too? Was he watching the candle cry?

"She was a good person, Dad. Some of her friends came to Grandma's and told good stories about her."

She moved her finger and thumb into the ashes, feeling them. "The ashes don't feel like her, do they?"

"No, they don't," he said.

"I miss her real self," she said. "She wasn't crazy, Dad. She got broken. I think we broke her."

"I did," he said. "Not you. I broke her."

"But, Dad," Grace said, "the morning she did it, I said awful things to her. Terrible things." Although Grandma said she wasn't responsible, that she'd just been acting like a thirteen-year-old when she swore at her mother that morning, she couldn't let go of it. She was responsible. "I swore at her, Dad. I was so awfully mean, and I'm so very sorry."

"Grace," he said, "I promise you, it wasn't anything you said that morning. She'd been planning to do it before that day. I don't know how long she'd been thinking about it, but it wasn't anything you said."

"Are you sure?"

"Grace, listen to me. You didn't break her. She loved you more than anything."

"But she just left us, she just left us and she didn't tell us what was wrong."

"Maybe she didn't know herself. Or maybe she told me, and I wasn't paying attention."

She carefully sealed the bag with the wire tie and then closed the box flaps. She rubbed her palm over the box surface—round and round—moving slow, wishing it was a genie lamp and if she rubbed long enough, her mother would whoosh out in a mist and talk to her. It was stupid thinking, she knew that, but kept rubbing. When her hand got tired, she leaned her face down, kissed the box, and handed it to her dad.

"I came to get some things, then I'm going back to Grandma's," she said.

She headed toward the back of the house. It was getting colder outside and she had a cute hat in the mudroom that used to be the old kitchen. As she came into the dining room, she noticed that the door that used to lead to the back yard and now was the door to the new kitchen and family room was closed. The door to the mudroom/ex-kitchen was closed too. Very odd.

She came back carrying her hat and stood in the hall and asked, "How come the doors are all shut?"

"I don't know," he said. "I just feel better with doors shut. Crazy, huh? Every time I leave a room, I shut the door. Maybe it's like the dripping candle. Remember how your mom wanted us to turn off the lights when we leave a room to save energy? I've been doing that too. Shutting the doors and turning off the lights."

She didn't know how to respond. She felt sorry for him, so she just nodded and put her face into a sympathetic expression. Maybe she should hold off on what she needed to say, but if not now, then when? She took a deep breath; what she needed to say was risky. She thought she might have an anxiety attack—even though she didn't know what happened to you when you had one. He could hate her forever. She might never get to listen to his heart again.

"The things they've been saying about her on TV, they aren't true. She wasn't bipolar or in a mental hospital in Mexico. If you're sorry, Dad, you have to make it right. You have to let people know who she really was."

Okay, so she did it now—he'd probably never speak to her again. But if she wanted him to take risks and do the right thing, she had to risk his deserting her and say the truth.

He didn't respond, or react, or do anything. She wondered if he'd heard her, so she said it again. "Your people are telling lies about my mother. Your people, Dad."

When he didn't speak, she turned and started up the stairs.

As she headed upstairs, where the bad thing happened, she was afraid. When she got to the upper hallway, she saw the door to her parents' bedroom was closed. Relieved, she exhaled the breath she'd been holding all the way up the steps. The door jam was still splintered where the police broke in.

She wondered why her fussy Dad hadn't had someone come to fix it yet. Sometimes her mom had called him "Mr. Clean," but she did it in a nice way, not like a put-down, but more just teasing or kidding around. It was weird that he let the candle drip on the coffee table. He didn't like messy, didn't like junk lying around. It seemed to make him nervous. Now he was shutting doors all over the place. Maybe it wasn't her mother who was the nutcase in the family?

Her bedroom door was closed too, just like all the other doors in the hallway. Thick carpet always made it difficult to open and close the door, and she pushed hard. Her room was little and cozy. Her mom liked cozy, so Grace liked cozy too. The room was just big enough for her twin bed and a big old dresser with a wide mirror. Last summer, after her mom's thirty-seventh birthday party, she discovered that her mother had plunked a photo in the center of the mirror. When Grace had discovered the photo there, her first reaction was to be mad. "Mom, you put this picture right in the very middle of my mirror!" But then she thought it was funny, so she left it there. They both had blowing faces, their lips puckered and their cheeks fat with air. Her mom had asked her to help blow out the birthday candles and also to share her wish. You're not supposed to tell your wishes, but Mom said that was just a superstition—as if blowing out candles and wishing weren't a superstition—so she told her mother how she wanted pierced ears and then her mother made her wish come true.

She never asked her mother what *her* wish was. It struck her now that she'd been a very self-centered kid last summer. She never even thought about what her mother might have wanted back then, only her own wish mattered. Maybe it was a clue for why she'd killed herself? Maybe she died because her wishes didn't come true, or worse, that no one even cared what she was wishing for?

Wishes. There were so many ways to make wishes: wishes on birthday candles; wishing your mom's box of ashes was a genie box and she'd pop out; wishing for stuff or fame or whatever. She decided that wishing was a waste space inside your brain.

She gathered some things from her closet and dresser drawers, then looked at the picture on the mirror again. Grace loved the picture. She carefully pulled it up, so the tape came loose without tearing the photo. She'd take it to Grandma's house and tape it right in the middle of the mirror in her bedroom there, right where her mom would put it. She didn't know if she'd return home. Her dad might not want to talk to her after what she said about the lies his people were saying about her mother.

As she started to leave her room, she glanced at her bed, and shook her head, puzzled. Her bed was made. Her mother didn't make her bed except when she changed the sheets. She wanted Grace to be a responsible person and make her own bed. Grace hadn't made it the morning she swore at her mother—the same terrible day that her mother died. It was very odd. Maybe her dad made it? But if he made it, it would be perfectly smooth and the blanket and sheets would have hospital corners. Yes, he taught her about hospital corners and having the sheet so tight and smooth that you could bounce a quarter on it like it was on a trampoline. It was how he wanted her mother to make their bed. It didn't look like her father had made the bed. It was lumpy, like the sheet was bunchy and someone had just pulled the blanket up. It was probably Grandma. Grandma had come to the house a few times to get her things. She probably just tossed the blanket over the messy sheets, so she could spread out the clothes and things that Grace had asked her to bring to her condo.

When she left her room, she turned off the light and closed the door even though it was odd for all the doors to be shut. She felt a bit like a guest complying with house rules.

As she came down the stairs and into the front hall, she saw Grandma's headlights shining in the driveway. She stopped in the living room doorway and looked at her dad, wondering if she'd lost him. She felt her heart thumping inside her.

"Grace," he said. "I love you. Please come home."

She nodded, smiled with relief, but then decided not to let him off the hook so easily.

"I love you too, Dad," she said. "Make it right, please."

28. LILY

Lily was including her husband Jagger in her experience; she told him about Dust's memorial in Christina's kitchen, and added that she was sorry he had to work and couldn't be there. She laid out the whole scene when she learned about her mother, Wanda. Loving means sharing who you are with your beloved. She exposed that most vulnerable core of herself to Jagger. She told him how she yearned for her mother, talked about her deserted little girl sorrow with him, confided to him that she was afraid to go meet Wanda. Who would her mother be? Would she reject her again? But no, that was wrong, her mother had not rejected her. It was hard to unthink embedded thoughts. The belief that she held for most of her life was wrong. Her mother didn't choose to leave her—she had been a mess and was sent away.

She talked to Jagger about her terror of flying, and he gave her statistics. "Driving a car is more risky than flying," he said. He wanted her to go. He wanted her to experience flight and to find her mother.

She confided that she wanted Dust to be proud of her, even though it was like cleaning the house after drop-in company had left the premises.

"You should go," Jagger had said.

In all its nakedness, she opened her heart to him. She even confessed that there was a time when she thought about killing herself, and how much she wished that Dust had waited, had given whatever was bothering her time to pass and change. Things change, she told Jagger. She decided that time could heal wounds.

***

It was dark in their bedroom. Lily knew Jagger was still awake beside her. She rolled toward him and slid her hand under his t-shirt, delicately touching the hairs on his chest.

"Lily, stop," Jagger said.

"You don't want me to touch you?" she pulled her hand away.

"We have to talk," he said.

"Why don't you want me to touch you?"

With her right ear muffled in the pillow, she thought she heard him say, "someone else." *Someone else, oh God, had he found out about Evan? How could he know?* She was always so careful. She ended the relationship and NOW he knew?

"Say again?" she whispered, trepidation paralyzing her.

"Lily, I'm sorry," he said. "You've been so good to me lately; I just can't take it anymore. Right before Dust died, I was going to tell you, but there never was a right time, and then she died and how could I tell you then? And lately you've been being so sweet to me that I feel like a real jerk."

"What?" she said, and found it hard to get that one word out.

"Lily, there's someone else," he said. "I'm in love with someone else."

Someone else? She couldn't speak. She rolled away from him. *Someone else?* She wondered if she should be carrying on like a crazed jealous person, but how could she? The words righteous indignation came into her head. How could she be righteous? What sort of indignation could she have without feeling like a fraud?

She had questions, but she couldn't speak.

"Lily," he said, "are you okay? Say something."

She was motionless and silent with her back to him.

"Lily," he said, "Lily, I'm sorry. I never meant for it to happen."

Wide awake and silent. Dumbstruck. Mute. Thoughts raced past each other, collided, then merged into a confused jumble. She was angry. She was sad. She was hurt. She felt herself closing—closing her oyster shell around this irritating grain of knowledge, covering it with layers of nacre, growing a hard pearl inside her gut.

"Please," he said. "Please, Lily. Talk to me."

She shook her head and realized that in the dark he wouldn't see it. Then she didn't move or speak. Minutes passed; her hip hurt. She thought of moving but lay still.

Eventually she heard him breathing evenly. He was asleep. How could he be asleep? If she couldn't sleep, he shouldn't either.

She had questions. Three years ago, when she'd been so depressed, did her remoteness drive him away? When her outside interests—college classes and later, Evan—became more interesting than him, was that when he sought another woman's company? Was it a woman? Probably. He said he was in love with someone else. He didn't say what sex "else" was. She dropped that idea. Her husband liked breasts and running his hands up her long legs—shaved and silky smooth—up and up. He liked tanned girls in white dresses. The song came into her head then.

"Girls in white dresses with blue satin sashes;
Snowflakes that stay on my nose and eyelashes;
Silver white winters that melt into springs;
These are a few on my favorite things."

She was Julie Andrews twirling on a mountain, singing about her favorite things. She was losing it. She should be upset, should be thinking about what she should do next, but she was humming. She should sing out loud, wake him up.

"When the dog bites,
When the bee stings,
When I'm feeling sad,
I simply remember my favorite things,
And then I don't feel so bad."

***

When she woke on Sunday morning, she wasn't thinking about Jagger, instead she thought about her favorite things. She dressed in a long sleeved t-shirt and her sweats—comfortable, favorite clothes. She dressed to please Lily.

She made coffee and sat at the dining room table writing her list of favorite things. Mostly her favorite things weren't things, they were people: first the twins and Dust, Daddy and Rose and Christina, and Grace—black-haired Goth Grace so precious and vulnerable. Lily added a second tier of people: Fred, Dust's neighbor was a good guy, who would have been on Dust's list, so she added him to hers. Then Carlos and her boss Amanda went on the list. Should Jagger go on her list? He wasn't evil. He had an affair. Fell in love. She had an affair. She'd known Jagger since she was Grace's age. She drew a line on the paper; someday she might add Jagger, but not now. She didn't add Evan to the list; Evan was only interested in safely married women. Married women didn't threaten his marriage. Evan was over.

Lily sat with her elbows on the dining room table and her hands clasped in front of her chin, thinking of more favorite things: Classes—especially the literature and psychology classes. She liked getting lost in a book. She wrote those things on the list.

A stair creaked; someone was up and she'd have to stop writing. If it was one of the twins, she could expect a sleepy-eyed, messy-haired boy to flop down on the living room couch and hit the TV's remote. Quiet—the lovely, but always fleeting quiet—would be lost. But then she heard kitchen cupboards open, cups clinking. Jagger was in the kitchen pouring coffee. He brought his cup into the dining room.

"What are you doing?" he said, as he sat down across from her.

"Making a list."

"Of what you want from me?" he asked.

"No," she said. "I'm making a list of what I have."

"Can I see?"

She pushed the paper across the table.

He pointed to a name on the list. "Dust is gone," he said.

"I'll always have her," she said.

"So who's this Fred?"

"Dust's next door neighbor."

Jagger nodded, "Oh, yeah, old black guy. I remember him."

He pushed the paper back to her.

"Lily, I'm sorry," he said. "I never meant for this to happen."

"I know," she said.

"You're being too reasonable. You should be screaming at me."

"I don't want to."

"Are you shutting down?" He looked alarmed. "You're not going to shoot yourself, are you?"

"No, Jagger. I am not going to shoot myself. First of all, we don't have any guns. My life is worth something, even without you. I have value."

"Aren't you going to ask me anything?" he said.

"What should I ask you?" she said.

"Well, don't you want to know how old she is? Or how we met? Or how long this has been going on?" He was flustered. She could see that he was dying to tell all.

"Do you want to tell me?" she said, feeling calm. She realized that those details didn't matter to her. What mattered was that he loved someone else, not her. Dust's suicide made every other pain minimal. Maybe it was because of Evan, too, that she understood the possibilities of attractions. She was in no position to judge him.

"Five years. She's thirty-two. She has a 1966 mustang." The statistics flew out of his mouth—numbers, like pointy darts, that he was shooting at her.

"Five years?" she said. Okay, so that got to her. "Five years?" she repeated and she started to cry. Five years ago, the boys were twelve, and when she tried to remember back that far, she only remembered being happy. Before the time of blackness and depression had sucked her in. Long before Evan, her husband was fucking another woman. Five years, that was longer than some marriages.

"I'll move out," he said, as though he was doing his duty to God and country. He would probably move in with her, the someone else. Maybe her name was Sally? Mustang Sally.

"You have to tell the boys," she said.

"Can we tell them together?"

She nodded.

"I should have told you months ago. I know this is terrible timing," he said.

How about years ago, she thought.

"I'm sorry to tell you now, now when you're going through all this about Dust." He sipped his coffee, wiped his mouth with the back of his hand. "I just, well, I was just afraid that if I kept waiting to tell you, something else would come up."

She just nodded at him, and thought, when people die, is it ever a convenient time?

29. FRED

At 7:45 a.m. on Wednesday, October 24, Fred went from window to window staring out into his yard at the fog, a white mist, hanging over the garden. It was 61 degrees and supposed to go up to 76 degrees today. His Hostas had all died; their leaves had turned yellow and lay flattened on the ground. Oak leaves covered the front lawn. He'd have to rake later in the day. He'd cleaned out the vegetable garden down to the black soil that he and Dust had been enriching with compost for years. The only things still standing were the ferns of the asparagus plants. Seasons were changing. Winter would come, then spring, then summer, and another fall—over and over. Seasons replaced seasons. Nothing would replace Dust.

Depressed, he went back to bed.

30. CHRISTINA

As a nurse, Christina had wrapped her arms around mothers whose young children had died from unthinkable illnesses. She'd patted the shoulders of fathers bent over with the pain of their loss. She understood the patterns of life—the fragile, tentative beginnings—learned in the years of neonatal nursing at Hutzel Women's Hospital. Babies—black babies, brown babies, Asian babies, Arab babies, white babies—tiny beings, tiny bodies with scrawny legs and arms, clinging to life. She'd started her nursing career there, a new, young nurse with the newest humans. Later, she moved to Children's Hospital, where the small lives she cared for were toddlers and preschool children. How many times over the years had she used her quiet, soothing voice to console parents as they watched their precious children suffer and die? She understood the mechanics of grief, knew that after a tragedy you aren't supposed to make any major changes in your life. Don't move to a different house. Don't quit your job. Give it a year. Two years. Pass time and don't make any abrupt movements. Speak quietly, soothingly, cry, pray, meditate. Take up yoga.

Yoga? Hardly. No yoga for her tired—very tired—body. Her body wouldn't, couldn't go into those exotic poses. She couldn't bend into a pretzel or catch her breath with her body in a downward dog position. She was lucky that one foot could move in a line with the other and she could walk.

Grace was off with Robert seeing the therapist again, and afterward, the two of them were going out to dinner. Christina knew it was important for Grace to be with her father. Grace had told her about Robert's candles and the box with Dusty's ashes, and that Robert said Dusty had requested no funeral. But Christina wanted to be angry about it. She didn't want to allow him any wiggle room. She wanted to blame Robert for Dusty's death. If the truth was that he caused Dusty such unhappiness that she wanted to die, then she, Christina, was off the hook. Would she feel any better if it were as simple as that? She was on the hook, too, so she struggled to soften toward her son-in-law.

She could choose not to believe Robert about Dusty's request for no funeral, but she knew it was true. Dusty was a no-muss, no-fuss gal. She didn't like big deals made over her, although at her birthday party last summer, she'd seemed pleased with all the love being lavished on her. Christina was grateful for that party. She could hold on to the image of her daughter in a sundress the color of sunshine, yellow ribbons braided into her long, red hair. When images came into Christina's head of the anguish that Dusty must have been feeling as she planned and then followed through on her suicide, she'd quickly shift her focus to the birthday party and her daughter's smiling face.

Christina told herself to speak softly and kindly to herself, just as she would tell grieving parents at the hospital. Be gentle. Hold on to the pretty pictures in your mind. Know the sorrow, but let it go and replace it with the good memories.

***

She met Lily at Somerset Mall for a walk and dinner. Nordstrom's Cafeteria was comfortable and quiet at dinnertime. From the third floor window along the side of their booth, they watched people coming and going from the parking lot far below. They looked out on Big Beaver Road and watched traffic passing the manicured median and perfectly pruned trees. Christina looked out the window and across the street at the original, upscale mall. When they expanded, they built a walkway over the street to connect the two massive buildings; Saks and Neiman Marcus were on the South mall, Macy's and Nordstrom's anchored the North mall.

"Dust hated this mall," Lily said, with an amused smile.

"Maybe we should boycott it for her," Christina said, and smiled too.

"She hated all the elegant consumerism. Hated that people would spend $300 on a purse or a blouse and then complain about taxes. If you walk all the floors on both sides of Big Beaver Road, it's almost two miles. We came out here together a couple of times. She'd talk about all the trucks and ships and fuel it must have taken to bring all the building materials in. But, you know, in bad weather it's a nice place to walk."

"I haven't been able to go to the gym yet," Christina said.

"Don't rush it, Christina," Lily said. "We can walk here, if you feel up to it."

Christina knew they wouldn't take the walkway over to the South mall. They would walk around the first, second, and maybe even the third floor on the North side, but even that might be too much for her tired feet and weary lungs.

Their food came, and they ate quietly for a while.

"So, Lily, there's something you want to tell me, but you're hesitating. I can take it, whatever it is. I'm a strong person, you know."

Lily sighed. "You're like a mother to me, Christina. You always have been. So I don't want you to hear this from someone else."

"Oh, Lily," Christina said. "This doesn't sound good."

"Jagger wants a divorce."

"Oh, dear. I'm so sorry. When did this happen?"

"He told me a couple of nights ago. He has a girlfriend."

"What will you do?"

"Divorce him," Lily said.

"Good." Christina heard herself and was surprised.

"Really, Christina?" Lily said. "You don't think it's terrible? In all those years, you never divorced Jay Jones. I'm so surprised."

"Oh, but, Lily, I should have divorced him. Sometimes it works out for people to stay together and work on a marriage, but in my case, Jay just wasn't there. I think of how much better it would have been for Dusty. Me too. Maybe I would have hooked up with your father?"

Lily laughed. "Hooked up?"

"Okay," Christina leaned in intimately, "so does that mean having sex, or getting married, or just dating? I like the sound of it. Hooking up. When I'm a grown-up, that's what I want to do. Hook up."

They spent the rest of their main course giggling, then during coffee they talked about Lily and Rose flying to New Mexico to see their mother.

"Did you talk to Wanda? Does she know you're coming?"

"Rose called her. She said she sounded pleased."

"Well, of course she is. I'm so glad you're doing this, Lily." Christina said. "I'm happy for your mother getting to see her girls again. I wish I could come," Christina said. "I'm very curious about Wanda."

"You could come," Lily said. "You could hold my hand on the plane."

"No, you need to do this with Rose," Christina said. "The two of you together. It's important. Rose will hold your hand. She needs to feel important to you."

Christina reached into her purse and said, "I have something for you to take on your trip."

She reached across the table and placed Dusty's pink rosary in Lily's hand. "When you run the beads through your fingers, you'll have some of Dusty there on the plane with you. She would be so proud of how brave you're being. Flying, I mean. And I want you to keep the rosary. I know you're not Catholic, Lily. Dusty wasn't either. But the beads gave her comfort, and I want you to have them."

31. CARLOS

The early morning flight was Carlos's idea. He thought that Lily seeing only darkness from the plane's window would ease her fears. He regretted that he hadn't been able to find them a direct flight to Albuquerque. On short notice, all he could find was a flight with a plane change in Denver. He was anxious about this trip, hopeful that Lily would be able to board the plane without having Rose drag her on board by the heels. He was plagued by a fear for Rose. Rose, who had felt rejected by her mother and whose insecurities made her feel less than she was. He wondered if it would have been better for them never to know about Wanda. He was very afraid that Rose would come home more hurt than when she left. He pushed for the sisters to take this trip and now he thought the plan was questionable.

He'd drive them to Detroit Metropolitan Airport at four in the morning, so Lily was spending the night. They were having a sleepover—a pajama party. Carlos had never been to a pajama party in his life. There were outfits to consider for a sleepover, Rose told him. Rose and Lily were flannelized up to their necks; his outfit was a sweatshirt and fleece pants—gray with red dots.

Lily's anxiety over flying crackled like an electric charge in the room. He and Rose were swatting at it with jokes, trying to make Lily laugh and relax. "You know what we call red dots in my business?" he asked, pointing at his pants, and then answered. "Pimples."

They were huddled up in front of the fireplace drinking hot chocolate with marshmallows. Lily would take a Xanax before they left for the airport in the morning. It wasn't nine o'clock yet, but they'd go to bed early. Carlos wondered if Lily would sleep at all. He doubted that any of them would sleep.

"So do you think Wanda ever remarried?" Rose said.

"Maybe we have more sisters?" Lily said. "She named us after flowers. What do you think their names would be?"

"Daisy?" Rose said.

"Iris. Jasmine. Violet," Carlos said. They looked at him surprised, "What? I've been thinking about this." He didn't admit that he'd just gone online on his cell phone and checked flower names for girl babies. "Okay, what other girls' names?"

"Flowers only?" Rose asked. "Poppy, Heather, Petunia, Fern."

"Hey, you two," Lily said. "No fair. You've been researching."

"How about other earthy things then?" Carlos said. "Willow. Ruby. Jade. Sandy."

"Sandy?" Lily said, and was alarmed. "Maybe we should cancel our trip. Hurricane Sandy has already hit Cuba. Maybe our flight will be canceled?"

"Wishful thinking, Lily," Rose said.

"Sandy is heading up the Eastern Seaboard," Carlos said. "It won't affect your trip. Lily, you'll be fine. Besides, it'll probably veer off over the Atlantic or dissipate and just turn into rain."

32. LILY

In Rose and Carlos's guest room, Lily woke up with a memory. She was with her parents, Ben and Wanda Abbott, in a park. Her mother was there, but she couldn't see her in the memory. There were swings and teeter-totters and a slide. She sat on one end of the teeter-totter and Daddy pushed the other end down. She went up. She didn't like it.

"Lily, let's go try the slide," they prodded her.

She didn't want to. It was high up in the air. Her father was standing at the side of the ladder telling her, "Just step up on the ladder. Just climb the ladder, do it once and you'll want to do it again. It's fun."

She climbed slowly, one rung, then two. Her knees felt weak. She was so scared.

"You're doing fine. One more step. Come on, Lily. All the kids go on the slide." *All the kids do it*, a phrase that normally came out of a kid's mouth, not a parent's.

She reached the top of the ladder and held the sides in a death grip. She couldn't look down or out or around. She was terrified. Too high. Too high. This ancient slide had no flat platform at the top, just a ladder and slide and no middle zone to get yourself arranged.

"Now, Lily, bring up one foot at a time, and move it in front of you. Move your legs around to the front, so you can sit down."

"I can't, Daddy. I can't. I'll fall."

"Damn it, Lily, move your feet."

"I can't, Daddy. I'm scared."

She tried to lift her right leg up. She'd seen other kids get to the top of the slide and then just lift themselves with their hands on the curved top bar—just hoist themselves with their arms and plop their butts down at the top of the slide. It looked easy. Shaking and quaking, she got one leg onto the sloped side, the slippery slide side. One leg over and then she was stuck—straddling one leg on the ladder, one on the slide.

"I can't do it! I can't. I can't."

"Lily, just bring your other leg up and over. Just don't even think about it. You're thinking too much. Just do it.

When she tried to bring the ladder leg up, the slide leg started slipping more. She shook and cried. Daddy came up the ladder. Picked her up and arranged her legs. He left her clutching the sides of the slide and went back to standing on the ground.

"Relax your grip."

"I'm afraid, Daddy. I don't want to let go. I'll fall."

"Keep holding on, but don't hold on so tight. Relax your hands. Hold gently like you're petting a puppy."

She thought about that, petted the puppy, and suddenly she was zooming down the slide. Screaming. She slid right off the end of the slide and landed in the dirt at the bottom with a hard thud.

It was the only time she ever got on a slide.

***

It was balmy when Carlos drove them to the airport. Dark. Lily hadn't slept, or maybe she did; she wasn't sure of anything. She took one of the Xanax tablets from the bottle of ten when she got up. As they neared the airport, she was surprised by the way she felt. Calm, but hyper-observant. In the airport, she followed Rose as they moved through the security lines. She worried about bathrooms. She was going to need a bathroom very soon.

Days ago, she'd argued with Rose about shoes. Rose told her to wear slip-on shoes; they were easier to deal with at check-in. But somewhere Lily had heard that heavy, lace-up shoes were better if the plane crashed and you had to escape by sliding down a wing. Then you wanted good shoes to protect your feet from the burning metal of the plane. She was also wearing her heaviest jeans, thick socks, a bulky, long-sleeved sweater, and a vest with deep pockets—clothes that would protect her skin when the plane crashed.

She told Rose that her thick-soled walking shoes would take up too much room in her borrowed carryon luggage, so when Rose handed her the bin for her shoes and purse, she had to stand there backing up the line while she untied her shoes.

She stood in a clear plastic, or was it glass, vertical tube and was scanned for weapons, then she gathered her belongings at the end of the conveyer belt. After getting her shoes back on, she walked beside Rose down the long corridor. Rose was talking, but she couldn't listen.

"Huh?" she said. Rose said something again, but she lost concentration. "Huh?"

They found a bathroom. She was worried. What if she couldn't pee enough now and had to go on the plane? She'd have to unhook her seat belt and walk through the moving plane to the bathroom on board. She wanted to stay securely belted for the whole flight.

Rose bought coffee. Lily was afraid that drinking anything would make her stomach feel even more unstable than it already felt, plus there was the bathroom issue. They went to the boarding area, where rows of chairs were already filled with dozens of people getting on this flight. No one looked afraid. Most looked bored or tired. She wanted to say, *Rose, Rose, I can't do this*, but she sat down on a black chair to wait with her sister.

Rose talked, more quietly than she usually did, almost whispering. She patted Lily's hand. Rose sipped her coffee. Minutes passed. Lily's stomach churned. She hurried back to the bathroom and, afraid that she was taking too long, skipped hand washing and hurried back to Rose.

Then, too soon for Lily, a voice on a loudspeaker said, "Now boarding Flight 245 for Denver." Rose stood, so Lily stood too. She followed Rose. A woman in a uniform checked their boarding passes. Then they walked down a long tube, pulling their carryon luggage behind them.

"You alright?" Rose asked.

Lily nodded. She was afraid to speak.

People were backed up as they moved into the plane. Lily saw the crack on the floor where the plane and the tube connected. A gap. She could see lights shining on the concrete far beneath her. She stepped briskly over the gap and onto the plane. She felt calm, numb, and very observant. She praised drugs with all her heart. People were stopping to lift their luggage up into bins over the rows of seats. Rose opened a bin and they hoisted their luggage inside.

A nun in a powder blue habit sat in the aisle seat of their row; she stood aside while Rose slid into the window seat. Lily sat in the middle between the nun and Rose. What order of nuns still wore full habits—pale blue habits? Lily was usually friendly and outgoing, normally she'd chat, ask the nun where she was from. She couldn't speak. She wasn't sure if the nun was a good or bad omen. She decided that she was just a passenger and not an omen of any kind, just a nun. But the nun was a good distraction. Better to wonder about the pale blue habit than to think about the airplane.

She buckled her seat belt.

The steward demonstrated how to put on the yellow life vests, and how to use the oxygen masks. No one seemed to be paying attention. Lily watched and listened carefully, while other passengers read books or appeared to nap. "Save yourself before you save your child," the flight attendant said. She thought of Dust and Grace. She wasn't sure how it applied, but she thought of them.

It was still dark outside as the plane started moving—driving like a bus down an expressway—heading west with the sunrise chasing them. As the plane taxied down the runway, Lily saw blue lights outside like Christmas decorations scattered on the ground, the pattern unknowable.

She didn't realize that she was holding her breath until Rose whispered to her, "You'll be fine. Breathe, Lily, or you'll faint."

Lily watched out the window from her center seat. In the darkness the plane taxied between rows of yellow lights, gaining speed. The liftoff was soft, barely perceptible. The cabin was dark. She sensed earth falling away beneath her. Lights on the ground were tiny and then they disappeared into a soot-colored cloud. White lights on the tip of the long, skinny wing flashed like a movie star had just arrived and the paparazzi were snapping pictures, then darkness, no clouds visible. Nothing. The light flashing on the wing was flashing red now in the black darkness.

The nun was quiet. She had thick, black eyebrows and a thick, gold wedding band. She was married to Christ. If they left the Church, did that mean they divorced Christ?.

Lily's gold wedding band was at home on her dresser. When they told the twins about the divorce, Henry got teary-eyed and Andrew argued with them that they should try harder. But then, very quickly, it seemed to her, they gave up. It was pointless and they all knew it. They went to Buddy's Pizza on Northwestern Highway for dinner. Celebrating? No, just eating.

Lily remembered that she put Dust's rosary in her vest pocket. She reached in and touched it with her fingers. Clots of blood floating in Dust's bathroom sink flashed in her memory as she touched the pink beads. Christina didn't know that part of the rosary story. Lily took her hand out of her pocket and took Rose's hand.

Carlos had called her at work and asked her to watch over her sister—to protect Rose. He was afraid that their mother would make

Rose feel even more insecure. He was worried. She told him that no matter what Wanda did, she would do her best to make Rose feel good about herself. Rose's job was to help her conquer her fear of flying. They each had their challenges.

It was pale gray outside the window when they arrived in Denver. The plane landed with a bump and a screeching noise. As they got off the plane, she felt elated. She did it. She didn't cry or carry on like a big scaredy-cat. She wasn't Lily Livered.

She didn't let go of the rope.

A memory. Summer vacation during high school, she was at someone's cottage and all her friends were waterskiing. Dust did it. Dust skied. Jagger skied and came back dripping water and laughing. Then it was Lily's turn. She stood on shore with her feet in the skis. She stared at the blue water, darker in the center of the lake, deep, dark water, and knew that she'd sink and never come back up. When the boat took off, she let go of the rope. Jagger was angry with her, but Dust had said, "Oh, leave her alone. You can take Lily's turn." She overheard some girl whisper, *Lily Livered*. She was humiliated, embarrassed in front of all those kids, but she just couldn't do it.

Lily flew in an airplane.

Rose said, "What are you smiling about?"

They waited again in a crowded boarding area, more crowded than at Detroit Metropolitan Airport. Planes were delayed; people from three flights were standing around looking crabby.

Xanax made her body calm. Watchful.

Then they were in the next plane, flying again. Heavy clouds. Snow on the ground. Lily could see the white teepees of Denver's airport blending into the gray-white sky as they flew away. The whole sky was white, no trace of blue in sight, a sky loaded with snow. The backside of the wing moved down, then up, then down again. They lifted up through snow clouds; the plane's wing disappeared into the whiteness, then higher, above the clouds into the bright blue sky. Looking down through the clouds, there were gaps—she could see towns like children's toys, and white caps on the Rocky Mountains. It's beautiful up here, she thought. She was so calm, observant, and acutely aware. Altitude muffled sound. Sound muted—plugged up. Fears muted—drugged up.

The back of the wing tipped downward as the plane turned toward the mountains. She gulped and closed her eyes. The ride became bumpy, like riding in an old bus without shocks down a dirt road in the country. Rose squeezed her hand and checked her for signs of panic.

"I'm alright," she said.

They were high, high above the Rocky Mountains. The ground turned sienna and brown. Earth had been pushed and shoved around during the Ice Age; glaciers had carved out valleys and plowed up mountains, making way for rivers to ribbon in and out between peaks. Tectonic plates pushed together and pulled apart. Topography gradually formed, shaped, and moved again. Now she saw piles of snow on mountain peaks beneath them. Bright, dazzling white. Painfully white, like looking at an eclipse with your bare eyes. Abruptly, the land was flat, the color of cocoa. The sky was clear and intense blue, hazy along the horizon. There were patterns—circles of green and dull gold—in the cocoa-colored landscape. Then shining squares reflected up at them.

"What is it?" she asked Rose, and pointed out the window.

"Solar panels."

Solar panels sucking up the sun's energy.

The ground was mottled shades of brown, like the patterns of slate or marble. There were squares of farm acreage and circles of irrigation. Nearing Albuquerque, the ground was like sand with dark freckles. Trees? Tumbleweeds? Grids of streets were another shade of sand color.

"The earth will survive. People will die, but the earth, pregnant with inner fire will keep shifting and moving, erupting and changing." Dust Steward, 2012.Lily decided to keep a notebook of things she remembered Dust saying.

"Yawn," Rose said. "It'll help clear your ears."

Lily yawned.

33. ROSE

Carlos had made reservations for them at the Hotel Santa Fe, a Native American—owned-and-operated hotel. Rose loved this place. It was where she and Carlos had stayed on their honeymoon and every anniversary so far. After checking in and putting their luggage in their room, the sisters rode in one of the hotel's purple shuttle buses into town. Rose was giddy with anticipation. She wanted to show Lily all the places she loved. They lunched at the French Pastry Shop and Creperie. They walked around town peering in shop windows and admiring the work of Native American vendors displayed on the sidewalk in front of the Palace of the Governors. Their wares, mostly jewelry, were spread out in front of them. Lily and Rose each bought necklaces—one yellow, one orange—made of strung, dried corn kernels for Grace, then a purple van came and took them back to the hotel.

Rose knew Lily must be tired. She was tired. They had been up since three in the morning. It had been a big day, a long day that had started in the night. She was proud of Lily and relieved. Nothing dramatic had happened. She'd held together—even smiled a few times when her face relaxed and she didn't look frozen.

Carlos was working at his clinic, but when she called and left his receptionist a message, he called back immediately and told her how happy he was.

They napped for an hour, then she led Lily through the hotel dining room and out to the patio to a large teepee. They stepped inside through a circular hole and pulled two wrought iron chairs with red cushions—that seemed incongruous to the space—close together.

She said, "What do you think Native Americans sat on inside their teepees? The bare ground? Cushions? Blankets? Buffalo skins?"

"Bean bag chairs," Lily said, and they both laughed.

The sisters sat on the stiff chairs facing the round cutout entry. On other trips here, Rose and Carlos came into the tepee for a powwow, sans peace pipe. They'd hold hands and say loving things, then go to their room and fuck each other's brains out.

"You're doing great," Rose said, while turning her chair and dragging it closer to Lily's so she could see her sister's expression as she spoke. She reached out and took Lily's hands as Carlos might have taken hers, "I was so proud of you on the plane."

"Good drugs, Rose," Lily said. "Thank you for getting us here. Thank you for making me fly. I think I like being high."

Rose laughed.

"No, seriously, I liked seeing the clouds from above. Good drugs and good views."

"Do you want the window seat on the way back home?"

"Hmm, let me think about that."

They sat quietly for a while, then Rose asked, "Lily, why do you think Dust did it?"

Lily shook her head, sighed, and shrugged, "I don't know."

"My first thought was that she had a crush on Carlos and he humiliated her," Rose said. "He told me she'd called and invited him to meet her for lunch, and he turned her down."

"Oh, Rose," Lily said, "you know she'd never do that to you. She'd never hurt you."

Rose knew from Carlos that her fears were unfounded, but it was good to hear this from Lily. It was true then. If you couldn't be honest here—during a powwow in a teepee on the patio of an expensive hotel—then where could you?

"I can't imagine being so unhappy that I'd want to kill myself," Rose said.

"I can."

Rose felt the horrified expression on her face and tried to hide it. "You've thought about killing yourself?"

"It was a few years ago. I don't know why. I was depressed." Lily stopped speaking, glanced up at the hole at the top of the teepee. Rose looked up too and only saw the vivid blue sky.

"I felt like I couldn't breathe," Lily said.

"Did Dust know about that?" Rose felt a twinge of the green-eyed monster inside her, feeling hurt that Dust probably knew her sister ever so much better than she did. She was always the outsider.

A minute passed while Rose waited for Lily to speak.

"No," Lily said, and shook her head. "I regret more than anything that I never told her about how I felt then. I didn't tell anyone. Why should I be so depressed that I'd consider ending my life? How could I be so ungrateful? I had sweet sons, a husband, a nice house, and a good job. I didn't understand where the depression came from. Maybe if I had told her, she would have felt safe telling me what she was planning. Maybe talking about it would have helped her...saved her."

"Dust never knew?"

Lily shook her head.

"Did you tell anyone?" Rose asked.

"No one. No, wait, I did tell Jagger just last week when I was trying to be the perfect wife. Now I wish I hadn't opened up to him."

"Oh, Lily, I'm glad you told me," Rose said. "It means so much that you'd confide in me."

"Rose, promise me you'll talk to me if you ever have any thoughts like that."

"Hopefully I won't," Rose said, "But, Lily, how are you doing about the divorce? Are you alright? You're not considering suicide, are you?"

"My wedding ring made my finger feel trapped. Claustrophobic." She held up her naked ring finger, smiled, and said, "All better now. I had to go to a jeweler and have it cut off." She wiggled her finger. "Feels so good," she said. "And I know I never would consider suicide again. Well, unless I was old with some terrible, incurable illness and was going to have to go through a brutal death, then I might. But otherwise, especially seeing how Dust's suicide has torn everyone up, I wouldn't do it. Life fluctuates, you know, Rose. Things get bad and they get good; it doesn't always stay bad. Things change, that's one thing you can count on. If the changes aren't in your life, then they're in the lives of people you love and then that changes your life, too. Sometimes I want to shout at her, 'Take it back, Dust! It gets better.'"

Rose could see Lily struggling, trying not to cry. Watching her, she felt her own eyes welling up. Then Lily was downright blubbering—tears poured out and her nose was running.

Rose scooted her chair closer and leaned forward to wrap her arms around her older sister. "I don't have any tissues," Rose said.

"Me either," Lily said, when she caught her breath. "Do you think anyone will notice if I wipe my nose on my sleeve?"

"I will," Rose said, and laughed. "Go ahead, people notice faces more than sleeves, and your face is disgustingly snotty."

34. LILY

They arrived at Wendy's on the outskirts of Taos late Saturday morning. When they came into the fast food restaurant, Lily spotted a woman sitting at a table for four at the far side of the room. The woman saw Lily and waved.

"Over there," Lily said, and nudged Rose.

Still standing at the entry, Rose turned, so her back was to the woman at the table, and whispered, "Oh, Lily, Oh, my God, Lily. Look at her. She looks like a bag lady."

"It'll be okay, Rose," Lily said. "Remember, she's lived a hard life."

They walked over to the table, and Lily said, "Are you Wanda?"

The woman's eyes darted around the room. She nodded and seemed nervous. "Are you going to buy my lunch?" the woman asked.

Lily was startled. "Oh. Well, yeah, sure. What would you like?"

"Wait a minute," Rose said, touching Lily's arm. "Do you know who we are?" Rose asked the woman.

"Why, sure, honey," the older woman said. "You're my sisters, Meg and Beth. Amy died, you know."

Lily clapped her hand over her mouth to hide a laugh.

"What's your name?" Rose asked.

"Why, honey, you know my name," she said. "Why it's Jo, Jo March, and I'd like a burger and fries."

Lily went up to the counter and ordered food for Jo March. The girl behind the counter took the order and then whispered to her,

"That's real nice of you. We let her sit inside. I feel sorry for her. She's harmless. Hungry. Thank you for doing this."

When Lily got back to the table with the lunch tray, Rose said, "Well, Miss March, it was nice meeting you," and headed back toward the door, where several people were coming in.

Jo March said, "Hey, don't I get a drink?"

"Sure," Lily said, and went back to the counter, where the girl handed her a paper cup that she took back to the homeless woman.

The sisters found another table closer to the door and watched the parking lot. A few cars and trucks pulled in. It was nearing lunchtime and getting busy. They assessed each person or group that entered the restaurant—too young, too Mexican, too Native American, too tall. Everyone coming in was Too Something—not their mother.

"Maybe we should get lunch?" Rose said. "I'm getting hungry."

"Let's give her a few more minutes."

They sat. They talked about Jo March. They checked their watches.

"Maybe we're late and she was already here and left?" Lily said.

"Or maybe we have the wrong place. Should we ask if there's another Wendy's in Taos?"

"Maybe you should call her?" Lily said.

They watched as a dusty red pickup truck pulled into the parking lot. An older woman with a white skunk stripe down the center of her dark hair climbed down from the driver's side. She wore a denim jacket and jeans and walked like Rose. Her short hair was brushed back behind her ears in almost the same style as Rose's. As she neared the door, Lily saw that she was wearing a half dozen silver bracelets and turquoise earrings. Her lips were very red. She wondered if her breath would smell like wine.

"She's here," Lily said, and stood. This stranger coming through the door was their mother. Lily was nervous. What would they say to each other?

Rose stood.

"Wanda?" Lily said, when the woman was inside.

"Lily?" her long lost mother said, staring up at her. "Oh, good heavens, you're so big! You're huge."

Lily sucked in her stomach and felt embarrassed. BIG. But then she realized that the last time her mother saw her, she was eight years old. She relaxed her stomach. Let it hang out, let it be whatever it was, but by that time, her stomach was irrelevant because Wanda had found Rose.

"Oh," Wanda said. "Oh, precious little Rosebud. You are so beautiful. So beautiful. I'm so lucky and so happy to see you. Dear beautiful Rose."

Her mother had the voice of a longtime smoker—raspy, grinding words out of damaged vocal cords. She had tiny cigarette-sucking pucker wrinkles around her mouth and deep creases at the edge of her eyes from years of squinting into the sun. In spite of a glaze of makeup, Lily could see Wanda's road map of purple and red broken blood vessels on her cheeks. Her skin was crackled and ancient; she could have been eighty. She looked twenty years older than Christina, even though they were the same age. Christina's weight filled out her wrinkles.

Mother and beautiful little daughter were both in tears, hugging each other. Lily watched them and again tried to scrunch down, get compressed so she'd fit in with this family gathering of short women. Her self-consciousness grew her taller than she was. Big boned, flat-butted, but thin, she wondered why she sucked in her stomach. Daddy's girl stood aside as the little people embraced. Wanda was now delicately touching Rose's face, a blind woman, reading the hills and valleys in the face of a long lost friend. No, not lost, Lily realized, someone Wanda had seen every day of her life; she might have been feeling her own face—tracking her own round cheeks and chin—as it was thirty years ago. Two sets of blue-eyes embraced each other. Brown-eyes considered going over and hanging out with Jo March.

Wanda turned from Rose and gave Lily a hug. Perfunctory? No. It was a decent, big hug and then a kiss on each cheek. Then she said, "I'm so sorry I was late."

Better late than never, Lily thought, but just shrugged and smiled. It's nothing, Wanda. You haven't seen us in thirty years, what's another half hour?

"I've fixed us a nice lunch," Wanda said. "Lily, why don't you follow me? You girls have a rental car, right? Rose, will you ride along with your Mama?"

Rose was ecstatic—a puppy licking and wagging and bouncing—and as Lily observed Rose's expression, any jealousy she felt evaporated. Her baby sister was getting attention from their mother. It was good. Carlos would be relieved and grateful that Rose wasn't being hurt.

"Is that okay?" Rose asked. "You good to follow?"

"Of course," Lily said. But as they headed out toward Wanda's truck and the rental car, Lily started feeling panicked. She pictured Wanda racing off in that red truck, leaving her lost in New Mexico. She'd left her in a bar once, so why should she trust Wanda now?

"Rose, you've got your cell phone on just in case I lose you?" Lily said, trying not to look as anxious as she felt, as she approached their car.

Wanda stopped and peered up at Lily, "Oh, my goodness, that's right. Lily, you were always such a scaredy-cat," she shook her head. "Huh, can't imagine where you got that. I'll drive slowly, I promise. Don't worry." She pointed at their rental car, "That your white car?

I'll keep it in view. Now, for goodness' sakes, don't you be a big ole scaredy-cat, just follow me."

Reprimanded, humiliated, Lily nodded and got into the white Escort. When Wanda's truck passed her, she backed out of her parking space and followed.

She had a flash memory from her childhood. She and Dust were running off to the park and Rose was trailing far behind. She was three years older than Rose, why should she have to include her in everything she did? But as Lily followed the twosome in the red truck, she realized how Rose must have felt. Left out. Sorry for herself.

Payback's a bastard.

They drove through town and stopped at a red light. Wanda waited for Lily to catch up before she made a left turn. Then Lily followed the truck as it drove past adobe businesses, past adobe houses, past more adobe and aluminum-sided businesses, then out into the flatland of the mesa. They passed sagebrush, sagebrush, dirt, and more sagebrush. The intense blue sky was vast and empty, except for two tiny clouds. Lily could see low mountains far ahead of her. And still they drove on. They turned off the paved highway and rumbled down a long, dirt road. There was no sign of humans, except that some human had created the dirt road. The land eased up and down. Sagebrush. Dry land. The truck's dust sprayed out in front of her, the rental car's dust chased her; she was in a cloud of dust. They turned again and the dirt road continued. They wound their way up a C-cup hill and stopped at a terra cotta-colored adobe house.

Lily left the suitcases in the car, unsure what would happen next. She trailed behind smitten Rose and Wanda through a gate that opened into a walled garden. Wanda stopped at the cobalt blue front door.

"Would you like to know why this door is blue?" she asked, her voice sounding of something blown up off an unpaved road—sand and stones and dirt.

They nodded.

"In ancient times, the Indians in this area built their houses without doors. They used a ladder to climb up onto the roof, where there was a hole that worked both as a chimney and an entry. They lifted the ladder up, put it down in the hole, and then entered their house. It was safe. Their enemies couldn't reach them unless they traveled with their own ladders." Wanda stopped then, and smiled. "My goodness, can you picture warriors from enemy tribes riding bareback on their horses carrying ladders. Ho," she said, and laughed. "But then, the Spaniards came along and introduced them to doors. They told the Indians to paint the doors in turquoise or blue to keep evil spirits out." She opened the cobalt blue door, and stood aside, "So welcome, daughters, to this home with no evil spirits."

Inside the house was dim and comfortable. Rounded arches. Every wall was a different classic warm color of the Southwest— peach and yellow and blue, warm blues with a hint of sunlight, and tan. The kitchen was in the center of the space with a curving counter of decorated Mexican tile. The living room was compact, but the vista out the picture window expanded the space for miles out into blue-gray sagebrush. It was lovely.

"Pull up a stool," Wanda said. "My goodness, you're probably starving. After lunch, I'll show you around."

They sat on stools at the curved counter and ate a hearty spicy soup and hunks of crusty bread, followed by cookies and grapes. As Lily ate, she absorbed the quiet beauty of this home, her mother's home. Wanda had lived here for twenty years. Twenty years when she could have made some contact with her daughters. Why didn't she? She wrote to Daddy and she wrote to Christina. She never even sent her children a birthday card.

Lily picked up on a bit of conversation between her mother and Rose. Heard her mother say, "My goodness." My goodness, an ironic phrase coming from a woman whose goodness had been questionable.

After lunch, Wanda showed them around the house and talked about her husband, Warren. She said how sorry she was that they wouldn't meet him during their short visit. Warren had left the day before with his grown son and a team of guys from the power company. They were headed to New York City to help out when Hurricane Sandy made landfall. Wanda was worried about their safety. She told her daughters that she met Warren after she had her act cleaned up. He was a fine man. She pulled out an album and showed them pictures. He had dark eyes and heavy eyebrows and was only a couple inches taller than Wanda. His son resembled him but still had black hair that his father probably once had. They were handsome, rugged men. Lily guessed that Warren probably had dark hair when he and Wanda had first become a couple. It was so many years ago.

There were no pictures of any daughters.

"Do you have any more children," Lily asked. A Delphinium? An Aster? A Tulip?

Wanda looked startled. "No," was all she said.

Lily didn't ask any more questions. She thought about being left in the bar when she was eight years old, while Wanda went off with some biker guy. Wanda had found herself another man, so she didn't need daughters.

Wanda told them how they had built this house with the help of friends, pouring and smoothing the slab, and how the outside walls were built from bales of straw covered in adobe mud. She showed them a picture of straw on the wall, framed with a tiny door that closed, but it wasn't a picture of straw, it was the actual inside of the wall. She took them outside and pointed out the solar panels, the power source for the house.

"Dust would love this," Lily said.

"Dust? You mean Dusty, Christina's little girl?" Wanda said. "How is she?"

Lily looked at Rose, and Rose said, "She shot herself three weeks ago."

"Oh, my goodness," Wanda whispered. "I didn't know this. How is Christina? I'll write her. Oh, dear, how awful. How sad. Tragic." Her hands made a flutter movement, and then she raised one hand in a halt motion that said, *Don't speak or follow me.*

Lily watched her mother inhale deeply, then turn and walk away from them. She went through the gate and down to the dirt driveway, as though her daughters no longer existed. She walked several yards away from the house, down the sloping road, and stood still. Then she slowly turned in a circle with her arms held out at her sides. Lily and Rose watched her from the distance.

When she returned to them, her eyes were damp.

"There's a power here, you know," Wanda said. "When I first crossed the border between Colorado into New Mexico, I felt it. I heard it. There's a vibration, a sort of low rumbling sound. I don't notice it too often anymore. But still, I know it's there, something spiritual down deep in the ground. Vibrating. I feel it now. I want to send this spirit to Christina. I want to wrap her in it and hold her. She must be in such terrible pain. The vibration. That's why I've stayed here all these years. When it comes, it fills me from my feet upward."

Lily thought, but didn't say, your daughters were in terrible pain, but in Detroit there's no spiritual vibration coming out of the earth. Did you ever do any voodoo for your little girls?

"When Warren and I first bought this land," Wanda was saying, "we camped out here. We had an old trailer, tiny like an Airstream, but hardly that fancy. I wanted to be in this remote place. I was in exile. I banished myself to this desolate land with nothing but sagebrush. Emptiness. It was what I deserved. But then, very quickly, I knew that this place was my salvation. This place was more beautiful than any place I had ever been in my life. Look at how much sky I have. It's mine. It belongs to me. All of it." She swung her outstretched arm up over her head and around in an arc. "I'm part of this land. It has forgiven me."

It was just grand that the land had forgiven her mother, but had Lily forgiven her? She didn't think so.

"And now you're here," Wanda said. "Now my girls have come. I am so lucky. There is nothing more I could want. Come here and stand with me, hold my hands and be very, very still."

Lily and Rose went to her and took her hands and each other's; they closed their eyes and were very, very still. Lily heard the wind shuffling among the sagebrush. She felt the ground solid under her feet.

She opened her eyes, and Wanda was smiling at her.

"Come on, girls, let's go see some sights," Wanda said.

Who were they to her? A couple Midwesterners come out for a visit with just enough time for two days worth of sightseeing? Lily wanted to meet Wanda. Sit and talk. Find out what she'd been doing all those years—almost thirty—when she hadn't been being their mother. Lily wasn't interested in learning about New Mexico. She was interested in learning about her mother, but it seemed that Wanda wanted to give them sights, not Wanda. They all piled into Wanda's red truck, and she drove them out to the big crack in the earth that was the Rio Grande River. She drove over the bridge and parked in the rest area at the side of the road.

"Let's walk across the bridge," Wanda said, and headed out onto the pedestrian walkway. Lily stepped onto the bridge just as a heavy truck rumbled by, causing the bridge to vibrate and quake. She felt shaky and unbalanced. This probably wasn't the vibration that Wanda had talked about. She could see far down into the crack in the earth, rough with gray-black shadowy rocks. At the bottom, a narrow stream of blue water reflected the sky. It was so far down; Lily couldn't guess how wide it was.

She stood still. Rose and Wanda crossed the bridge without her. She stood there. Didn't move. Wanda looked back at her and seemed to smirk, shook her head, turned away and continued on across the bridge, chatting with Rose. Lily took a picture of their backs with her cell phone. Then she took a picture of their fronts as they headed back toward her.

"Alright," Wanda said. "Now I have to show you the Earthships. My goodness, you just can't come all the way out here and miss seeing the Earthships."

My goodness, Lily thought, what the hell is an Earthship? Next thing you know, Voodoo Wanda will be putting us into a ship and shooting us out into space.

They drove past more gray earth and sagebrush. Eventually, across miles and miles of dirt, Lily could see raised mounds of earth and piles of old tires at construction sites scattered far apart. As they got closer she could see houses or buildings in the distance that looked like they could be on mars—sensuous, rounded buildings with all their faces aiming south into the sun—sculptures that people lived in. They parked next to the Earthship Welcome Center, a pale-green serpentine building, and Wanda led them to a shady entryway with walls dotted with circles of glass.

"That's the bottoms of recycled bottles," Wanda said, pointing at the glass. "Earthships are houses built with old tires packed with sand, then covered with adobe mud or concrete. They're off the grid.

All their power comes from solar panels." Wanda pointed around as she spoke. "Water comes from rain caught on their roofs and kept in cisterns."

Lily wondered how many other people Wanda—chatting and informing and *oh my goodness*ing—had brought on tours here.

They took pictures of each other standing in the long corridor greenhouse, where palms and lemon trees and tomato plants grew under a wall of slanted windows.

Lily couldn't help but think of Dust as she checked out how black water and gray water systems worked. If Dust were still alive, she could have come out here and built a house of tires with colorful wine bottles embedded in the walls. This would have been the perfect place for her.

Back outside, the air was cool as they climbed the berm behind the visitors' center to check out the sloping, pale-green metal roof where rain would run down into the cistern. The sun was hot on her head, and Lily thought about Dust's skin cancer. She remembered complimenting her on the floppy brimmed pink hat she had worn last summer. Dust had said something like, *Cute, huh? I got it online.* Why didn't she tell her about the cancer? Was it of little consequence, or had she been terrified of it?

Returning to planet Earth, Lily heard Rose ask Wanda why she'd picked a straw bale house instead of an Earthship.

"Look around at the view," Wanda said. "Earthships only face the south. It's more energy efficient. We wanted to see the view all the way around our house."

They went back to Wanda's house with the 360 degree view, and as she suggested, got dusted off and prettied up, then headed back into Taos for an elegant dinner at El Meze.

A charming waiter gushed over them. His personality reminded Lily of Carlos. Lily thought back to her conversation with Rose in the tepee in Santa Fe. Rose thought that Dust had been humiliated when she invited Carlos to lunch, but then Rose had since dismissed it as a motive for Dust's suicide, and Lily pretended that she agreed. "No, Rose, it wouldn't have anything to do with Carlos," she'd said, protecting Rose. But Lily remembered seeing Carlos playing with Dust's bangs at the birthday party. Checking the skin cancer scar? She remembered catching Dust staring at Carlos in a dreamlike state as he walked away from her and again when he stood across the room during her birthday party. She'd seen Dust craning her neck, seeking out a glimpse of Carlos. Lily had picked up on that look, seen that hungry, longing on Dust's face. She recognized a woman wanting a man who wasn't available.

Now remembering, it shook her. At the time, she'd brushed it aside. She never brought it up to Dust; if she had, then she would have had to talk about Evan, Evan her lover, who was married to a woman she'd never met. She didn't mention it to Dust, didn't want to embarrass her or let her know that her attraction was so visible. Carlos was taken. He belonged to Rose, whom Dust had cared about for all of Rose's life. What had Dust done with those feelings? It was an untenable situation for her. Carlos had seen her as his patient. Each time he touched Dust's forehead or searched her body for signs of more cancer, had a rush of desire flooded through her? A week or two weeks before she died, she invited Carlos to lunch. He turned her down. He did the right thing. Carlos did the right thing; he stopped the infatuation from going further. Dust did the wrong thing and asked him to lunch, and when he refused, she could have blown it off. She could have laughed about it. Maybe she did? Maybe it wasn't a big deal? Or maybe she was deeply humiliated or ashamed. Lily had no way to know what Dust's truths were.

Thousands of text messages, tweets, phone calls, and intimate lunches were happening between people all the time, but was anyone talking to anyone else? What Lily did know was only what Dust had told her—Robert wouldn't divorce her. If she left him, he'd keep

Grace from her. He didn't beat her. Didn't abuse her. She never needed a restraining order. But she'd been stuck. Stuck. Dust had talked about Robert's damn addition on the house. He could have added a room, a reasonable sized family room, and she would have accepted it. But the monster addition was a blatant smack down of Dust's environmental concerns.

Wanda insisted that they all begin their dinner at El Meze with a salad of grilled romaine lettuce topped with shaved parmesan cheese. "You have to try this," she said. They did. It was delicious. Later, the grilled lettuce would be the part of the dinner that Lily most remembered. They ate their Southwestern entrees. Lily ordered buffalo tamales covered in green chili verde. She laughed and chatted with Rose and Wanda. She pulled out pictures of her boys— Wanda's grandsons, Henry and Andrew.

"Hendrew and Andry, Dust used to call them," and there she was—Dust had joined them at the table. You could fly thousands of miles away, you could meet your mother for the first time in nearly thirty years, but grief came along on the trip.

"My grandsons," Wanda said, and smiled. For the first time since meeting her mother after so many years, Lily saw the sense of loss in Wanda's sad smile. She had grandsons that she only saw in a picture when they were seventeen years old.

"Who's this cute man with my grandsons?" Wanda asked.

"That's Jagger, my soon to be ex-husband," Lily said. "I should cut him out of the picture. Can I use your knife?" Then she laughed and put the picture away, intact.

"Oh, my goodness, I'm sorry," Wanda said, with warmth and compassion.

"I'll be fine," Lily said. "I have Rose and two sweet sons." She thought about saying she had Daddy and Christina, decided that might be hurtful and added, "and now I have you too." She didn't know about that, but thought it sounded like a nice thing to say.

"Thank you for that," Wanda said.

"Rose," Lily said, "did you show Wanda a picture of Carlos?" Neither of them had called Wanda *Mom*. It would feel too weird.

"I did, when you were in the ladies room," Rose said, then turned to Wanda. "Wanna see him again?"

Wanda laughed, "Oh, my goodness, yes, of course. Pull out your pictures, Rose."

The waiter came over and wooed them into having dessert. "I don't know, lovely ladies," he said, slowly shaking his head. "You could share one with three forks, but wouldn't you rather have something sweet all for yourself?"

Had Dust wanted some dessert all for herself? Carlos?

By the time they left the restaurant, it was black dark. Wanda drove them back to her place and parked in her driveway. They gazed up at the stars, diamond studs in a black velvet sky. Lily stood very still hoping to feel the earth pulse. She decided that it wasn't a vibration that she was hoping for, but a pulse, as though the heart of the planet were under her feet. The ground stayed firm and solid. She went inside.

The house had two small guest rooms. Lily chose the smaller room with a single bed so that Rose could have the larger room with a double bed. It was good. Lily was good with it all. Rose looked so much like a young Wanda, no one could ever doubt whose womb she'd come from. Lily looked like her father—the man who had sent Wanda away to build her life all by herself. After Wanda left, Rose had spent her childhood looking like she belonged to another family, like the stork had gotten the wrong address.

Rose, who was very happily married to a kind and loving man— yes, Carlos was a flirt, but he was a decent, good guy—needed to be special to Wanda. Lily, who was dumped by her husband and whose best friend was dead, didn't need Wanda's adoration. It struck her as very strange. She felt at peace. She flew in an airplane, by God. She could do anything. Well, maybe not go on escalators or swim or go down slides, or walk on a bridge over the Rio Grande River. But she could fly!

She decided to cut Wanda a break. During dinner, she thought about asking Wanda why she never wrote or called them. But the mood had been light. Carefree. Congenial. That question would have been a dirt bomb thrown into the middle of the white tablecloth, an ugly, unavoidable centerpiece. It was obvious that Wanda didn't want to talk about her past. Maybe she was simply done with it.

Lily decided that she was going to try to like her mother. It wouldn't take much effort or energy. When she had decided she was going to be Jagger's loving wife, it was grueling. To like Wanda, all she had to do was drop her hostile thoughts. It would involve no housecleaning. No football watching. Just be nice. If Wanda were only going to be a tour guide and charming hostess, well then, Lily would take that.

Lily curled up in the twin bed and felt calm and happy. She remembered when the twins were born, pictured their little chins. She put her finger on her chin, remembering how she hated it when she was growing up. She had a dent in the middle of her chin like someone had poked it with the eraser end of a pencil. Dents in things were bad—a dent in the car, a dent in the wall where the doorknob smacked it, the new refrigerator came with a dent and they sent it back to the store—so when some kid asked how she got that dent in her chin, she felt broken. She'd spent her whole life hating her chin, until the twins were born. Her two matching babies inherited her chin. How could she hate her chin if her babies had chins like hers? Chins tied them all together.

Whatever Wanda had hated about herself was probably erased when she caught sight of her grown-up Rosebud, looking healthy and pretty with her dark hair and blue eyes.

Lily scooted over to the edge of the twin bed and reached her hand down to the floor, waiting and hoping to feel the New Mexico vibration that Wanda described.

35. CHRISTINA

Christina watched the digital numbers on her bathroom scale. It was momentarily indecisive about half a pound—point five or not point five. The numbers settled and stopped at two hundred and one point five pounds. In the three weeks since her daughter died, she'd gained nine point five pounds. Three pounds a week plus a point five. Was she trying to commit a slow, sugarcoated death? There was an ice cream flavor—death by chocolate, suicide by food.

There were so many ways to kill yourself.

She pictured herself getting ever bigger and bigger—her beached walrus body splayed out on a heavy-duty, king-sized bed—unable to turn over, or wash herself, or wipe her bottom when she went to the toilet. And how would she even get into the bathroom? She wouldn't be able to fit through the door. And if she could squeeze through the door into the bathroom, when she sat down, the toilet would crack under her weight. She pictured herself needing a special supersized casket carried by eight or ten burly pallbearers, or maybe the casket would have to be moved by a crane.

Three weeks since her daughter died. Just three weeks. The pain Christina felt hadn't even developed a scab yet. She was using food as a salve—an antibiotic cream—on her wound. It was nothing new; it was how she coped.

She stood naked in front of her bedroom mirror. She was suddenly a short-waisted woman. Now wasn't that odd? She'd never been short-waisted in her life. If fact, before the fat, she'd been nicely proportioned. She was getting old. Then a thought occurred to her. She put a hand under each of her large, heavy breasts and lifted them up. Ah, so she wasn't short-waisted, she was droopy-boobed.

Dusty would never have old, sagging breasts. She'd never have age spots, or bat wings under her upper arms. She'd never get fallen arches, or ugly varicose veins in her legs. Her hair would never get so thin that she could see her pink scalp. She'd never worry about getting dementia when she forgot her keys or someone's name that she'd known all her life. Dusty would never get old.

Christina mourned all the possibilities of life that Dusty would miss: Grace's graduation, wedding, grandchildren, a retirement in Florida. Florida? Christina had no interest in moving south for the winters. She liked the snow. Dusty might have wanted that. But what difference did any of it make? Dusty had shot all her options.

36. FRED

On Saturday, October 27, Fred was lonely. Margaret was visiting her sister for the morning. Dust was dead. He had no one to play with. He was lost in his own house. Depressed. Sorry for himself. He needed to get out. Out of his house, out of himself. He was sick of feeling pathetic. He decided to drive into Detroit and just look around. If you live in a nice house in a tidy suburb, driving into the city could make your wah-wahs seem ludicrous.

He drove south down Woodward Avenue into Detroit. Woodward Avenue—M1, the first major street in America—ran from Hart Plaza on the Detroit River for twenty-one miles north to Pontiac. He drove on the overpass above Eight Mile Road and then he was in Detroit and the gloom set in, or maybe the problem was that the median—the grassy green and treed median—ended soon after you entered the city and lanes converged, tightening the road down to four lanes and a center turn lane.

On his left he passed the old state fairgrounds, but fairs were just a memory. No more pie contests, or pigs and goats being judged. No more needlecrafts or cakes winning blue ribbons. No more musicians playing. No more singers singing. No Ferris wheel or merry-go-round rides. Palmer Woods, where elegant, old houses still stood, was on his right, mostly hidden by the trees along Woodward Avenue. As he drove past Palmer Park, he remembered his childhood, when his parents brought him to feed ducks on Lake Frances and his father took photos of the lighthouse. Why there was a lighthouse on a tiny island in a tiny lake inside the city was perplexing. When he was young, the lighthouse had colored lights that shone on the lake.

On his left, someone had started building a huge cathedral and had probably run out of money. It was just the same as the last time he drove down here. Progress had stagnated. Perhaps poor folks wanting salvation decided that eating was more important than praising the Lord in a lavish monstrosity that sucked the bucks from their pockets. He drove past an old movie theater that ran porn films like *Deep Throat* in the seventies; now it was painted purple and housed the Revival Tabernacle. He passed a car dealership and a Powerhouse Gym, another church, a car wash, then new strip malls on both sides of the street—clean, busy. Fred smiled at that.

People were outside, standing around or crossing Woodward in random, erratic patterns having nothing to do with the white lines on the concrete roadway. People standing around, waiting for buses, or walking to a store, or just outside moving around. Black people like him, but not like him—he was encased in his minivan, gawking like a tourist.

Continuing south on Woodward, there were storefronts boarded up or with iron grates; a tall building where someone had crudely spray painted "DYKE" in two-story letters; apartment buildings with lower floor storefronts boarded up, but upper stories seeming lived in; a beige brick building that had probably been an architectural gem at one time now looked like its insides had been bombed out; a red building that had been some sort of storage facility was missing most of the bricks and windows on the upper stories; the Cathedral of the Most Blessed Sacrament was elegant, beautiful, and intact; the Boston Edison neighborhood with grand homes appeared to be reviving; Woodward Nursing Center was covered in graffiti. As he neared Wayne State University's campus, there were more churches and new condos. At the Detroit Institute of Arts, Fred turned left onto Kirby, then right, and came up behind the art museum. He slowed down and stared at the entrance to the Detroit Film Theater at the rear of the museum.

He remembered a film that he and Margaret had seen down here. He couldn't remember if it was last summer or the year before. It was a film about urban farming in Detroit. He remembered telling Dust about the film. He thought about looking into it back then, but time had slipped away, and with it, the urgency to do something passed.

Now he wound his way through residential neighborhoods. There were so many streets with just one or two houses. Mayor Bing wanted to shrink the city. Tighten it up. Move people in closer, so city services could function more efficiently. There were other ideas floating around too—environmental ideas: solar panels and windmills on rooftops, green plantings on flat roofs, better land management, and people hired to insulate houses. Young artists from around the world were taking up residence in the city, where the costs were cheap and a gritty, new art was emerging.

As he drove, he thought of kids—poor kids whose groceries came from quick marts and gas stations. Kids whose nutrition came from pop and chips—sugar water and grease. How could they learn anything, how could they concentrate in school? Much of Detroit was being called a food or a nutrition desert. With vacant lots and few grocery stores, urban farming sounded like a good answer. If all that empty land could be farmed, it could change people's lives. He wondered about toxins in the soil—they had talked about that in the movie. He couldn't remember the solutions they came up with.

He was excited to explore this.

He wanted to help. He craved doing something of value, something useful with his life. He wished Dust were still alive. They could go down and work on farms together. Maybe the loss of her own garden—both of their gardens—wouldn't hurt so much. How he wished he'd thought of this months ago. She could have done this without affecting Robert's career. She could have done something hopeful.

During the cold months that were coming, when he'd normally be studying seed catalogs and then starting his tomatoes and cabbages under grow lights in the basement, he could be researching urban farming. Talk to some people. Make some calls. He felt better, could see something good in his future. There was something he could do that had value.

***

It was late, nearly midnight. Margaret had already gone to bed, and Fred was still fooling around with the iPad. Margaret told everyone they knew that it had become an extension of her husband's arm. Fred Googled "Urban Farming in Detroit," and up came a long list of entries. He scrolled down to "Images for urban farming Detroit," on the iPad and found dozens of photos. His eyes were tired. He'd been staring at the screen for too many hours.

It was time to hit the sack. He headed toward the kitchen to turn out the lights and lock the side door. When he stopped to grab a glass of water to take upstairs with him, something outside caught his attention, something wrong. The night outside his window should be black with shades of gray. It wasn't. A golden light was coming from Dust's house, Robert's house. Fire? He stared hard. Yes! FIRE! He dropped the glass into the sink.

He ran to the desk and fumbled for Dust's key, then yelled up the stairs at Margaret, "Fire! Fire! The house next door is on fire. Dust's house is on fire. Call 911!"

He ran out of his front door in his shirtsleeves, chilly air hitting his face and arms. He took the shortest route across their yards and trampled through the garden that he and Dust had worked on for so many years. The late fall mums collapsed and crunched under his feet. He was sixty years old and yet ran up Dust's porch steps two at a time. The front door had an old-fashioned knocker; he banged iron against iron and shouted, "Fire!"

No one came to the door, so he fumbled with Dust's key. He hesitated before opening the door. He'd seen on some TV show that opening a door feeds oxygen to the fire and creates a killer fireball. He cracked open the door quickly, squeezed inside, and shut it fast. The front hall was filled with smoke. He opened his mouth wide and shouted, "Fire!" Smoke choked him and stung his eyes. He stood still, getting his bearings, held his hand over his nose and mouth. He heard the TV on upstairs. It was loud. Sirens. Was that on the TV or had the fire department arrived?

Sweet Jesus, did Margaret wake up? Did she call 911? Was she still asleep? After living with her for nearly forty years, he knew her well. When she finally fell asleep after tossing and turning and keeping him awake some nights, she slept like a rock. He should have called 911 himself.

The house was dark and the smoke dense; he couldn't see as he climbed the stairs. He carefully felt his way up each step, smoke in his lungs now slowing him down. He'd been in the house many times, fixing fuses and such, when Robert was gone campaigning. He knew the house, knew the new addition. Margaret had asked for a tour, so Dust had shown them the new kitchen and family room and then led them upstairs to the new master suite. He'd been up in the old bathroom when the hairdryer blew a fuse, but the smoke was disorienting. It was like moving through a thick gray fog that bit at his eyes and throat.

He remembered thinking that Robert should burn in hell. He still thought that was fine by him, he just didn't want him to burn in the house. It was a grizzly thought. Maybe he didn't want anyone to burn in hell. It was a stupid phrase. He didn't even believe in hell.

The smoke was confusing him. Why was he here? Saving Dust. No, he couldn't save Dust. She was gone. Robert? It was Robert he had to save. Save him for Grace and for Dust. Grace was at Christina's, wasn't she? He thought she was. He hadn't seen her around the house. *Sweet Jesus, let Grace not be here.*

In the upper hall, he felt along the wall. He banged on a door and tried to shout, but the smoke closed his throat. He moved through the smoke, found another door. He was getting angry. Why did Robert have the damn TV on so loud? Why didn't he hear him? At the smashed doorframe of the master suite, a sharp, jagged splinter of wood stabbed into his palm. He yelped with pain, but didn't stop feeling around the door. Knocking hard, kicking the door with his foot, he searched for the doorknob. He yelled, "Fire!" forcing the word from his painful throat. Robert must have fallen asleep with the TV on. Fred's chest ached. It felt heavy; he could barely breathe. He wondered just how much smoke he'd inhaled. He'd wanted a cigarette, wanted a smoke for weeks. The irony of it got caught up in his thinking. What was he doing here? Why was he standing in all this smoke? Where was he?

Then he remembered.

He keep feeling around for the doorknob, finally found it, turned it and pushed in, remembering just at that moment that Robert had guns in the house.

As he pushed in the door, he choked out, "It's Fred, don't shoot." He heard a loud boom and then his body hit the off-white carpet.

37. ROBERT

In spite of the screaming TV, Robert had fallen asleep. The loud volume shut out the nagging conflict in his head. Grace was right, they shouldn't be telling lies about Dust. But Dust was gone. Fixing the lies wouldn't bring her back. The repercussions of admitting the falsehoods would destroy his career, and any integrity he ever had would be questionable. Lies. Corruption. Scandal. If he admitted that the stories about his wife's mental health were false, then those damning original questions would reappear. What had he done to her? What kind of man was he? It was a lose-lose situation.

He dreamed about a burning building—a vivid dream. So vivid that he smelled smoke. It confused him because the scent was so real and painful. But then he woke up and opened his eyes.

There was banging at his bedroom door. The door opened and there was his neighbor Fred rasping, "Don't shoot."

Boom!

The room shook. Something in the kitchen beneath them exploded, and Fred fell to the floor. Robert leapt out of bed, dragged Fred into the room, and shut the door. He yanked an afghan from a chair and pushed it against the bottom of the door, hoping to stop more smoke from coming in the room. Then he carried Fred out to the balcony, and laid him there while he ran back in the room for his cell phone. He dialed 911, and shouted, "Fire! Ambulance! Help!"

He'd taken a class in CPR, but it was so long ago that he wasn't confident about what he was doing. Fred wasn't coughing or moving. Robert began chest compressions, pushing down in the center of Fred's chest, pumping hard and pumping fast, counting as he pressed down thirty times. He tilted Fred's head back and lifted his chin, then he pinched Fred's nose and blew into his mouth while watching for his chest to rise.

He shouted at him, "Don't die, Fred. Please, wake up. Wake up."

He was terrified. Beneath them windows in the new family room and kitchen were exploding with loud bangs and shattering glass sounds. He ran back inside and pulled the comforter and pillows off the bed and took them outside. The wool carpet was smoking. Flames were eating through the bedroom floor. If the fire was burning through the bedroom floor, then the whole kitchen must be in flames. The floor was hot to his feet. He ran back outside and wrapped Fred in the comforter. He tried to arrange the pillows as cushioning around them. He pulled the comforter over their heads.

He wondered how long the balcony would hold. Flames were eating the supports. He peeked out and the heat stung his eyes. The porch wobbled. He covered his head again, and wondered if the comforter was flammable. Had he made a mistake? Rolled up in the goose down and cotton, were they at even more risk of igniting. He laughed then. Maybe their goose was cooked? It was too late to do anything different. He closed his eyes tight and held onto Fred. He prayed out loud, begged, and tears ran down his cheeks. In seconds he would be dead. But then in his terror, resignation came over him, and he became still and just listened to the noise of the fire—a monster chewing on his house with a terrible gluttonous noise, spitting, burping, chomping on boards. The flaming orange mouth of the beast crackled, cackled, and laughed with its omnipotent power.

Motion: shaking, trembling, quaking, then the porch dropped away beneath them, collapsing with a boom. They hit the ground with a force like being hit by a truck. Scattered, shattered burning boards surrounded them. The comforter was smoldering—feathers smelling like burning hair. Tangled, he pushed his way out of it. His left arm was screaming at him, but he ignored it, and dragged Fred away from the burning boards.

Sirens? He stopped. Listened. The sound was coming closer.

He dragged Fred further back into the yard, and then he passed out.

38. LILY

Lily was curled up on Wanda's twin bed. Darkness. Dreams. Her eyes darted about under her closed lids. Dust was there with Lily in her fake-pine paneled attic bedroom. They were little girls surrounded by cardboard boxes. They had sharp knives—butcher and paring—snuck upstairs from her parent's kitchen. Blades flashed, stabbing into cardboard, then slicing, cutting out the windows and doors for the houses they were making with the boxes. Partitions made of cardboard were taped in for walls. They were laughing as they colored stripes and flowers on sheets of typing paper that they'd paste in for wallpaper. *Ooh, ooh, let's do a pink baby's room with teddy bears on the wallpaper.* Little houses. Happy little houses. Happy little girls. Lily was smiling in her sleep.

"Lily." She heard her mother call. Oh, no, will she be mad about the knives?

Then her mother's voice was saying, "Wake up, Lily. Wake up."

She felt a shake on her shoulder. Lily's eyes popped open. It was still dark. She was fuzzy and confused, still half in the dream, waking up in a strange bed in a strange room. She wasn't ten years old anymore. Her mother's lips weren't red and she didn't smell like wine. Her breath wafted coffee when she leaned down and kissed Lily's forehead.

"Lily, dear, wake up. Come on. Get dressed. Hurry or we'll miss it."

As Wanda left the room, she called back, "Dress warm."

Lily hastily got into her heavy sweater and jeans, splashed water on her face, combed her hair, and rushed out to the kitchen where

Rose and Wanda sat at the counter sipping their coffee from thermos mugs.

"I couldn't sleep," Rose said, "I got up an hour ago and then Wanda got up and made coffee."

Wanda handed Lily a loaded travel mug. "Rose said you take it with a little cream. Are you ready?" she said. Lily nodded and Wanda grabbed her truck keys and led them outside in the early morning dim.

As they headed back into Taos, they listened to reports of Super Storm Sandy on the radio. The storm had become a category one hurricane and had turned in toward the eastern coastline. They tried to remember if any storm this big and bad had ever hit along those northern coasts; there were none that they recalled. Lily felt empathetic terror as she imagined the ocean rushing into the cities and towns along the shore, rampaging through streets, washing away houses and businesses, ravaging bodies, and tearing a violent path through devastated lives.

Wanda talked about her husband and stepson with a frightened edge to her voice. "They're getting close to New York; they'll probably arrive just as the storm hits. He checks in with me a couple times a day, just so I won't worry," she said. "I worry anyway."

Lily wondered if she should think about a career change. Leave the insurance business. This is what Dust had predicted. It was happening. Had already begun. Violent storms. Droughts. Wildfires.

Wanda drove through town and, at the city hall, turned toward a big, empty field and parked the truck. It was barely light out, and yet the field was filling with people and pickup trucks and balloons— huge, hot air balloons laid out on tarps that were as big as the foundations of houses. The balloons were spread out flat on the tarps, and their baskets were tipped over on their sides. Someone held a line that was attached to the top of a balloon, while other members of the team aimed giant fans into the circular opening. Gas hissed and a long yellow flame shot into the round opening of a balloon that was the colors of a rainbow.

Balloons all around them were filling up, like strange, flattened beings, wobbling and becoming lumpy, shaking, quaking, waking up and growing fatter and fatter until finally they were filled and upright. It was a spectacle. The three women roamed the field, watching as more balloons were filled and lifted into the sky. They oohed and ahhed, sounding like people watching fireworks.

Years ago, Dust had floated up in a hot air balloon in Michigan; she had begged Lily to come too, probably knowing that she wouldn't. Now, Lily imagined Dust laughing and excited as she climbed into that big, yellow balloon. Dust was happy. Lily stood mesmerized as the balloon lifted up and up and up, floating higher and getting smaller and farther and farther away, and then she couldn't see her anymore. Dust was gone.

Tears ran down Lily's cheeks. She brushed them away, but Wanda had seen her and came up close beside her.

"Watching them, I sometimes feel so awed, it brings me to tears, too," she said.

"I was picturing Dust in that yellow balloon," Lily said. "She looked so happy." She pointed into the distance, where the yellow balloon was just a dot in the sky. "And then she just floated away."

Wanda patted Lily's shoulder. "I remember a time when you were little girls. The two of you blew up a balloon that you covered with papier-mâché," Wanda said. "Somehow the balloon popped and you were both devastated. I took all three of you little girls to the store, and we bought a new balloon. We all worked on it together. Do you remember that, Lily?"

It was strange that she always remembered the balloon popping, but had forgotten that her mother had helped them make a new one. Her mother's recollection brought back the memory; she could see her mother blowing up the balloon. Hidden in the dark recesses of her memory, her mother had been there in her early childhood. After Wanda left, had Lily blocked all her connections with her?

Wanda took Lily's hand and said, "Dusty was a lovely little girl. I'm sorry I never knew her as an adult."

Rose had wandered off and was watching the red Spiderman balloon lift off. They could see her staring up with her eyes big and awed, watching the balloon lift higher. Rose waved to the people in the balloon. With Rose out of hearing distance, Wanda touched Lily's arm, and said, "I hope you don't think I'm neglecting you, Lily. Rose's husband called before you got here and told me how he was concerned for Rose. He was afraid she might feel left out or neglected. I just hope I haven't gone too far. I don't want you to feel bad while I've been trying to make her feel good."

Lily thought of her boys. It was tricky balancing attention so each one felt as loved as the other. Sometimes one was more needy. Henry was more sensitive and more affectionate. Andrew was the comedian, but sometimes under the humor she saw his vulnerability. Parenting wasn't easy.

"I love you both," Wanda said. "I want you to know that."

"I know that," Lily said, and put her arm around Wanda's shoulder. She wasn't ready yet to say, *love*, to Wanda. She barely knew her. But she could see the possibilities.

PART THREE—SURVIVORS

39. ROBERT

Robert's wife was dead; half of his house was destroyed; his left arm had a compound fracture—shattered bone had pierced through his skin. But then, who said life was supposed to be fair? He was alive. He'd been in surgery for five hours. His left ankle was sprained. He thought of a Nietzsche quote, *What doesn't kill you makes you stronger.* He didn't believe it.

Robert was in Fred's hospital room. Fred was still on oxygen—plastic tubing ran from the wall into his nose. His voice box was scarred. Speaking was difficult. Robert's left arm was in a cast and his left foot was in a stabilizing boot. He sat on a chair beside Fred's bed. They were both alive.

He was still a state senator. The election was just days away. Polling numbers were all over the place. There was a possibility—a slim possibility—that he could win the election. The hospital staff was allowing just one reporter into the room. There had been a drawing from a jar of tongue depressors; only one had a red dot. Alice Copenheimer from WDIV was the red dot winner. Her cinematographer followed her into the room.

The reporter was calling Robert a hero; Robert saved Fred's life. He was a hero. Everyone knew that Fred had tried to save him, but he'd saved Fred. He was a hero. Brave.

"No, no," Robert said. "You're wrong. Fred saved my life. Fred ran into my burning house, inhaled toxic smoke. He ran up the stairs unable to see where he was going, barely able to breathe and came into my room and woke me up." He didn't mention that Fred thought he fired a gun at him when something in the kitchen below them exploded, something loud that shook the floor.

"If it weren't for Fred Williams, I'd be dead right now." That was true.

"Senator Steward, has the fire chief determined the cause of the fire?"

"Yes, Alice," he said, "the culprit was me," he hesitated for effect. "Me and the toaster." All those toasted peanut butter and jelly sandwiches. He'd slipped out of his need for order—his OCD over clean counters—maybe because he had to clean the counters himself, maybe because he was depressed? He left the toaster out and plugged in, and sometimes, thinking he'd probably want another sandwich, he also left the bread bag opened and the peanut butter and jelly on the counter. He never put the toaster back into the cupboard.

"The fire chief told me that home appliances cause around one hundred fifty thousand fires a year. So when you're not using an appliance with a heat element, unplug it."

"Important information for everyone," reporter Alice said. "Senator," she went on, "this has been an incredibly difficult month for you with not only the fire, but also the tragedy of your wife's suicide. Your campaign has given the media information about your wife's mental illness, but you've not made any public statement yourself. Would you like to say something now, Senator Steward?"

Dust. They wanted him to talk about her. He flashed back to the months before she died. She'd begged him to break with his party's attitude on climate change. There were other parts of the party platform that she hated—most of them, but climate change was the biggie. He always laughed. Laughed. Told her that it was all nonsense. He wondered, and had been wondering for days, was the motive for her suicide to sabotage his political career? Could that be possible? Or was he using that crazy possibility as an excuse not to expose the lies his campaign had told about her mental health? He heard Dust say, *It's not always about you, Robert.* When she wanted a divorce, he'd threatened to take Grace away. He trapped her. But by shooting herself, she lost Grace anyway. She left Grace with him. It didn't make any sense.

She left him a puzzle, why did she do it? What's a seven letter word for killing yourself? Dust loved puzzles, is that why she didn't leave a note? Was she so angry with him that not leaving a suicide note was a form of not speaking to him, ignoring him when he spoke to her, walking away, giving him the cold shoulder? She'd planned it, she wanted out. Maybe she didn't know herself why she wanted to do this. Maybe the puzzle was one that even she couldn't find an answer to.

He would tell the reporter the truth.

"Alice," he said to the reporter, "my wife was a wonderful woman. She was beautiful. She was kind." For Grace and for Fred, he added, "She

cared deeply about the environment. She believed that it was urgent that we do something about climate change."

"Do you agree? Are you breaking with your party on climate change, Senator Steward?"

He glanced at Fred, saw him smile and nod, urging him on.

"Well, Alice," he said. "I think that it's obvious that we have a climate problem. And as far as breaking with my party, ask anyone in New Jersey or New York how they feel about climate change. Ask farmers in the Midwest. Ask the hundreds of people whose homes burned down out West and in the Southwest."

He remembered Dust talking about carbon emissions, and how carbon dioxide's molecular structure traps heat—ergo, a hot planet. He'd laughed at her. "Maybe if the carbon in the atmosphere gets hot enough, it'll rain diamonds," he had said. "The facts aren't in.

Not all scientists believe climate change is man-made. It isn't a hundred percent."

Dust said, "If you went to a hundred doctors and ninety-eight said you had cancer, but two doctors said you didn't, who would you believe?"

He said, "The planet's been warming since the ice age."

Dust said, "A few very wealthy men are spending billions to convince the population that climate change isn't man-made. It's intentional—their motive is to avoid carbon taxes. If they hire the right congress, they'll keep their tax credits and profit margins high."

Reporter Alice cleared her throat, reminding him whom he was supposed to be having a conversation with.

She said. "What about her mental health, Senator?"

Grace wanted him to come clean about the mental illness misinformation—no actually, the lies. She'd come up with schemes. They could set up a camera—a hidden camera, and he could tell someone, maybe Fred, the truth while the film was recording. They could expose the lies that his campaign people told reporters. Then they'd put the video on YouTube. He was startled by her thinking, didn't realize that even thirteen-year-olds would know about Mitt Romney's hidden camera fiasco. He told her that would be cowardly and deceitful. A strong person, an honest person, would stand up and tell the truth.

He wished now that he hadn't told her that. He also told her that nothing he said would bring her mother back. He was convinced that a scandal would be worse for his daughter. He pictured headlines, STEWARD LIED ABOUT WIFE'S MENTAL ILLNESS. What would the kids at Grace's school do with that? What would happen to his parents and sister with LIAR plastered all over the news? And what would happen to him? His political career would be destroyed. Even if he won this election, he'd always carry that black mark. He told himself that what he was about to say was for Grace. Maybe so. Maybe not so.

"I'm sorry, Alice. I'm not going there. All I'm going to say is that I loved my wife and I miss her terribly."

Fred started choking and coughing.

The reporter wrapped up the segment and left the room.

Alone in the room with Fred, he saw his next door neighbor slowly shaking his head. Fred knew. They both knew. Robert wasn't brave.

40. CHRISTINA

The cracked saucer that had held her father's pipe went into the trash. It was broken—Dusty had been broken; Christina was broken; Grace was broken—on this day, Christina accepted it all. Everything was broken. It was a fact and she accepted it, but she didn't want to save a broken saucer anymore. Accept what is and then clean up what pieces you can. No one would want the broken saucer, and she remembered her father without having to see it.

She gathered all the framed family pictures from around the condo and took them to the kitchen table. With a tiny screwdriver, she loosened the frame backs and removed the photos. The frames would go to the Salvation Army for resale. The photos would go into albums that she might keep on her coffee table, or not. She hadn't decided that yet.

She gathered all the Hummel figurines that had been her mother's and wrapped each one in bubble wrap. There was a nurse she knew who was into eBay, maybe the little figures would be valuable to someone else, some collector.

Christina knew the rules of grief, knew she shouldn't make any major changes in her life. And yet here she was filling cardboard boxes. Someone outside herself might wonder if she was suicidal, or they might wonder if this was some form of giving up or depression. It was none of that. She just wanted to breathe—clear out cobwebs. She craved clean, visual space. She didn't want to devote her life to taking care of things that no longer mattered to her.

She took down the print of Da Vinci's *Last Supper* and put it in the box. The Jesus plate that Jay Jones had given her on their first anniversary was wrapped in bubble wrap and nestled in the box beside the marble Madonna and the crucifixes that she'd gathered from every room. The painting of the shepherds on the hill came off the wall and went into the box. She'd keep the little clay manger that Dusty made, but it would go into a dresser drawer. The wooden crèche was wrapped and placed in the box. The portrait of Christ— Christ looking like a blond rock star in the seventies, surely the real Jesus had dark hair and dark eyes—went into the box. She found the Bible she'd been given as a child and put it in the box. Whenever Christina went to Somerset Mall, she saw a black woman who sat at a table next to Starbuck's studying her Bible. The woman underlined and highlighted passages. Christina hadn't opened her Bible in years. No, it was more like decades.

She'd filled a large box with her religion—artifacts that might comfort someone else. She thought about the monks and nuns who lived in empty cells—devout without artifice. She thought about the Vatican, gilded, golden, and bejeweled. What did it mean? Did the splendor help anyone? How did it honor the man who washed the feet of his disciples? She thought about Sister Simone Campbell and the Nuns on the Bus, and how they campaigned for the less fortunate.

Rules of Grief: Don't move to a different house. Don't quit your job. Give it a year. Two years.

She'd been hearing rumors at the hospital. The nonprofit Detroit Medical Center had been taken over by a for-profit company and the rumor was that they were going to fire all licensed practical nurses. Every nurse would have to have a Bachelor of Science in nursing degree, so Christina expected to lose her job before long. Since she'd already been considering retiring, she wasn't concerned for herself, but she was worried about others on the staff. They were already overworked. How would they take good care of the patients with the cutbacks? What quality of care and attention would the sick children or any patient be getting? When the LPNs were all discarded, it would take a while to fill those empty positions, but maybe that was the whole point. It would look like the for-profit company's goal was to increase the quality of care in the hospital, when actually they were cutting back on staff. Employees cut into profit, don't you know. She decided (for the sake of the staff and the patients) that she'd continue to work until they fired her, however long that might be.

On her last day off, she had told Ben Abbott about the rumors at the hospital; she told him how much she'd miss the little children. She told him how she'd miss walking through the blue tunnels in the hospital complex on her missions to see the art collection. She had never mentioned that she did that to anyone before; it was a private pleasure that she just did for herself.

Ben sat listening without comment; he didn't say anything. When she stopped speaking, he went to her hall closet and took out the coat she wore most often. He held it up to her and said only, "Let's go."

She was puzzled but let him help her with her coat and followed him to his car, not knowing what would come next. He drove to Interstate 75 and headed south into Detroit, then exited the expressway at Warren. Was he taking her to the DMC, the Detroit Medical Center? No. He circled the Detroit Institute of Arts and parked in the lot beside the Scarab Club. Then he took her hand as they walked away from the car and across John R. Street.

When they entered the museum, several people called out, "Hi, Ben. You working today?"

"Nope," he said, "just having a tour with my friend."

"You work here?" Christina asked. He never mentioned anything about this that she could recall.

"I volunteer," he said. "I come down a couple times a month." He motioned his thumb at his chest and added, "I'm the guy who tells people where the bathrooms are."

As they wandered together in the art, she kept glancing at him. She'd known him most of her adult life and this was unexpected.

Ben led her to the court just beyond the main entrance of the museum—the Rivera Court. He stood with her in the center of the space, pointing around them, and said, "Diego Rivera painted twenty-seven panels in here." Rivera's Detroit Industry fresco surrounded them—huge scenes and smaller images were all framed with the original white marble—some of it carved into columns and some carved with figures—that had been there before Rivera came to town with his paint pots and brushes.

Christina was drawn to the painting of a plump baby curled up in a fetal position inside a bulb surrounded by roots. She pointed up at it.

Ben said, "That's 'The Baby in the Bulb.' See those small panels of fruits and vegetables on either side of the baby panel? Rivera only used Michigan-grown produce in the images. Right above them, he painted fertility figures. Rivera was saying that everything we do is linked to nature and the earth."

Dusty would have agreed with him, Christina thought, and sighed. She looked up at the image of a bare-breasted woman, her naked legs crossed. She held shafts of wheat in her lap. At the other side of the wall, her counterpart held apples.

They turned west to the wall that opened out to the museum's main entry hall. Two narrow panels were on either side of the opening. On the left, Rivera painted a worker at the bottom of the panel with a huge steam turbine looming above him. Christina thought that part of the turbine resembled a huge drooping penis, maybe, not so subtly, conveying the impotence of the workers at the time the murals were painted.

"See the dove in the small panel above him," Ben said. "And that's a passenger plane in the panel closest to the ceiling." They moved to the right of the entry. "See, here this man looks like a manager. Notice, Christina, he's equal in size to the worker in the left panel. That's symbolic. Everything in this room is symbolic. The manager sits before a turbine that converts steam into electricity. Look at how the turbine takes on the appearance of a huge ear. Henry Ford used henchmen to spy on his workers at home. If he found out they smoked, they were fired. In the small panel directly above the panel of the manager and turbine is a hawk and above that, a warplane. The passenger plane and the war plane symbolize that industry can be used for good or evil."

Ben bought her lunch in the cafeteria: bowls of soup and salad on glass plates. When they finished eating, he took her hand and they went upstairs to the contemporary collection. She stared at the squares with blurring edges in Rothko's *Orange Brown* painting for a long time. Mark Rothko, 1903—1970. She remembered reading about his suicide, and was somehow weirdly comforted, knowing that she wasn't the only survivor of a loved one's choosing death. She moved on through the galleries, and then she got caught up in Charles McGee's huge collage—*Noah's Arc: Genesis*. At first glance, it just looked like an abstract, but then she found images—snakes, a spotted dog, and a rat. Maybe the dog was a leopard? The main focus was two black women. Both figures wore skirts, but that didn't mean anything. Maybe it wasn't two women, but Adam and Eve?

Christina came home with a poster of the Charles McGee collage. It was still rolled up. She'd get a frame for it and hang it in her newly pristine space. Although she'd cleared away all the religious artifacts, she would hang *Noah's Arc: Genesis*. Not so far from where she started, just different. She needed different.

41. LILY

The plane taking them home was slowly rolling down the runway. Lily had taken her Xanax and—congratulating herself for being excessively brave—chose the window seat. As the plane pulled out of its parking space, a toddler across the aisle started bouncing up and down, straining forward against her seat belt. "Faster, plane. Faster," she shouted. Then, as if on the child's command, the plane started racing down the runway. Lily, with her back pressed into the seat, thought about the Roadrunner cartoon.

"Meep-meep," she said to Rose.

Rose looked perplexed.

Faster. Faster. It left the ground. She could feel the lift, just like when she was small and her father would swing her up off the ground and put her on his shoulders. The liftoff sensation filled her body. She was in the air. Buildings and cars below shrank.

There was a bump beneath her. Panicked, she grabbed Rose's hand.

"Don't worry," Rose said, and squeezed Lily's hand. "They just folded up the wheels. Like a bird folds up its legs to fly."

"Meep-meep."

Lily felt closer to Rose than she ever had. They had traveled to find their mother, and they found her. It was all good. Wanda was good. *Oh my goodness*, yes she was. Maybe in the summer she'd come back with the twins and introduce them to their grandmother. Grandma Wanda could give them a tour of the sights around Taos. But the best part, Lily thought, was that on this trip, she'd found her sister. The Rose she'd known all her life always tried so hard to be noticed that Lily stopped paying attention, maybe as long ago as grade school. But on this trip, Lily saw how loving and kind her sister was. She understood Rose's insecurity and jealousy. She got it.

They were above the clouds. The sky was bright blue, and the clouds—glaringly white foam—were far below them. People under the clouds were probably seeing gray and shadows, maybe it was raining. Up here, it was so beautiful. She didn't believe in heaven or angels. She believed in Dust. Dust loved her. The text message had read, "I love you. Be."

Lily looked out the window into the clouds—cotton batting, white fuzz. She put her hand into her purse and felt around until she had Dust's rosary in her fingers. She moved the beads one by one, as though she was counting them. Dust loved these beads. Lily blocked out the beads in the death scene and replaced it with an earlier memory of her friend. Dust was maybe twelve years old, chanting as she fingered the beads. With the touch of each bead, Lily recited in her head, *Corrina Dustina Malibu Jones, Corrina Dustina Malibu Jones.*

I love you. Be

Be? Maybe Dust was telling her to be—just be. Be whatever you are and whatever you want to be. Just be. She would go home and be Lily, see her boys and her father, and hang out with Rose and Christina and Grace.

42. GRACE

Grace was curious—curiosity killed the cat—but she wasn't afraid since she wasn't a cat. She was going home to check out the fire damage. No one said she shouldn't. She figured that it hadn't even crossed their minds that she'd want to see her house, since she'd been so leery of coming home after her mother died.

Grandma was working at the hospital this weekend, and her dad was living at his parents' house until the repairs were done, so Grace had plenty of time. It was chilly and she walked fast.

She approached her house from the side street, coming at it from the back, and all she could see was the blue tarp; the whole back of the house was gone. The original red brick house still stood; a wolf huffing and puffing couldn't blow her house down. Workmen had cleared away the rubble, but since it was Sunday, the house was deserted.

She walked around to the front, and then shifted around on the sidewalk until she found a position where the house looked normal. If you stood exactly in this spot, you couldn't see any blue tarp. The house looked just like it had always looked. Her parents bought this house before she was born. It was her house, she had worn diapers in this house, had skinned her knee on this very front sidewalk, played tag, and hide and go seek in this front yard. It was her house for her whole life. Suddenly, it seemed important to her. Is that what happens when you almost lose something, or when you've lost something that you took for granted and can never get back, like for instance, your mom.

Dad had been talking about selling the house because it had too many sad memories. Her memories were good—good memories when they were all together, quiet, good memories of sitting in her mother's living room, and studying (texting), or watching TV with her mom. He was talking about buying another house, maybe one of those big ones north or west of here. Sometimes she wondered if he'd learned anything. She'd have to change schools, and like her mom—she didn't want a monster house. They weren't good for the planet. But he didn't listen to much of what she said. Grandma said that he probably wouldn't be able to sell the house easily anyway, what with the events that had happened here. Her dad told her that he wasn't going to have the addition rebuilt—he said he felt superstitious about it—so the house would go sort of back to what it was before. The whole thing would be painted inside, maybe white, because that was easier to sell. Maybe when it was clean and fresh, he'd change his mind and want to live here again? Maybe.

It was odd standing on the sidewalk, looking at her house. The sense of longing to be back here was making her feel weepy. She wanted to live here again. The part where her mother died was gone, so she didn't feel afraid of it anymore. The house that they had been happy in was all that was left.

Grace had been upset that her dad hadn't told the reporter the truth about her mother. She had cried and yelled at him. He told her that he was responsible for what his campaign did; he was the leader. The staff wouldn't be guilty. He would be the culprit. It would be a big scandal and she, Grace, would get fallout from that. She'd pretended that she wasn't listening, but she sort of thought that maybe he did the right thing. She still wasn't sure.

The election was over. Dad didn't seem to be very upset about losing the election, since he'd already lost the most important thing—her mom. He went back to Lansing for the lame duck session in the State Senate. Her lame dad, lame with his broken wing, was in a lame duck session. That struck her funny, but it probably wasn't funny at all. In January, he'd go back to being a plain old lawyer, although she overheard him saying something to someone on his cell phone about being a lobbyist. She didn't know what he'd lobby for or against.

Their neighbor Fred was home from the hospital. His lungs were hurt, but he was, as he'd said when she and Grandma had visited him, *on the mend*. He was getting physical therapy and had joined the Breather's Club at Beaumont Hospital. After she'd checked out the house, she'd go next door and say hi. Her mother would like her to do that.

Her friend Max had offered to walk with her to check out the house, but she wanted to do this alone. Her old girlfriends were starting to be more normal and friendly. Since the fire, people were texting her again, but maybe she changed too, since she was texting back. She was nice to them, but mostly her loyalty was to Max.

At Grace's request, Grandma took her to a salon. Her hair was red again, but not quite her real color. Eventually it would grow out and she'd be back to having her mother's hair color.

She walked up her front sidewalk, and as she climbed the stairs of the front porch, she could smell charred wood and smoke. When she unlocked the front door and stepped inside, the house smelled even worse, like an old dog that had rolled around in wet soot, or like the stinky smell when you stick your head inside the fireplace after a rainy day. Yes, she'd done that once. The house was damp and chilly inside, with the heat kept low to save energy.

She shivered and just stood in the front hall thinking about how Fred had rushed in here in the smoke. He was so brave. She didn't think she could ever run into a burning house, also she knew it wasn't the smartest thing to do, but he saved her father's life. They had saved each other's lives.

What her dad said on the TV news interview—stuff about her mom's concern for the environment—that pleased Fred, even though Dad hadn't fessed-up about the mental hospital lies. So they could be, maybe not good friends, but good neighbors. They'd saved each other's lives, for God's sake, Dad even said that by summer when they were both (hopefully) a little more healed, that maybe he could help Fred down in Detroit. Maybe they'd do some urban farming together? Maybe she could go, too, since she'd be out of school? Maybe Fred would take her and Max with him and they could all help?

Grace went into her mother's living room. Everything looked normal in here except that it was dirty with black and gray soot on everything. Obviously, a bunch of stuff—her beloved squishy chair and the loveseats—would have to be thrown out. They could probably keep the coffee table. The cardboard box with her mother's ashes was still there, but now it was covered with oily gray ash—ashes on the ashes. The candles were arranged just like they had been the night she came and sat with her father. When she heard about the fire, she was sure that it had been the candles that started it. She ran her finger over the table, leaving a trail, and then she wrote *Grace was here.*

The jigsaw puzzle that they'd all been working on for weeks was still on the dining room table. But the tabletop was so thick with ashes that it was hard to make out the pieces, especially the upside-down ones that were the same gray color as the ash. The back wall of the room was charred around the door to the addition and the floor was buckled from the water from fire hoses.

The mudroom was a mess of burnt and broken cupboards. The fire had burst through the old kitchen window, but with the addition being gone, they'd need a whole new kitchen anyway. She headed back toward the front of the house.

The stairs creaked when she climbed them, but then they had always done that. In the upper hallway, boards covered the opening where the door into her parents' room used to be. The door was gone and the wall around it was burnt black. The hall carpet had been pulled up, and the floor was watermarked and warped from the firefighters putting out the fire. Workmen had boarded up the hole in the roof so rain wouldn't come in. The other doors in the hall were all closed. Her dad turning into a nutcase and shutting doors had saved most of the old house.

She opened the door to her room, shoving hard. The thick carpet made a tight fit since they'd never shaved the bottom of her door after they put new carpet in here. It smelled smoky, but there wasn't as much soot on everything as there was downstairs. Her bedroom looked nearly the same as it always had, although the smell was bad.

She was glad that she'd taken the photo—the one of her and her mom blowing out the birthday candles—back to Grandma's condo. She'd taped it right in the center of the mirror over her dresser, exactly where her mother would have put it. What if the fire had burned down the whole house? The precious photo would have been lost.

Grace felt nauseated from the smoke smell and maybe from a big sadness inside her. She sat down on her bed and heard a crunchy sound. Weird. She wiggled her butt. More crunchy sound. What? What was it? She stood up and pulled back her blanket.

Colored squares were splattered all over her rumpled sheet—green and pink and orange and blue Post-it notes. There must be twenty, or maybe even a fifty. She remembered telling everyone at her mother's memorial in Grandma's kitchen how she loved her mother's Post-it notes. Maybe Grandma or Lily had done this. They both had keys. Maybe Fred? She even told her Dad about missing her mother's notes on one of their trips to the psychologist's office.

Any one of them could have done it, but no one had said anything about her coming back into the house after the fire. No one gave any hints that she should check her bed.

She was pretty sure that the writing was her mother's. She carefully picked up each Post-it and read it before adding another to the pile in her palm. There were so many messages. She slowly examined each one. The notes said *I heart you, Hugs & Kisses, I love Grace, Be Green, Be Kind, Be Yourself, Be Happy, I'm Sorry.* Then she found a note that said, *Surreptitious Texter*, and she knew for sure that the notes were from her mother.

Maybe her mother had been writing the notes for days or weeks, adding to the stack as she thought of messages for her? The Post-its were put here that Friday morning after Grace left for school, the day she swore at her mother and was so mean to her. Her mother had forgiven her. With the stack of Post-its resting in her hand, Grace kissed them and said, "I heart you too, Mom."

THE END

ACKNOWLEDGEMENTS

First I'd like to thank my husband, John Bogner, who's always supportive, whether it's lugging my paintings around the country, or reading my manuscripts for the zillionth time. Who—when I have an idea—usually says, "Do it." I can count on John for an honest opinion. When I wanted to go to New Mexico for research for this book, he was right there with me.

Then there's all the readers who were so giving of their time: my family—Sue Schoettle, Kristen Schoettle, Bonnie Schoettle, and Alison Ruble; and friends—Ann Amenta, Barbara Aylward, Pat Burke, Jim DeLorey, Mary Cay Dietz (who read it twice!), Colette Dywasuk, Carol Lee, Joy Powell, and Ed Sharples. I'm indebted to them all for their honesty, comments, and the suggestions that helped me write a better novel.

Anthony Cardellio, DO, read pages of my manuscript, offered some good information, and on a return visit when he read my revisions, wrote a large, red A+ on my pages.

Former Pleasant Ridge Police Chief Kurt Swieczkowski and Officer Robert Ried answered questions with kindness and openness.

I'm grateful to my copyeditor, Susan Franco, who tamed my commas and helped me feel secure about showing the world my novel. The use of "Okay" instead of "OK" was my choice.

Nancy Massa designed the Spring Forward Publishing logo and spent hours helping me tweak the cover design. I am grateful.

ABOUT THE AUTHOR

Lynn Arbor was born in Ann Arbor, Michigan, and has lived in California, Massachusetts, Colorado, and Illinois. She's spent her life writing and making art. When her daughter and son were little she wrote children's books: *Grandpa's Long Red Underwear* was published by Lothrop, Lee & Shepard Books. She contributed to a decorating column in the *Detroit News* and wrote two unpublished novels. For twenty-five years she made her living as a graphic designer, but after serious illness, she turned to fine art. She's best known in the Detroit area as a painter. When she created a website for her paintings, she wanted to include a link to her blog—which meant she had to write a blog. The blog reminded her of the pleasure of writing, which has occupied most of her time for the past four years. She lives in Pleasant Ridge, Michigan, with her architect husband, John Bogner.

Made in the USA
Charleston, SC
03 February 2015